THE WITCH of PORTOBELLO

HarperCollins*Publishers*

THE
WITCH
OF
PORTOBELLO

A Novel

PAULO COELHO

TRANSLATED
FROM THE PORTUGUESE
BY MARGARET JULL COSTA

THE WITCH OF PORTOBELLO. Copyright © 2006 by Paulo Coelho.
English translation copyright © 2007 by Margaret Jull Costa.
All rights reserved. Printed in the United States of America.
No part of this book may be used or reproduced in any manner
whatsoever without written permission except in the case of brief quotations
embodied in critical articles and reviews. For information, address
HarperCollins Publishers, 10 East 53rd Street, New York, NY 10022.

Designed by Jennifer Ann Daddio

Library of Congress Cataloging-in-Publication Data is available upon request.

ISBN-13: 978-0-7394-9021-1

FOR S.F.X.,

a sun who spread light and

warmth wherever he went,

and was an example to all those

who think beyond their horizons

O Mary conceived without sin,

pray for those who turn to you.

Amen.

No man, when he hath lighted a candle,

putteth it in a secret place,

neither under a bushel, but on a candlestick,

that they which come in may see the light.

—LUKE 11:33

THE WITCH OF PORTOBELLO

Before these statements left my desk and followed the fate I eventually chose for them, I considered using them as the basis for a traditional, painstakingly researched biography, recounting a true story. And so I read various biographies, thinking this would help me, only to realize that the biographer's view of his subject inevitably influences the results of his research. Since it wasn't my intention to impose my own opinions on the reader, but to set down the story of "the Witch of Portobello" as seen by its main protagonists, I soon abandoned the idea of writing a straight biography and decided that the best approach would be simply to transcribe what people had told me.

HERON RYAN, FORTY-FOUR, JOURNALIST

No one lights a lamp in order to hide it behind the door: the purpose of light is to create more light, to open people's eyes, to reveal the marvels around.

No one sacrifices the most important thing she possesses: love.

No one places her dreams in the hands of those who might destroy them.

No one, that is, but Athena.

A long time after Athena's death, her former teacher asked me to go with her to the town of Prestonpans in Scotland. There, taking advantage of certain ancient feudal powers that were due to be abolished the following month, the town had granted official pardons to eighty-one people—and their cats—who were executed in the sixteenth and seventeenth centuries for practicing witchcraft.

According to the official spokeswoman for the Barons Courts of Prestoungrange & Dolphinstoun: "Most of those persons condemned … were convicted on the basis of spectral evidence—that is to say, prosecuting witnesses declared that they felt the presence of evil spirits or heard spirit voices."

There's no point now in going into all the excesses committed by the Inquisition, with its torture chambers and its bonfires lit by hatred and vengeance; however, on our way to Prestonpans, Edda said several times that there was something about that gesture which she found unacceptable: the town and the Fourteenth Baron of Prestoungrange & Dolphinstoun were "granting pardons" to people who had been brutally executed.

"Here we are in the twenty-first century, and yet the descendants of the real criminals, those who killed the innocent victims, still feel they have the right to grant pardons. Do you know what I mean, Heron?"

I did. A new witch hunt is starting to gain ground. This time the weapon isn't the red-hot iron, but irony and repression. Anyone who happens to discover a gift and dares to speak of their abilities is usually regarded with distrust. Generally speaking, their husband, wife, father, or child, or whoever, instead of feeling proud, forbids all mention of the matter, fearful of exposing their family to ridicule.

Before I met Athena, I thought all such gifts were a dishonest way of exploiting people's despair. My trip to Transylvania to make a documentary on vampires was also a way of proving how easily people are deceived. Certain superstitions, however absurd they may seem, remain in the human imagination and are often used by unscrupulous people. When I visited Dracula's castle, which has been reconstructed merely to give tourists the feeling that they're in a special place, I was approached by a government official who implied that I would receive a "significant" (to use his word) gift when the film was shown on the BBC. In the mind of that official, I was helping to propagate the myth and thus deserved a generous reward. One of the guides said that the number of visitors increased each year, and that any mention of the place would prove positive, even a program saying that the castle was a fake, that Vlad Dracula was a historical figure who had nothing to do with the myth, and that it was all merely a product of the wild imaginings of one Irishman [*Editor's note: Bram Stoker*], who had never even visited the region.

I knew then that, however rigorous I was with the facts, I was unwittingly collaborating with the lie; even if the idea behind my script was to de-mythologize the place, people would believe what they wanted to believe; the guide was right, I would simply be helping to generate more publicity. I immediately abandoned the project, even though I'd already spent quite a lot of money on the trip and on my research.

And yet my journey to Transylvania was to have a huge impact on my life, for I met Athena there when she was trying to track down her mother. Destiny—mysterious, implacable Destiny—brought us face-to-face in the insignificant foyer of a still more insignificant hotel. I was witness to her first conversation with Deidre—or Edda, as she likes to be called. I watched, as if I were a spectator of my own life, as my heart struggled vainly not to allow itself to be seduced by a woman who didn't belong to my world. I applauded when reason lost the battle, and all I could do was surrender and accept that I was in love.

That love led me to see things I'd never imagined could exist—rituals, materializations, trances. Believing that I was blinded by love, I doubted everything, but doubt, far from paralyzing me, pushed me in the direction of oceans whose very existence I couldn't admit. It was this same energy which, in difficult times, helped me to confront the cynicism of journalist colleagues and to write about Athena and her work. And since that love remains alive, the energy remains, even though Athena is dead, even though all I want now is to forget what I saw and learned. I could only navigate that world while hand in hand with Athena.

These were her gardens, her rivers, her mountains. Now that she's gone, I need everything to return as quickly as possible to how it used to be. I'm going to concentrate more on traffic problems, Britain's foreign policy, on how we administer taxes. I want to go back to thinking that the world of magic is merely a clever trick, that people are superstitious, that anything science cannot explain has no right to exist.

When the meetings in Portobello started to get out of control, we had endless arguments about how she was behaving, although I'm glad now that she didn't listen to me. If there is any possible consolation in the tragedy of losing someone we love very much, it's the necessary hope that perhaps it was for the best.

I wake and fall asleep with that certainty; it's best that Athena left when she did rather than descend into the infernos of this world. She would never have regained her peace of mind after the events that earned her the nickname "the Witch of Portobello." The rest of her life would have been a bitter clash between her personal dreams and collective reality. Knowing her as I did, she would have battled on to the end, wasting her energy and her joy on trying to prove something that no one, absolutely no one, was prepared to believe.

Who knows, perhaps she sought death the way a shipwrecked victim seeks an island. She must have stood late at night in many a Tube station, waiting for muggers who never came. She must have walked through the most dangerous parts of London in search of a murderer who never appeared or perhaps tried to provoke the anger of the physically strong, who refused to get angry.

Until, finally, she managed to get herself brutally murdered. But, then, how many of us will be saved the pain of seeing the most important things in our lives disappearing from one moment to the next? I don't just mean people, but our ideas and dreams too: we might survive a day, a week, a few years, but we're all condemned to lose. Our body remains alive, yet sooner or later our soul will receive the mortal blow. The perfect crime—for we don't know who murdered our joy, what their motives were, or where the guilty parties are to be found.

Are they aware of what they've done, those nameless guilty parties? I doubt it, because they too—the depressed, the arrogant, the impotent, and the powerful—are the victims of the reality they created.

They don't understand and would be incapable of understanding Athena's world. Yes, that's the best way to think of it—Athena's world. I'm finally coming to accept that I was only a temporary inhabitant, there as a favor, like someone who finds himself in a beautiful mansion, eating exquisite food, aware that this is only a party, that the mansion belongs to someone else, that the food was bought by someone else, and that the time will come when the lights will go out, the owners will go to bed, the servants will return to their quarters, the door will close, and we'll be out in the street again, waiting for a taxi or a bus to restore us to the mediocrity of our everyday lives.

I'm going back, or, rather, part of me is going back to that world where only what we can see, touch, and explain makes sense. I want to get back to the world of speeding tickets, people arguing with bank cashiers, eternal complaints about the weather, to horror films, and Formula I racing. This is the universe I'll have to live with for the rest of my days. I'll get married, have children, and the past will become a distant memory, which will, in the end, make me ask myself: How could I have been so blind? How could I have been so ingenuous?

I also know that, at night, another part of me will remain wandering in space, in contact with things as real as the pack of cigarettes and the glass of gin before me now. My soul will dance with Athena's soul; I'll be with her while I sleep; I'll wake up sweating and go into the kitchen for a glass of water. I'll understand that in order to combat ghosts you must use weapons that form no part of reality. Then, following the advice of my grandmother, I'll place an open pair of scissors on my bedside table to snip off the end of the dream.

The next day, I'll look at the scissors with a touch of regret, but I must adapt to living in the world again or risk going mad.

ANDREA MCCAIN, THIRTY-TWO, ACTRESS

"No one can manipulate anyone else. In any relationship, both parties know what they're doing, even if one of them complains later on that they were used."

That's what Athena used to say, but she herself behaved quite differently, because she used and manipulated me with no consideration for my feelings. And given that we're talking about magic here, this makes the accusation an even more serious one; after all, she was my teacher, charged with passing on the sacred mysteries, with awakening the unknown force we all possess. When we venture into that unfamiliar sea, we trust blindly in those who guide us, believing that they know more than we do.

Well, I can guarantee that they don't. Not Athena, not Edda, nor any of the people I came to know through them. She told me she was learning through teaching, and although, at first, I refused to believe this, later I came to think that perhaps it was true. I realized it was one of her many ways of getting us to drop our guard and surrender to her charm.

People who are on a spiritual quest don't think, they simply want results. They want to feel powerful and superior to the anonymous masses. They want to be special. Athena played with other people's feelings in a quite terrifying way.

I understand that she once felt a profound admiration for St. Thérèse of Lisieux. I have no interest in the Catholic faith, but from what I've heard, Thérèse experienced a kind of mystical and physical union with God. Athena mentioned once that she would like to share a similar fate. Well, in that case, she should have joined a convent and devoted her life to prayer or to the service of the poor. That would have been much more useful to the world and far less dangerous than using music and rituals to induce in people a kind of intoxicated state that brought them into contact with both the best and the worst of themselves.

I sought her out when I was looking for some meaning to my life, although I didn't say as much at our first meeting. I should have realized from the start that Athena wasn't very interested in that; she wanted to live, dance, make love, travel, to gather people around her in order to demonstrate how wise she was, to show off her gifts, to provoke the neighbors, to make the most of all that is profane in us—although she always tried to give a spiritual gloss to that search.

Whenever we met, whether it was to perform some magical

ceremony or just have a drink, I was conscious of her power. It was so strong I could almost touch it. Initially, I was fascinated and wanted to be like her. But one day, in a bar, she started talking about the "Third Rite," which has to do with sexuality. She did this in the presence of my boyfriend. Her excuse was that she was teaching me something. Her real objective, in my opinion, was to seduce the man I loved.

And, of course, she succeeded.

It isn't good to speak ill of people who have passed from this life onto the astral plane. However, Athena won't have to account to me, but to all those forces that she turned to her own benefit, rather than channeling them for the good of humanity and for her own spiritual enlightenment.

The worst thing is that if it hadn't been for her compulsive exhibitionism, everything we began together could have worked out really well. Had she behaved more discreetly, we would now be fulfilling the mission with which we were entrusted. But she couldn't control herself; she thought she was the mistress of the truth, capable of overcoming all barriers merely by using her powers of seduction.

And the result? I was left alone. And I can't leave the work half-finished—I'll have to continue to the end, even though sometimes I feel very weak and often dispirited.

I'm not surprised that her life ended as it did: she was always flirting with danger. They say that extroverts are unhappier than introverts and have to compensate for this by constantly proving to themselves how happy and contented and at ease with life they are. In her case, at least, this is absolutely true.

Athena was conscious of her own charisma, and she made all those who loved her suffer.

Including me.

Deidre O'Neill, thirty-seven, doctor, known as Edda

If a man we don't know phones us up today and talks a little, makes no suggestions, says nothing special, but nevertheless pays us the kind of attention we rarely receive, we're quite capable of going to bed with him that same night, feeling relatively in love. That's what we women are like, and there's nothing wrong with that—it's the nature of the female to open herself to love easily.

It was this same love that opened me up to my first encounter with the Mother when I was nineteen. Athena was the same age the first time she went into a trance while dancing. But that's the only thing we had in common—the age of our initiation.

In every other aspect, we were totally and profoundly different, especially in the way we dealt with other people. As her teacher, I always did my best to help her in her inner search. As her friend—although I'm not sure my feelings of friendship were reciprocated—I tried to alert her to the fact that the world wasn't ready for the kind of transformations she wanted to provoke. I remember spending a few sleepless nights before deciding to allow her to act with total freedom and follow the demands of her heart.

Her greatest problem was that she was a woman of the

twenty-second century living in the twenty-first, and making no secret of the fact either. Did she pay a price? She certainly did. But she would have paid a still higher price if she had repressed her true exuberant self. She would have been bitter and frustrated, always concerned about "what other people might think," always saying "I'll just sort these things out, then I'll devote myself to my dream," always complaining that "the conditions are never quite right."

Everyone's looking for the perfect teacher, but although their teachings might be divine, teachers are all too human, and that's something people find hard to accept. Don't confuse the teacher with the lesson, the ritual with the ecstasy, the transmitter of the symbol with the symbol itself. The Tradition is linked to our encounter with the forces of life and not with the people who bring this about. But we are weak: we ask the Mother to send us guides, and all she sends are signs to the road we need to follow.

Pity those who seek for shepherds, instead of longing for freedom! An encounter with the superior energy is open to anyone but remains far from those who shift responsibility onto others. Our time on this earth is sacred, and we should celebrate every moment.

The importance of this has been completely forgotten: even religious holidays have been transformed into opportunities to go to the beach or the park or skiing. There are no more rituals. Ordinary actions can no longer be transformed into manifestations of the sacred. We cook and complain that it's a waste of time, when we should be pouring our love into making that food. We work and believe it's a divine curse, when we should be using our skills to bring pleasure and to spread the energy of the Mother.

Athena brought to the surface the immensely rich world we all carry in our souls, without realizing that people aren't yet ready to accept their own powers.

We women, when we're searching for a meaning to our lives or for the path of knowledge, always identify with one of four classic archetypes.

The Virgin (and I'm not speaking here of a sexual virgin) is the one whose search springs from her complete independence, and everything she learns is the fruit of her ability to face challenges alone.

The Martyr finds her way to self-knowledge through pain, surrender, and suffering.

The Saint finds her true reason for living in unconditional love and in her ability to give without asking anything in return.

Finally, the Witch justifies her existence by going in search of complete and limitless pleasure.

Normally a woman has to choose from one of these traditional feminine archetypes, but Athena was all four at once.

Obviously we can justify her behavior, alleging that all those who enter a state of trance or ecstasy lose contact with reality. That's not true: the physical world and the spiritual world are the same thing. We can see the Divine in each speck of dust, but that doesn't stop us from wiping it away with a wet sponge. The Divine doesn't disappear; it's transformed into the clean surface.

Athena should have been more careful. When I reflect upon

the life and death of my pupil, it seems to me that I had better change the way I behave too.

LELLA ZAINAB, SIXTY-FOUR, NUMEROLOGIST

Athena? What an interesting name! Let's see ... her Maximum number is nine. Optimistic, sociable, likely to be noticed in a crowd. People might go to her in search of understanding, compassion, generosity, and for precisely that reason, she should be careful, because that tendency to popularity could go to her head and she'll end up losing more than she gains. She should also watch her tongue, because she tends to speak more than common sense dictates.

As for her Minimum number eleven, I sense that she longs for some leadership position. She has an interest in mystical subjects and through these tries to bring harmony to those around her.

However, this is in direct conflict with the number nine, which is the sum of the day, month, and year of her birth reduced to a single figure: she'll always be subject to envy, sadness, introversion, and impulsive decisions. She must be careful not to let herself be affected by negative vibrations: excessive ambition, intolerance, abuse of power, extravagance.

Because of that conflict, I suggest she take up some career that doesn't involve emotional contact with people, like computing or engineering.

Oh, she's dead? I'm sorry. So what *did* she do?

What did Athena do? She did a little of everything, but if I had to summarize her life, I'd say: she was a priestess who understood the forces of nature. Or, rather, she was someone who, by the simple fact of having little to lose or to hope for in life, took greater risks than other people and ended up being transformed into the forces she thought she mastered.

She was a supermarket checkout girl, a bank employee, a property dealer, and in each of these positions she always revealed the priestess within. I lived with her for eight years, and I owed her this: to recover her memory, her identity.

The most difficult thing in collecting together these statements was persuading people to let me use their real names. Some said they didn't want to be involved in this kind of story, others tried to conceal their opinions and feelings. I explained that my real intention was to help all those involved to understand her better, and that no reader would believe in anonymous statements.

They finally agreed because they all believed that they knew the unique and definitive version of any event, however insignificant. During the recordings, I saw that things are never absolute, they depend on each individual's perceptions. And the best way to know who we are is often to find out how others see us.

This doesn't mean that we should do what others expect us to do, but it helps us to understand ourselves better. I owed it to Athena to recover her story, to write her myth.

SAMIRA R. KHALIL, FIFTY-SEVEN, HOUSEWIFE, ATHENA'S MOTHER

Please, don't call her Athena. Her real name is Sherine. Sherine Khalil, our much-loved, much-wanted daughter, whom both my husband and I wish we had engendered.

Life, however, had other plans—when fate is very generous with us, there is always a well into which all our dreams can tumble.

We lived in Beirut in the days when everyone considered it the most beautiful city in the Middle East. My husband was a successful industrialist, we married for love, we traveled to Europe every year, we had friends, we were invited to all the important social events, and once, the president of the United States himself visited my house. Imagine that! Three unforgettable days, during two of which the American Secret Service scoured every corner of our house (they'd been in the area for more than a month already, taking up strategic positions, renting apartments, disguising themselves as beggars or young lovers). And for one day, or rather, two hours, we partied. I'll never forget the look of envy in our friends' eyes, and the excitement of having our photo taken alongside the most powerful man on the planet.

We had it all, apart from the one thing we wanted most—a child. And so we had nothing.

We tried everything: we made vows and promises, went to places where miracles were guaranteed, we consulted doctors, witch doctors, took remedies and drank elixirs and magic potions. I had artificial insemination twice and lost the baby both times. On the second occasion, I also lost my left ovary, and after that, no doctor was prepared to risk such a venture again.

That was when one of the many friends who knew of our plight suggested the one possible solution: adoption. He said he had contacts in Romania, and that the process wouldn't take long.

A month later, we got on a plane. Our friend had important business dealings with the dictator who ruled the country at the time, and whose name I now forget [*Editor's note: Nicolae Ceausescu*], and so we managed to avoid the bureaucratic red tape and went straight to an adoption center in Sibiu, in Transylvania. There we were greeted with coffee, cigarettes, mineral water, and with the paperwork signed and sealed. All we had to do was choose a child.

They took us to a very cold nursery, and I couldn't imagine how they could leave those poor children in such a place. My first instinct was to adopt them all and carry them off to Lebanon, where there was sun and freedom, but obviously that was a crazy idea. We walked up and down between the cots, listening to the children crying, terrified by the magnitude of the decision we were about to make.

For more than an hour, neither I nor my husband spoke a word. We went out, drank coffee, smoked, and then went back in again—and this happened several times. I noticed that the woman in charge of adoptions was growing impatient; she wanted an immediate decision. At that moment, following an instinct I would dare to describe as maternal—as if I'd found a child who should have been mine in this incarnation, but who had come into the world in another woman's womb—I pointed to one particular baby girl.

The woman advised us to think again. And she'd been so impatient for us to make a decision! But I was sure.

Nevertheless—trying not to hurt my feelings (she thought we had contacts in the upper echelons of the Romanian government)—she whispered to me, so that my husband wouldn't hear: "I know it won't work out. She's the daughter of a gypsy."

I retorted that culture isn't something that's transmitted through the genes. The child, who was barely three months old, would be our daughter, brought up according to our customs. She would go to our church, visit our beaches, read books in French, study at the American School in Beirut. Besides, I knew nothing about gypsy culture—and I still know nothing. I only know that they travel a lot, don't wash very often, aren't to be trusted, and wear earrings. Legend has it that they kidnap children and carry them off in their caravans, but here, exactly the opposite was happening: they had left a child behind for me to take care of.

The woman tried again to dissuade me, but I was already signing the papers and asking my husband to do the same. On the flight back to Beirut, the world seemed different: God had given me a reason for living, working, and fighting in this vale of tears. We now had a child to justify all our efforts.

Sherine grew in wisdom and beauty—I expect all parents say that, but I really do think she was an exceptional child. One afternoon, when she was five, one of my brothers said that if, in the future, she wanted to work abroad, her name would always betray her origins, and he suggested changing it to one that gave nothing away, like Athena, for example. Now, of course, I know that Athena refers not only to the capital of Greece, but that it is also the name of the Greek goddess of wisdom, intelligence, and war.

Perhaps my brother knew not only that but was aware too

of the problems an Arab name might bring in the future, for he was very involved in politics, as were all our family, and wanted to protect his niece from the black clouds that he, and only he, could see on the horizon. Most surprising of all was that Sherine liked the sound of the word. That same afternoon, she began referring to herself as Athena and no one could persuade her to do otherwise. To please her, we adopted the nickname too, thinking that it would be a passing fancy.

Can a name affect a person's life? Time passed, and the name stuck.

From very early on, we discovered that she had a strong religious vocation—she spent all her time in the church and knew the Gospels by heart; this was at once a blessing and a curse. In a world that was starting to be divided more and more along religious lines, I feared for my daughter's safety. It was then that Sherine began telling us, as if it were the most natural thing in the world, that she had a series of invisible friends—angels and saints whose images she was accustomed to seeing in the church we attended. All children everywhere have visions, but they usually forget about them after a certain age. They also treat inanimate objects, such as dolls or fluffy tigers, as if they were real. However, I really did feel she was going too far when I picked her up from school one day, and she told me that she'd seen "a woman dressed in white, like the Virgin Mary."

Naturally, I believe in angels. I even believe that the angels speak to little children, but when a child starts seeing visions of grown-ups, that's another matter. I've read about various shepherds and country people who claimed to have seen a woman in white, and how this eventually destroyed their lives, because others sought them out, expecting miracles; then the priests took over, their village became a center of pilgrimage, and the poor children ended their lives in a convent or a monastery. I was, therefore, very concerned about this story. Sherine was at an age when she should have been more concerned with makeup kits, painting her nails, watching soppy TV soaps and children's programs. There was something wrong with my daughter, and I consulted an expert.

"Relax," he said.

According to this pediatrician specializing in child psychology—and according to most other doctors in the field—invisible friends are a projection of a child's dreams and a safe way of helping the child to discover her desires and express her feelings.

"Yes, but a vision of a woman in white?"

He replied that perhaps Sherine didn't understand our way of seeing or explaining the world. He suggested that we should gradually begin preparing the ground to tell her that she was adopted. In the pediatrician's words, the worst thing that could happen would be for her to find out by herself. Then she would begin to doubt everyone, and her behavior might become unpredictable.

From then on, we changed the way we talked to her. I don't know how much children remember of what happens to them, but we started trying to show her just how much we loved her and that there was no need for her to take refuge in an imaginary world. She needed to see that her visible universe was as beautiful as it could possibly be, that her parents would protect her from any danger, that Beirut was a lovely city and its beaches full of sun and people. Without ever mentioning "the woman in white," I began spending more time with my daughter; I invited her school friends to come to our house; I seized every opportunity to shower her with affection.

The strategy worked. My husband used to travel a lot, and Sherine always missed him. In the name of love, he resolved to change his way of life a little. Her solitary conversations began to be replaced by games shared by father, mother, and daughter.

Everything was going well. Then, one night, she came into our room in tears, saying that she was frightened and that hell was close at hand.

I was alone at home. My husband had had to go away again, and I thought perhaps this was the reason for her despair. But hell? What were they teaching her at school or at church? I decided to go and talk to her teacher the next day.

Sherine, meanwhile, wouldn't stop crying. I took her over to the window and showed her the Mediterranean outside, lit by the full moon. I told her there were no devils, only stars in the sky and people strolling up and down the boulevard outside our apartment. I told her not to worry, that she needn't be afraid, but she continued to weep and tremble. After spending almost half an hour trying to calm her, I began to get worried. I begged her to stop; after all, she was no longer a child. I thought perhaps her first period had started and discreetly asked if there was any blood.

"Yes, lots."

I got some cotton wool and asked her to lie down so that I could take care of her "wound." It wasn't important. I would explain tomorrow. However, her period hadn't started. She cried for a while longer, but she must have been tired, because then she fell asleep.

And the following morning, there was blood.

Four men had been murdered. To me, this was just another of the eternal tribal battles to which my people have become accustomed. To Sherine, it clearly meant nothing, because she didn't even mention her nightmare.

Meanwhile, from that date onward, hell came ever closer, and it hasn't gone away since. On that same day, twenty-six Palestinians were killed on a bus, as revenge for the murders. Twenty-four hours later, it was impossible to walk down the street because of shots coming from every angle. The schools closed, Sherine was hurried home by one of her teachers, and the situation went from bad to worse. My husband interrupted his business trip halfway through and came home, where he spent whole days on the phone to his friends in government, but no one said anything that made any sense. Sherine heard the shots outside and my husband's angry shouts indoors, but to my surprise, she didn't say a word. I tried to tell her that it wouldn't last, that soon we'd be able to go to the beach again, but she would simply look away or ask for a book to read or a record to play. While hell gradually put down roots, Sherine read and listened to music.

But, if you don't mind, I'd prefer not to dwell on that. I don't want to think about the threats we received, about who was right, who was guilty, and who was innocent. The fact is that a few months later, if you wanted to cross a particular street, you had to catch a boat across to the island of Cyprus, get on another boat, and disembark on the other side of the street.

For nearly a year, we stayed pretty much shut up indoors, always hoping that the situation would improve, always thinking it was a temporary thing, and that the government would take control. One morning, while she was listening to a record on her little portable record player, Sherine started dancing and saying things like: "This is going to last for a long, long time."

I tried to stop her, but my husband grabbed my arm. I realized that he was listening to what she was saying and taking it seriously. I never understood why, and we've never spoken about it since. It's a kind of taboo between us.

The following day, he began taking unexpected steps, and two weeks later we were on a boat bound for London. Later, we would learn that, although there are no reliable statistics, during those years of civil war about 44,000 people died, 180,000 were wounded, and thousands made homeless. The fighting continued for other reasons, the country was occupied by foreign troops, and the hell continues to this day.

"It's going to last for a long, long time," said Sherine. Unfortunately, she was right.

LUKÁS JESSEN-PETERSEN, THIRTY-TWO, ENGINEER, EX-HUSBAND

When I first met Athena, she already knew that she was adopted. She was just nineteen and about to have a stand-up fight with a fellow student in the university cafeteria because the fellow student, assuming Athena to be English (white skin, straight hair, eyes that were sometimes green, sometimes gray), had made some insulting remark about the Middle East.

It was the first day of term for these students and they knew nothing about one another. But Athena got up, grabbed the other girl by the collar, and started screaming: "Racist!"

I saw the look of terror in the girl's eyes and the look of excitement in the eyes of the other students, eager to see what would happen next. I was in the year above, and I knew exactly what the consequences would be: they would both be hauled up before the vice chancellor, an official complaint would be made, and that would probably be followed by expulsion from the university and a possible police inquiry into alleged racism, etc., etc. Everyone would lose.

"Shut up!" I yelled, without really knowing what I was saying.

I knew neither of the girls. I'm not the savior of the world, and to be perfectly honest, young people find the occasional fight stimulating, but I couldn't help myself.

"Stop it!" I shouted again at the pretty young woman who now had the other equally pretty young woman by the throat. She shot me a furious glance. Then, suddenly, something changed. She smiled, although she still had her hands around her colleague's throat.

"You forgot to say 'please,'" she said.

Everyone laughed.

"Stop," I asked again. "Please."

She released the other girl and came over to me. All heads turned to watch.

"You have excellent manners. Do you also have a cigarette?"

I offered her my pack of cigarettes, and we went outside for a smoke. She had gone from outrage to nonchalance, and minutes later, she was laughing, discussing the weather, and asking if I liked this or that pop group. I heard the bell ringing for class and solemnly ignored the rule I'd been brought up to obey all my life: do your duty. I stayed there chatting, as if there were no university, no fights, no canteens, no wind or cold or sun. There was only that young woman with the gray eyes, saying the most boring and pointless things, but capable, nonetheless, of holding my interest for the rest of my life.

Two hours later, we were having lunch together. Seven hours later, we were in a bar, having supper and drinking whatever our limited budgets allowed us to eat and drink. Our conversations grew ever more profound, and in a short space of time, I knew practically everything about her life—Athena recounted details of her childhood and adolescence with no prompting from me. Later, I realized she was the same with everyone, but that day I felt like the most important man on the face of the earth.

She had come to London fleeing the civil war that had broken out in Lebanon. Her father, a Maronite Christian [*Editor's note: a branch of the Catholic Church, which, although it comes under the authority of the Vatican, does not require priests to be celibate and uses both Middle Eastern and Orthodox rituals*], had started to receive death threats because he worked for the Lebanese government, but despite this, he couldn't make up his mind to leave and go into exile.

Then Athena, overhearing a phone conversation, decided that it was time she grew up, that she assumed her filial responsibilities and protected those she loved.

She performed a kind of dance and pretended that she'd gone into a trance (she had learned all about this kind of thing at school when she studied the lives of the saints), and started making various pronouncements. I don't know how a mere child could possibly persuade adults to make decisions based on what she said, but that, according to Athena, was precisely what happened. Her father was very superstitious, and she was convinced that she'd saved the lives of her family.

They arrived here as refugees, but not as beggars. The Lebanese community is scattered all over the world, and her father soon found a way of reestablishing his business, and life went on. Athena was able to study at good schools, she attended dance classes—because dance was her passion—and when she'd finished at secondary school, she chose to take a degree in engineering.

Once they were living in London, her parents invited her out to supper at one of the most expensive restaurants in the city and explained, very carefully, that she had been adopted. Athena pretended to be surprised, hugged them both, and said that nothing would change their relationship.

The truth was, though, that a friend of the family, in a moment of malice, had called her "an ungrateful orphan" and put her lack of manners down to the fact that she was "not her parents' 'real' daughter." She had hurled an ashtray at him, cutting his face, and then cried for two whole days, after which she quickly got used to the idea that she was adopted. The malicious family friend was left with an unexplained scar and took to saying that he'd been attacked in the street by muggers.

I asked if she would like to go out with me the next day. She told me that she was a virgin, went to church on Sundays, and had no interest in romantic novels—she was more concerned with reading everything she could about the situation in the Middle East.

She was, in short, busy. Very busy.

"People think that a woman's only dream is to get married and have children. And given what I've told you, you probably think that I've suffered a lot in life. It's not true, and, besides, I've been there already. I've known other men who wanted to 'protect' me from all those tragedies. What they forget is that, from Ancient Greece on, the people who returned from battle were either dead on their shields or stronger, despite or because of their scars. It's better that way: I've lived on a battlefield since I was born, but I'm still alive and I don't need anyone to protect me."

She paused.

"You see how cultured I am?"

"Oh, very, but when you attack someone weaker than yourself, you make it look as if you really do need protection. You could have ruined your university career right there and then."

"You're right. Okay, I accept the invitation."

We started seeing each other regularly, and the closer I got to her, the more I discovered my own light, because she always encouraged me to give the best of myself. She had never read any books on magic or esoterics. She said they were things of the

Devil, and that salvation was only possible through Jesus—end of story. Sometimes, though, she said things that didn't seem entirely in keeping with the teachings of the Church.

"Christ surrounded himself with beggars, prostitutes, tax collectors, and fishermen. I think what he meant by this was that the divine spark is in every soul and is never extinguished. When I sit still, or when I'm feeling very agitated, I feel as if I'm vibrating along with the whole Universe. And I know things then that I don't know, as if God is guiding my steps. There are moments when I feel that everything is being revealed to me."

Then she would correct herself:

"But that's wrong."

Athena always lived between two worlds: what she felt was true and what she had been taught by her faith.

One day, after almost a semester of equations, calculations, and structural studies, she announced that she was going to leave university.

"But you've never said anything to me about it!" I said.

"I was even afraid of talking about it to myself, but this morning I went to see my hairdresser. She worked day and night so that her daughter could finish her sociology degree. The daughter finally graduated and, after knocking on many doors, found work as a secretary at a cement works. Yet even today, my hairdresser said very proudly: 'My daughter's got a degree.' Most of my parents' friends and most of my parents' friends' children also have degrees. This doesn't mean that they've managed to find the kind of work they wanted. Not at all; they went to university because someone, at a time when universities seemed important, said that in order to rise in the world, you had to have a degree. And thus the world was deprived of some excellent gardeners, bakers, antique dealers, sculptors, and writers."

I asked her to give it some more thought before taking such a radical step, but she quoted these lines by Robert Frost:

Two roads diverged in a wood, and I—
I took the one less traveled by,
And that has made all the difference.

The following day, she didn't turn up for class. At our following meeting, I asked what she was going to do.

"I'm going to get married and have a baby."

This wasn't an ultimatum. I was twenty, she was nineteen, and I thought it was still too early to take on such a commitment.

But Athena was quite serious. And I needed to choose between losing the one thing that really filled my thoughts—my love for that woman—and losing my freedom and all the choices that the future promised me.

To be honest, the decision was easy.

FATHER GIANCARLO FONTANA, SEVENTY-TWO

Of course I was surprised when the couple, both of them much too young, came to the church to arrange the wedding ceremony. I hardly knew Lukás Jessen-Petersen, but that same day, I learned that his family—obscure aristocrats from Denmark—was totally opposed to the union. They weren't just against the marriage, they were against the Church as well.

According to his father—who based himself on frankly un-answerable scientific arguments—the Bible, on which the whole religion is based, wasn't really a book, but a collage of sixty-six different manuscripts whose authors' real names or identities re-main unknown; he said that almost a thousand years had elapsed between the writing of the first book and the last, longer than the time that has elapsed since Columbus discovered America. And no living being on the planet—from monkeys down to parrots—needs Ten Commandments in order to know how to behave. All that it takes for the world to remain in harmony is for each being to follow the laws of nature.

Naturally, I read the Bible and know a little of its history, but the human beings who wrote it were instruments of Divine Power, and Jesus forged a far stronger bond than the Ten Com-mandments: love. Birds and monkeys, or any of God's creatures, obey their instincts and merely do what they're programmed to do. In the case of the human being, things are more complicated because we know about love and its traps.

Oh dear, here I am making a sermon, when I should be tell-ing you about my meeting with Athena and Lukás. While I was talking to the young man—and I say talking, because we don't share the same faith, and I'm not, therefore, bound by the secret of the confessional—I learned that, as well as the household's general anticlericalism, there was a lot of resistance to Athena because she was a foreigner. I felt like quoting from the Bible, from a part that isn't a profession of faith, but a call to common sense: "Thou shalt not abhor an Edomite, for he is thy brother; thou shalt not abhor an Egyptian, because thou wast a stranger in his land."

I'm sorry, there I am quoting the Bible again, and I promise I'll try to control myself from now on. After talking to the young man, I spent at least two hours with Sherine, or Athena as she preferred to be called.

Athena had always intrigued me. Ever since she first started coming to the church, it seemed to me that she had one clear ambition: to become a saint. She told me—although her fiancé didn't know this—that shortly before civil war broke out in Beirut, she'd had an experience very similar to that of St. Thérèse of Lisieux: she had seen the streets running with blood. One could attribute this to some trauma in childhood or adolescence, but the fact is that, to a greater or lesser extent, all creative human beings have such experiences, which are known as "possession by the sacred." Suddenly, for a fraction of a second, we feel that our whole life is justified, our sins forgiven, and that love is still the strongest force, one that can transform us forever.

But at the same time we feel afraid. Surrendering completely to love, be it human or divine, means giving up everything, including our own well-being or our ability to make decisions. It means loving in the deepest sense of the word. The truth is that we don't want to be saved in the way God has chosen; we want to keep absolute control over our every step, to be fully conscious of our decisions, to be capable of choosing the object of our devotion.

It isn't like that with love—it arrives, moves in, and starts directing everything. Only very strong souls allow themselves to be swept along, and Athena was a strong soul. So strong that she spent hours in deep contemplation. She had a special gift for music; they say that she danced very well too, but since the church isn't really the appropriate place for that, she used to bring her guitar each morning and spend some time there singing to the Holy Virgin before going off to her classes.

I can still remember the first time I heard her. I'd just finished celebrating morning mass with the few parishioners prepared to get up that early on a winter's morning, when I realized that I'd forgotten to collect the money left in the offering box. When I went back in, I heard some music that made me see everything differently, as if the atmosphere had been touched by the hand of an angel. In one corner, in a kind of ecstasy, a young woman of about twenty sat playing her guitar and singing hymns of praise, with her eyes fixed on the statue of the Holy Virgin.

I went over to the offering box. She noticed my presence and stopped what she was doing, but I nodded to her, encouraging her to go on. Then I sat down in one of the pews, closed my eyes, and listened.

At that moment, a sense of paradise, of "possession by the sacred," seemed to descend from the heavens. As if she understood what was going on in my heart, the young woman began to intersperse music with silence. Each time she stopped playing, I would say a prayer. Then the music would start up again.

And I was conscious that I was experiencing something unforgettable, one of those magical moments which we only understand when it has passed. I was entirely in the present, with no past, no future, absorbed in experiencing the morning, the music, the sweetness, and the unexpected prayer. I entered a state of worship and ecstasy and gratitude for being in the world, glad that I'd followed my vocation despite my family's opposition. In the simplicity of that small chapel, in the voice of that young woman, in the morning light flooding everything, I understood once again that the grandeur of God reveals itself through simple things.

After many tears on my part and after what seemed to me an eternity, the young woman stopped playing. I turned round and realized that she was one of my parishioners. After that, we became friends, and whenever we could, we shared in that worship through music.

However, the idea of marriage took me completely by surprise. Since we knew each other fairly well, I asked how she thought her husband's family would react.

"Badly, very badly."

As tactfully as I could, I asked if, for any reason, she was being forced into marriage.

"No, I'm still a virgin. I'm not pregnant."

I asked if she'd told her own family, and she said that she had, and that their reaction had been one of horror, accompanied by tears from her mother and threats from her father.

"When I come here to praise the Virgin with my music, I'm not bothered about what other people might think, I'm simply sharing my feelings with her. And that's how it's always been, ever since I was old enough to think for myself. I'm a vessel in

which the Divine Energy can make itself manifest. And that energy is asking me now to have a child, so that I can give it what
my birth mother never gave me: protection and security."

"No one is secure on this earth," I replied. She still had
a long future ahead of her; there was plenty of time for the
miracle of creation to occur. However, Athena was determined:

"St. Thérèse didn't rebel against the illness that afflicted her;
on the contrary, she saw it as a sign of God's glory. St. Thérèse
was only fifteen, much younger than me, when she decided to
enter a convent. She was forbidden to do so, but she insisted. She
decided to go and speak to the pope himself—can you imagine?
To speak to the pope! And she got what she wanted. That same
Glory is asking something far simpler and far more generous of
me—to become a mother. If I wait much longer, I won't be able
to be a companion to my child, the age difference will be too
great, and we won't share the same interests."

She wouldn't be alone in that, I said.

But Athena continued, as if she wasn't listening:

"I'm only happy when I think that God exists and is listening to me; but that isn't enough to go on living, when nothing
seems to make sense. I pretend a happiness I don't feel; I hide
my sadness so as not to worry those who love me and care about
me. Recently, I've even considered suicide. At night, before I
go to sleep, I have long conversations with myself, praying for
this idea to go away; it would be such an act of ingratitude, an
escape, a way of spreading tragedy and misery over the earth.
In the mornings, I come here to talk to St. Thérèse and to ask
her to free me from the demons I speak to at night. It's worked

so far, but I'm beginning to weaken. I know I have a mission, which I've long rejected, and now I must accept it. That mission is to be a mother. I must carry out that mission or go mad. If I don't feel life growing inside me, I'll never be able to accept life outside me."

LUKÁS JESSEN-PETERSEN, EX-HUSBAND

When Viorel was born, I had just turned twenty-two. I was no longer the student who had married a fellow student, but a man responsible for supporting his family, and with an enormous burden on my shoulders. My parents, who didn't even come to the wedding, made any financial help conditional on my leaving Athena and gaining custody of the child (or, rather, that's what my father said, because my mother used to phone me up, weeping, saying I must be mad, but saying too how much she'd like to hold her grandson in her arms). I hoped that, as they came to understand my love for Athena and my determination to stay with her, their resistance would gradually break down.

It didn't. And now I had to provide for my wife and child. I abandoned my studies at the Engineering Faculty. I got a phone call from my father, a mixture of stick and carrot: he said that if I continued as I was, I'd end up being disinherited, but that if I went back to university, he'd consider helping me, in his words, "provisionally." I refused. The romanticism of youth demands that we always take very radical stances. I could, I said, solve my problems alone.

During the time before Viorel was born, Athena began helping me to understand myself better. This didn't happen through
sex—our sexual relationship was, I must confess, very tenta-
tive—but through music.

As I later learned, music is as old as human beings. Our
ancestors, who traveled from cave to cave, couldn't carry many
things, but modern archaeology shows that, as well as the little
they might have with them in the way of food, there was always
a musical instrument in their baggage, usually a drum. Music
isn't just something that comforts or distracts us, it goes beyond
that—it's an ideology. You can judge people by the kind of music they listen to.

As I watched Athena dance during her pregnancy and listened to her play the guitar to calm the baby and make him feel
that he was loved, I began to allow her way of seeing the world
to affect my life too. When Viorel was born, the first thing we
did when we brought him home was to play Albinoni's Adagio.
When we quarreled, it was the force of music—although I can't
make any logical connection between the two things, except in
some kind of hippyish way—that helped us get through difficult times.

But all this romanticism didn't bring in the money. Since I
played no instrument and couldn't even offer my services providing background music in a bar, I finally got a job as a trainee
with a firm of architects, doing structural calculations. They
paid me a very low hourly rate, and so I would leave the house
very early each morning and come home late. I hardly saw my
son, who would be sleeping by then, and I was almost too

exhausted to talk or make love to my wife. Every night, I asked myself: When will we be able to improve our financial situation and live in the style we deserve? Although I largely agreed with Athena when she talked about the pointlessness of having a degree in engineering (and law and medicine, for example), there are certain basic technical facts that are essential if we're not to put people's lives at risk. And I'd been forced to interrupt my training in my chosen profession, which meant abandoning a dream that was very important to me.

The rows began. Athena complained that I didn't pay enough attention to the baby, that he needed a father, that if she'd simply wanted a child, she could have done that on her own, without causing me all these problems. More than once, I slammed out of the house, saying that she didn't understand me, and that I didn't understand either how I'd ever agreed at twenty to the "madness" of having a child, before we had even a minimum of financial security. Gradually, out of sheer exhaustion and irritation, we stopped making love.

I began to slide into depression, feeling that I'd been used and manipulated by the woman I loved. Athena noticed my increasingly strange state of mind, but instead of helping me, she focused her energies on Viorel and on music. Work became my escape. I would occasionally talk to my parents, and they would always say, as they had so many times before, that she'd had the baby in order to get me to marry her.

She also became increasingly religious. She insisted on having our son baptized with a name she herself had decided on—Viorel, a Romanian name. Apart from a few immigrants, I doubt that anyone else in England is called Viorel, but I thought it showed imagination on her part, and I realized too that she was making some strange connection with a past she'd never known—her days in the orphanage in Sibiu.

I tried to be adaptable, but I felt I was losing Athena because of the child. Our arguments became more frequent, and she threatened to leave because she feared that Viorel was picking up the "negative energy" from our quarrels. One night, when she made this threat again, I was the one who left, thinking that I'd go back as soon as I'd calmed down a bit.

I started wandering aimlessly round London, cursing the life I'd chosen, the child I'd agreed to have, and the wife who seemed to have no further interest in me. I went into the first bar I came to, near a Tube station, and downed four glasses of whiskey. When the bar closed at eleven, I searched out one of those shops that stay open all night, bought more whiskey, sat down on a bench in a square, and continued drinking. A group of youths approached me and asked to share the bottle with me. When I refused, they attacked me. The police arrived, and we were all carted off to the police station.

I was released after making a statement. I didn't bring any charges, saying that it had been nothing but a silly disagreement; after all, I didn't want to spend months appearing at various courts, as the victim of an attack. I was still so drunk that, just as I was about to leave, I stumbled and fell sprawling across an inspector's desk. The inspector was angry, but instead of arresting me on the spot for insulting a police officer, he threw me out into the street.

And there was one of my attackers, who thanked me for not taking the case any further. He pointed out that I was covered in mud and blood and suggested I get a change of clothes before returning home. Instead of going on my way, I asked him to do me a favor: to listen to me, because I desperately needed to talk to someone.

For an hour, he listened in silence to my woes. I wasn't really talking to him but to myself: a young man with his whole life before him, with a possibly brilliant career ahead of him—as well as a family with the necessary contacts to open many doors—but who now looked like a beggar—drunk, tired, depressed, and penniless. And all because of a woman who didn't even pay me any attention.

By the end of my story I had a clearer view of my situation: a life that I had chosen in the belief that love conquers all. And it isn't true. Sometimes love carries us into the abyss, taking with us—to make matters worse—the people we love. In my case, I was well on the way to destroying not only my life, but Athena's and Viorel's too.

At that moment, I said to myself once again that I was a man, not the boy who'd been born with a silver spoon in his mouth, and that I'd faced with dignity all the challenges that had been placed before me. Athena was already asleep, with the baby in her arms. I took a bath, went outside again to throw my dirty clothes in the bin, and lay down, feeling strangely sober.

The next day, I told Athena that I wanted a divorce. She asked me why.

"Because I love you. Because I love Viorel. And because all

I've done is to blame you both because I had to give up my
dream of becoming an engineer. If we'd waited a little, things
would have been different, but you were only thinking about
your plans and forgot to include me in them."

Athena said nothing, as if she had been expecting this, or as
if she had unconsciously been provoking such a response.

My heart was bleeding because I was hoping that she'd ask
me, please, to stay. But she seemed calm and resigned, concerned
only that the baby might hear our conversation. It was then that
I felt sure she had never loved me, and that I had merely been
the instrument for the realization of her mad dream to have a
baby at nineteen.

I told her that she could keep the house and the furniture,
but she wouldn't hear of it. She'd stay with her parents for a
while, then look for a job and rent her own apartment. She asked
if I could help out financially with Viorel, and I agreed at once.

I got up, gave her one last, long kiss, and insisted again that
she should stay in the house, but she repeated her resolve to go
to her parents' house as soon as she'd packed up all her things. I
stayed at a cheap hotel and waited every night for her to phone
me, asking me to come back and start a new life. I was even
prepared to continue the old life if necessary, because that separation had made me realize that there was nothing and no one
more important in the world than my wife and child.

A week later, I finally got that call. All she said, however, was
that she'd cleared out all her things and wouldn't be going back.
Two weeks after that, I learned that she'd rented a small attic
flat in Basset Road, where she had to carry the baby up three

flights of stairs every day. A few months later, we signed the final divorce papers.

My real family left forever. And the family I'd been born into received me with open arms.

After my separation from Athena and the great suffering that followed, I wondered if I hadn't made a bad, irresponsible decision, typical of people who've read lots of love stories in their adolescence and desperately want to repeat the tale of Romeo and Juliet. When the pain abated—and time is the only cure for that—I saw that life had allowed me to meet the one woman I would ever be capable of loving. Each second spent by her side had been worthwhile, and given the chance, despite all that had happened, I would do the same thing over again.

But time, as well as healing all wounds, taught me something strange too: that it's possible to love more than one person in a lifetime. I remarried. I'm very happy with my new wife, and I can't imagine living without her. This, however, doesn't mean that I have to renounce all my past experiences, as long as I'm careful not to compare my two lives. You can't measure love the way you can the length of a road or the height of a building.

Something very important remained from my relationship with Athena: a son, her great dream, of which she spoke so frankly before we decided to get married. I have another child by my second wife, and I'm better prepared for all the highs and lows of fatherhood than I was twelve years ago.

Once, when I went to fetch Viorel and bring him back to spend the weekend with me, I decided to ask her why she'd reacted so calmly when I told her I wanted a separation.

"Because all my life I've learned to suffer in silence," she replied.

And only then did she put her arms around me and cry out all the tears she would like to have shed on that day.

FATHER GIANCARLO FONTANA

I saw her when she arrived for Sunday mass, with the baby in her arms as usual. I knew that she and Lukás were having difficulties, but until that week, these had all seemed merely the sort of misunderstandings that all couples have, and since both of them were people who radiated goodness, I hoped that, sooner or later, they would resolve their differences.

It had been a whole year since she last visited the church in the morning to play her guitar and praise the Virgin. She devoted herself to looking after Viorel, whom I had the honor to baptize, although I must admit I know of no saint with that name. However, she still came to mass every Sunday, and we always talked afterward, when everyone else had left. She said I was her only friend. Together we had shared in divine worship; now, though, it was her earthly problems she needed to share with me.

She loved Lukás more than any man she had ever met; he was her son's father, the person she had chosen to spend her life with, someone who had given up everything and had courage enough to start a family. When the difficulties started, she tried to convince him that it was just a phase, that she had to devote herself to their son, but that she had no intention of turning Viorel into a spoiled brat. Soon she would let him face certain of life's challenges alone. After that, she would go back to being the wife and woman he'd known when they first met, possibly with even more intensity, because now she had a better understanding of the duties and responsibilities that came with the choice she'd made. Lukás still felt rejected; she tried desperately to divide herself between her husband and her child, but she was always obliged to choose, and when that happened, she never hesitated: she chose Viorel.

Drawing on my scant knowledge of psychology, I said that this wasn't the first time I'd heard such a story, and that in such situations men do tend to feel rejected, but that it soon passes. I'd heard about similar problems in conversations with my other parishioners. During one of our talks, Athena acknowledged that she had perhaps been rather precipitate; the romance of being a young mother had blinded her to the real challenges that arise after the birth of a child. But it was too late now for regrets.

She asked if I could talk to Lukás, who never came to church, perhaps because he didn't believe in God or perhaps because he preferred to spend his Sunday mornings with his son. I agreed to do so, as long as he came of his own accord. Just when Athena was about to ask him this favor, the major crisis occurred, and he left her and Viorel.

I advised her to be patient, but she was deeply hurt. She'd been abandoned once in childhood, and all the hatred she felt for her birth mother was automatically transferred to Lukás, although later, I understand, they became good friends again. For Athena, breaking family ties was possibly the gravest sin anyone could commit.

She continued attending church on Sundays, but always went straight back home afterward. She had no one now with whom to leave her son, who cried lustily throughout mass, disturbing everyone else's concentration. On one of the rare occasions when we could speak, she said that she was working for a bank, had rented an apartment, and that I needn't worry about her. Viorel's father (she never mentioned her husband's name now) was fulfilling his financial obligations.

Then came that fateful Sunday.

I learned what had happened during the week—one of the parishioners told me. I spent several nights praying for an angel to bring me inspiration and tell me whether I should keep my commitment to the Church or to flesh-and-blood men and women. When no angel appeared, I contacted my superior, and he said that the only reason the Church has survived is because it's always been rigid about dogma, and if it started making exceptions, we'd be back in the Middle Ages. I knew exactly what was going to happen. I thought of phoning Athena, but she hadn't given me her new number.

That morning, my hands were trembling as I lifted up the host and blessed the bread. I spoke the words that had come down to me through a thousand-year-old tradition, using the power passed on from generation to generation by the apostles. But then my thoughts turned to that young woman with her child in her arms, a kind of Virgin Mary, the miracle of motherhood and love made manifest in abandonment and solitude, and who had just joined the line as she always did, and was slowly approaching in order to take communion.

I think most of the congregation knew what was happening. And they were all watching me, waiting for my reaction. I saw myself surrounded by the just, by sinners, by Pharisees, by members of the Sanhedrin, by apostles and disciples and people with good intentions and bad.

Athena stood before me and repeated the usual gesture: she closed her eyes and opened her mouth to receive the body of Christ.

The body of Christ remained in my hands.

She opened her eyes, unable to understand what was going on.

"We'll talk later," I whispered.

But she didn't move.

"There are people behind you in line. We'll talk later."

"What's going on?" she asked, and everyone in the line could hear her question.

"We'll talk later."

"Why won't you give me communion? Can't you see, you're humiliating me in front of everyone? Haven't I been through enough already?"

"Athena, the Church forbids divorced people from receiving the sacrament. You signed your divorce papers this week. We'll talk later," I said again.

When she still didn't move, I beckoned to the person behind her to come forward. I continued giving communion until the last parishioner had received it. And it was then, just before I turned to the altar, that I heard that voice.

It was no longer the voice of the girl who sang her worship of the Virgin Mary, who talked about her plans, who was so moved when she shared with me what she'd learned about the lives of the saints, and who almost wept when she spoke to me about her marital problems. It was the voice of a wounded, humiliated animal, its heart full of loathing.

"A curse on this place!" said the voice. "A curse on all those who never listened to the words of Christ and who have transformed his message into a stone building. For Christ said: 'Come unto me all ye that labor and are heavy laden, and I will give you rest.' Well, I'm heavy laden, and they won't let me come to him. Today I've learned that the Church has changed those words to read: 'Come unto me all ye who follow our rules, and let the heavy laden go hang!'"

I heard one of the women in the front row of pews telling her to be quiet. But I wanted to hear, I needed to hear. I turned to her, my head bowed—it was all I could do.

"I swear that I will never set foot in a church ever again. Once more, I've been abandoned by a family, and this time it has nothing to do with financial difficulties or with the immaturity of those who marry too young. A curse upon all those who slam the door in the face of a mother and her child! You're just like those people who refused to take in the Holy Family, like those who denied Christ when he most needed a friend!"

With that, she turned and left in tears, her baby in her arms.

I finished the service, gave the final blessing, and went straight to the sacristy—that Sunday, there would be no mingling with the faithful, no pointless conversations. That Sunday, I was faced by a philosophical dilemma: I had chosen to respect the institution rather than the words on which that institution was based.

I'm getting old now, and God could take me at any moment. I've remained faithful to my religion, and I believe that for all its errors, it really is trying to put things right. This will take decades, possibly centuries, but one day, all that will matter is love and Christ's words: "Come unto me all ye that labor and are heavy laden, and I will give you rest." I've devoted my entire life to the priesthood and I don't regret my decision for one second. However, there are times, like that Sunday, when, although I didn't doubt my faith, I did doubt men.

I know now what happened to Athena, and I wonder: Did it all start there, or was it already in her soul? I think of the many Athenas and Lukáses in the world who are divorced and because of that can no longer receive the sacrament of the Eucharist; all they can do is contemplate the suffering, crucified Christ and listen to his words, words that are not always in accord with the laws of the Vatican. In a few cases, these people leave the church, but the majority continue coming to mass on Sundays, because that's what they're used to, even though they know that the miracle of the transmutation of the bread and the wine into the flesh and the blood of the Lord is forbidden to them.

I like to imagine that, when she left the church, Athena met Jesus. Weeping and confused, she would have thrown herself into his arms, asking him to explain why she was being excluded just because of a piece of paper she'd signed, something of no importance on the spiritual plane, and which was of interest only to registry offices and the tax man.

And looking at Athena, Jesus might have replied: "My child, I've been excluded too. It's a very long time since they've allowed me in there."

PAVEL PODBIELSKI, FIFTY-SEVEN,
OWNER OF THE APARTMENT

Athena and I had one thing in common: we were both refugees from a war and arrived in England when we were still children, although I fled Poland over fifty years ago. We both knew that despite the physical change, our traditions continue to exist in exile—communities join together again, language and religion remain alive, and in a place that will always be foreign to them, people tend to look after one another.

Traditions continue, but the desire to go back gradually disappears. That desire needs to stay alive in our hearts as a hope with which we like to delude ourselves, but it will never be put into practice; I'll never go back to live in Czestochowa, and Athena and her family will never return to Beirut.

It was this kind of solidarity that made me rent her the third floor of my house in Basset Road—normally, I'd prefer tenants without children. I'd made that mistake before, and two things had happened: I complained about the noise they made during the day, and they complained about the noise I made during the night. Both noises had their roots in sacred elements—crying and music—but they belonged to two completely different worlds, and it was hard for them to coexist.

I warned her, but she didn't really take it in and told me not to worry about her son. He spent all day at his grandmother's house anyway, and the apartment was conveniently close to her work at a local bank.

Despite my warnings, and despite holding out bravely at first, eight days later the doorbell rang. It was Athena, with her child in her arms.

"My son can't sleep. Couldn't you turn the music down at least for one night?"

Everyone in the room stared at her.

"What's going on?"

The child immediately stopped crying, as if he were as surprised as his mother to see that group of people, who had stopped in mid-dance.

I pressed the pause button on the cassette player and beckoned her in. Then I restarted the music so as not to interrupt the ritual. Athena sat down in one corner of the room, rocking her child in her arms and watching him drift off to sleep despite the noise of drums and brass. She stayed for the whole ceremony and left along with the other guests, but—as I thought she would—she rang my doorbell the next morning, before going to work.

"You don't have to explain what I saw—people dancing with their eyes closed—because I know what that means. I often do the same myself, and at the moment, those are the only times of peace and serenity in my life. Before I became a mother, I used to go to clubs with my husband and my friends, and I'd see people dancing with their eyes closed there too. Some were just trying to look cool, and others seemed to be genuinely moved by a greater, more powerful force. And ever since I've been old enough to think for myself, I've always used dance as a way of getting in touch with something stronger and more powerful than myself. Anyway, could you tell me what that music was?"

"What are you doing this Sunday?"

"Nothing special. I might go for a walk with Viorel in Regent's Park and get some fresh air. I'll have plenty of time later on for a social calendar of my own; for the moment, I've decided to follow my son's."

"I'll come with you, if you like."

On the two nights before our walk, Athena came to watch the ritual. Her son fell asleep after only a few minutes, and she merely watched what was going on around her without saying a word. She sat quite still on the sofa, but I was sure that her soul was dancing.

On Sunday afternoon, while we were walking in the park, I asked her to pay attention to everything she was seeing and hearing: the leaves moving in the breeze, the waves on the lake, the birds singing, the dogs barking, the shouts of children as they ran back and forth, as if obeying some strange logic incomprehensible to grown-ups.

"Everything moves, and everything moves to a rhythm. And everything that moves to a rhythm creates a sound. At this moment, the same thing is happening here and everywhere else in the world. Our ancestors noticed the same thing when they tried to escape from the cold into caves: things moved and made noise. The first human beings may have been frightened by this at first, but that fear was soon replaced by a sense of awe: they understood that this was the way in which some Superior Being was communicating with them. In the hope of reciprocating that communication, they started imitating the sounds and movements around them—and thus dance and music were born. A few days ago, you told me that dance puts you in touch with something stronger than yourself."

"Yes, when I dance, I'm a free woman, or, rather, a free spirit who can travel through the universe, contemplate the present, divine the future, and be transformed into pure energy. And that gives me enormous pleasure, a joy that always goes far beyond everything I've experienced or will experience in my lifetime. There was a time when I was determined to become a saint, praising God through music and movement, but that path is closed to me forever now."

"Which path do you mean?"

She made her son more comfortable in his stroller. I saw that she didn't want to answer that question and so I asked again: when mouths close, it's because there's something important to be said.

Without a flicker of emotion, as if she'd always had to endure in silence the things life imposed on her, she told me about what had happened at the church, when the priest—possibly her only friend—had refused her communion. She also told me about the curse she had uttered then, and that she had left the Catholic Church forever.

"A saint is someone who lives his or her life with dignity," I explained. "All we have to do is understand that we're all here for a reason and to commit ourselves to that. Then we can laugh at our sufferings, large and small, and walk fearlessly, aware that each step has meaning. We can let ourselves be guided by the light emanating from the Vertex."

"What do you mean by the Vertex? In mathematics, it's the topmost angle of a triangle."

"In life too it's the culminating point, the goal of all those who, like everyone else, make mistakes, but who, even in their darkest moments, never lose sight of the light emanating from their hearts. That's what we're trying to do in our group. The Vertex is hidden inside us, and we can reach it if we accept it and recognize its light."

I explained that I'd come up with the name "The Search for the Vertex" for the dance she'd watched on previous nights, performed by people of all ages (at the time there were ten of us, aged between nineteen and sixty-five). Athena asked where I'd found out about it.

I told her that, immediately after the end of World War II, some of my family had managed to escape from the Communist regime that was taking over Poland, and decided to move to England. They'd been advised to bring with them art objects and antiquarian books, which, they were told, were highly valued in this part of the world.

Paintings and sculptures were quickly sold, but the books remained, gathering dust. My mother was keen for me to read and speak Polish, and the books formed part of my education. One day, inside a nineteenth-century edition of Thomas Malthus, I found two pages of notes written by my grandfather, who had died in a concentration camp. I started reading, assuming it would be something to do with an inheritance or else a passionate letter intended for a secret lover, because it was said that he'd fallen in love with someone in Russia.

There was, in fact, some truth in this. The pages contained a description of his journey to Siberia during the Communist revolution. There, in the remote village of Diedov, he fell in love with an actress. [*Editor's note: It has not been possible to locate this village on the map. The name may have been deliberately changed, or the place itself may have disappeared after Stalin's forced migrations.*] According to my grandfather, the actress was part of a sect that believed they had found the remedy for all ills through a particular kind of dance, because the dance brought the dancer into contact with the light from the Vertex.

They feared that the tradition would disappear; the inhabitants of the village were soon to be transported to another place. Both the actress and her friends begged him to write down what they had learned. He did but clearly didn't think it was of much importance, because he left his notes inside a book, and there they remained until the day I found them.

Athena broke in:

"But dance isn't something you write about, you have to do it."

"Exactly. All the notes say is this: Dance to the point of exhaustion, as if you were a mountaineer climbing a hill, a sacred mountain. Dance until you are so out of breath that your organism is forced to obtain oxygen some other way, and it is that, in the end, that will cause you to lose your identity and your relationship with space and time. Dance only to the sound of percussion; repeat the process every day; know that, at a certain moment, your eyes will, quite naturally, close, and you will begin to see a light that comes from within, a light that answers your questions and develops your hidden powers."

"Have you developed some special power?"

Instead of replying, I suggested that she join our group, since her son seemed perfectly at ease in the room with the dancers, even when the noise of the cymbals and the other percussion instruments was at its loudest. The following day, at the usual time, she was there for the start of the session. I introduced her to my friends, explaining that she was my upstairs neighbor. No one said anything about their lives or asked her what she did. When the moment came, I turned on the music, and we began to dance.

She started dancing with the child in her arms, but he soon fell asleep, and she put him down on the sofa. Before I closed my eyes and went into a trance, I saw that she had understood exactly what I meant by the path of the Vertex.

Every day, except Sunday, she was there with the child. We would exchange a few words of welcome, then I would put on the music a friend of mine had brought from the Russian steppes, and we would all dance to the point of exhaustion. After a month of this, she asked me for a copy of the tape.

"I'd like to do the dancing in the morning, before I leave Viorel at my mum's house and go to work."

I tried to dissuade her.

"I don't know, I think a group that's connected by the same energy creates a kind of aura that helps everyone get into the trance state. Besides, doing the dancing before you go to work is just asking to get the sack, because you'll be exhausted all day."

Athena thought for a moment, then said:

"You're absolutely right when you talk about collective energy. In your group, for example, there are four couples and your wife. All of them have found love. That's why they can share such a positive vibration with me. But I'm on my own, or, rather, I'm with my son, but he can't yet manifest his love in a way we can understand. So I'd prefer to accept my loneliness. If I try to run away from it now, I'll never find a partner again. If I accept it, rather than fight against it, things might change. I've noticed that loneliness gets stronger when we try to face it down but gets weaker when we simply ignore it."

"Did you join our group in search of love?"

"That would be a perfectly good reason, I think, but the answer is no. I came in search of a meaning for my life, because, at present, its only meaning is my son, Viorel, and I'm afraid I might end up destroying him, either by being overprotective or by projecting onto him the dreams I've never managed to realize. Then one night, while I was dancing, I felt that I'd been cured. If we were talking about some physical ailment, we'd probably call it a miracle, but it was a spiritual malaise that was making me unhappy, and suddenly it vanished."

I knew what she meant.

"No one taught me to dance to the sound of that music," Athena went on, "but I have a feeling I know what I'm doing."

"It's not something you have to learn. Remember our walk in the park and what we saw there: nature creating its own rhythms and adapting itself to each moment."

"No one taught me how to love either, but I loved God, I loved my husband, I love my son and my family. And yet still there's something missing. Although I get tired when I'm dancing, when I stop, I seem to be in a state of grace, of profound ecstasy. I want that ecstasy to last throughout the day and for it to help me find what I lack: the love of a man. I can see the heart of that man while I'm dancing, but not his face. I sense that he's close by, which is why I need to remain alert. I need to dance in the morning so that I can spend the rest of the day paying attention to everything that's going on around me."

"Do you know what the word *ecstasy* means? It comes from the Greek and means 'to stand outside yourself.' Spending the whole day outside yourself is asking too much of body and soul."

"I'd like to try anyway."

I saw that there was no point arguing and so I made her a copy of the tape. And from then on, I woke every morning to the sound of music and dancing upstairs, and I wondered how she could face her work at the bank after almost an hour of being in a trance. When we bumped into each other in the corridor, I suggested she come in for a coffee, and she told me that she'd made more copies of the tape and that many of her colleagues at work were also now looking for the Vertex.

"Did I do wrong? Was it a secret?"

Of course it wasn't. On the contrary, she was helping me preserve a tradition that was almost lost. According to my grandfather's notes, one of the women said that a monk who visited the region had once told them that each of us contains our ancestors and all the generations to come. When we free ourselves, we are freeing all humanity.

"So all the men and women in that village in Siberia must be here now and very happy too. Their work is being reborn in this world, thanks to your grandfather. There's one thing I'd like to ask you: What made you decide to dance after you read those notes? If you'd read something about sports instead, would you have decided to become a footballer?"

This was a question no one had ever asked me.

"Because, at the time, I was ill. I was suffering from a rare form of arthritis, and the doctors told me that I should prepare myself for life in a wheelchair by the age of thirty-five. I saw that I didn't have much time ahead of me and so I decided to devote myself to something I wouldn't be able to do later on. My grandfather had written on one of those small sheets of paper that the inhabitants of Diedov believed in the curative powers of trances."

"And it seems they were right."

I didn't say anything, but I wasn't so sure. Perhaps the doctors were wrong. Perhaps the fact of being from an immigrant family, unable to allow myself the luxury of being ill, acted with such force upon my unconscious mind that it provoked a natural reaction in my body. Or perhaps it really was a miracle, although that went totally against what my Catholic faith preaches: dance is not a cure.

I remember that, as an adolescent, I had no idea what the right music would sound like, and so I used to put on a black hood and imagine that everything around me had ceased to exist: my spirit would travel to Diedov, to be with those men and women, with my grandfather and his beloved actress. In the silence of my bedroom, I would ask them to teach me to dance, to go beyond my limits, because soon I would be paralyzed forever. The more my body moved, the more brightly the light in my heart shone, and the more I learned—perhaps on my own, perhaps from the ghosts of the past. I even imagined the music they must have listened to during their rituals, and when a friend visited Siberia many years later, I asked him to bring me back some records. To my surprise, one of them was very similar to the music I had imagined would accompany the dancing in Diedov.

It was best to say nothing of all this to Athena; she was easily influenced and, I thought, slightly unstable.

"Perhaps what you're doing is right," was all I said.

We talked again, shortly before her trip to the Middle East. She seemed contented, as if she'd found everything she wanted: love.

"My colleagues at work have formed a group, and they call themselves the Pilgrims of the Vertex. And all thanks to your grandfather."

"All thanks to you, you mean, because you felt the need to share the dance with others. I know you're leaving, but I'd like to thank you for giving another dimension to what I've been doing all these years in trying to spread the light to a few interested people, but always very tentatively, always afraid people might find the whole story ridiculous."

"Do you know what I've learned? That although ecstasy is the ability to stand outside yourself, dance is a way of rising up into space, of discovering new dimensions while still remaining in touch with your body. When you dance, the spiritual world and the real world manage to coexist quite happily. I think classical ballet dancers dance on pointe because they're simultaneously touching the earth and reaching up to the skies."

As far as I can remember, those were her last words to me. During any dance to which we surrender with joy, the brain loses its controlling power, and the heart takes up the reins of the body. Only at that moment does the Vertex appear. As long as we believe in it, of course.

PETER SHERNEY, FORTY-SEVEN, MANAGER
OF A BRANCH OF [NAME OF BANK OMITTED]
IN HOLLAND PARK, LONDON

I only took on Athena because her family was one of our most important customers; after all, the world revolves around mutual interests. She seemed a very restless person, and so I gave her a dull clerical post, hoping that she would soon resign. That way, I could tell her father that I'd done my best to help her but without success.

My experience as a manager had taught me to recognize

people's states of mind, even if they said nothing. In a management course I attended, we learned that if you wanted to get rid of someone, you should do everything you can to provoke them into rudeness, so that you would then have a perfectly good reason to dismiss them.

I did everything I could to achieve my objective with Athena. She didn't depend on her salary to live and would soon learn how pointless it was: having to get up early, drop her son off at her mother's house, slave away all day at a repetitive job, pick her son up again, go to the supermarket, spend time with her son before putting him to bed, and then, the next day, spend another three hours on public transport, and all for no reason, when there were so many other more interesting ways of filling her days. She grew increasingly irritable, and I felt proud of my strategy. I would get what I wanted. She started complaining about the apartment where she lived, saying that her landlord kept her awake all night, playing really loud music.

Then, suddenly, something changed. At first it was only Athena, but soon it was the whole branch.

How did I notice this change? Well, a group of workers is like a kind of orchestra; a good manager is the conductor, and he knows who is out of tune, who is playing with real commitment, and who is simply following the crowd. Athena seemed to be playing her instrument without the least enthusiasm; she seemed distant, never sharing the joys and sadnesses of her personal life with her colleagues, letting it be known that, when she left work, her free time was entirely taken up with looking after her son. Then, suddenly, she became more relaxed, more communicative, telling anyone who would listen that she had discovered the secret of rejuvenation.

Rejuvenation, of course, is a magic word. Coming from someone who was barely twenty-one, it sounded pretty ridiculous, and yet other members of the staff believed her and started to ask her for the secret formula.

Her efficiency increased, even though her workload remained unchanged. Her colleagues, who up until then had never exchanged more than a "good morning" or a "good night" with her, started asking her out to lunch. When they came back, they seemed very pleased, and the department's productivity made a giant leap.

I know that people who are in love do affect the environment in which they live, and so I immediately assumed that Athena must have met someone very important in her life.

I asked, and she agreed, adding that she'd never before gone out with a customer, but that, in this case, she'd been unable to refuse. Normally this would have been grounds for immediate dismissal—the bank's rules are clear: personal contact with customers is forbidden. But, by then, I was aware that her behavior had infected almost everyone else. Some of her colleagues started getting together with her after work, and a few of them had, I believe, been to her house.

I had a very dangerous situation on my hands. The young trainee with no previous work experience, who up until then had seemed to veer between shyness and aggression, had become a kind of natural leader among my workers. If I fired her, they would think it was out of jealousy, and I'd lose their respect. If I kept her on, I ran the risk, within a matter of months, of losing control of the group.

I decided to wait a little, but meanwhile, there was a definite increase in the "energy" at the bank (I hate that word *energy*, because it doesn't really mean anything, unless you're talking about electricity). Anyway, our customers seemed much happier and were starting to recommend other people to come to us. The employees seemed happy too, and even though their workload had doubled, I didn't need to take on any more staff because they were all coping fine.

One day, I received a letter from my superiors. They wanted me to go to Barcelona for a group meeting, so that I could explain my management techniques to them. According to them, I had increased profit without increasing expenditure, and that, of course, is the only thing that interests executives everywhere.

But what techniques?

At least I knew where it had all started, and so I summoned Athena to my office. I complimented her on her excellent productivity levels, and she thanked me with a smile.

I proceeded cautiously, not wishing to be misinterpreted.

"And how's your boyfriend? I've always found that anyone who is loved has more love to give. What does he do?"

"He works for Scotland Yard." [*Editor's note: Police investigation department linked to London's Metropolitan Police.*]

I preferred not to ask any further questions, but I needed to keep the conversation going and I didn't have much time.

"I've noticed a great change in you and—"

"Have you noticed a change in the bank too?"

How to respond to a question like that? On the one hand, I would be giving her more power than was advisable, but on the other, if I wasn't straight with her, I would never get the answers I needed.

"Yes, I've noticed a big change, and I'm thinking of promoting you."

"I need to travel. I'd like to get out of London and discover new horizons."

Travel? Just when everything was going so well in my branch, she wanted to leave? Although, when I thought about it, wasn't that precisely the way out I needed and wanted?

"I can help the bank if you give me more responsibility," she went on.

Yes, she was giving me an excellent opportunity. Why hadn't I thought of that before? "Travel" meant getting rid of her and resuming my leadership of the group without having to deal with the fallout from a dismissal or a rebellion. But I needed to ponder the matter, because rather than her helping the bank, I needed her to help me. Now that my superiors had noticed an increase in productivity, I knew that I would have to keep it up or risk losing prestige and end up worse off than before. Sometimes I understand why most of my colleagues don't do very much in order to improve: if they don't succeed, they're called incompetent. If they do succeed, they have to keep improving all the time, a situation guaranteed to bring on an early heart attack.

I took the next step very cautiously: it's not a good idea to frighten the person in possession of a secret before she's revealed that secret to us; it's best to pretend to grant her request.

"I'll bring your request to the attention of my superiors. In fact, I'm having a meeting with them in Barcelona, which is why I called you in. Would it be true to say that our performance has improved since, shall we say, the other employees began getting on better with you?"

"Or shall we say, began getting on better with themselves."

"Yes, but encouraged by you—or am I wrong?"

"You know perfectly well that you're not."

"Have you been reading some book on management I don't know about?"

"I don't read that kind of book, but I would like a promise from you that you really will consider my request."

I thought of her boyfriend at Scotland Yard. If I made a promise and failed to keep it, would I be the object of some reprisal? Could he have taught her some cutting-edge technology that enables one to achieve impossible results?

"I'll tell you everything, even if you don't keep your promise, but I can't guarantee that you'll get the same results if you don't practice what I teach."

"You mean the 'rejuvenation technique'?"

"Exactly."

"Wouldn't it be enough just to know the theory?"

"Possibly. The person who taught me learned about it from a few sheets of paper."

I was glad she wasn't forcing me to make decisions that went beyond my capabilities or my principles. But I must confess that I had a personal interest in that whole story, because I too dreamed of finding some way of "recycling" my potential. I promised that I'd do what I could, and Athena began to describe the long, esoteric dance she performed in search of the so-called Vertex (or was it Axis, I can't quite remember now). As we talked, I tried to set down her mad thoughts in objective terms. An hour proved not to be enough, and so I asked her to come back the following day, and together we would prepare the report to be presented to the bank's board of directors. At one point in our conversation, she said with a smile: "Don't worry about describing the technique in the same terms we've been using here. I reckon even a bank's board of directors are people like us, made of flesh and blood, and interested in unconventional methods."

Athena was completely wrong. In England, tradition always speaks louder than innovation. But why not take a risk, as long as it didn't endanger my job? The whole thing seemed absurd to me, but I had to summarize it and put it in a way that everyone could understand. That was all.

Before I presented my "paper" in Barcelona, I spent the whole morning repeating to myself: "My" process is producing results, and that's all that matters. I read a few books on the subject and learned that in order to present a new idea with the maximum impact, you should structure your talk in an equally provocative way, and so the first thing I said to the executives gathered in that luxury hotel were these words of St. Paul's: "God hid the most important things from the wise because they cannot understand what is simple." [*Editor's note: It is impossible to know here whether he is referring to a verse from Matthew 11:25: "I thank thee, O Father, thou hast hid these things from the wise and prudent, and hast revealed them unto babes," or from St. Paul (1 Corinthians 1:27): "But God hath chosen the foolish*

*things of the world to confound the wise, and God hath chosen the weak things
of the world to confound the things which are mighty."*]

When I said this, the whole audience, who had spent the last
two days analyzing graphs and statistics, fell silent. It occurred
to me that I had almost certainly lost my job, but I carried on.
First, because I had researched the subject and was sure of what
I was saying and deserved credit for this. Second, because although, at certain points, I was obliged to omit any mention
of Athena's enormous influence on the whole process, I was,
nevertheless, not lying.

"I have learned that, in order to motivate employees nowadays, you need more than just the training provided by our own
excellent training centers. Each of us contains something within
us which is unknown, but which, when it surfaces, is capable of
producing miracles.

"We all work for some reason: to feed our children, to earn
money to support ourselves, to justify our life, to get a little
bit of power. However, there are always tedious stages in that
process, and the secret lies in transforming those stages into an
encounter with ourselves or with something higher.

"For example, the search for beauty isn't always associated
with anything practical and yet we still search for it as if it were
the most important thing in the world. Birds learn to sing, but
not because it will help them find food, avoid predators, or drive
away parasites. Birds sing, according to Darwin, because that is
the only way they have of attracting a partner and perpetuating
the species."

I was interrupted by an executive from Geneva, who called

for a more objective presentation. However, to my delight, the director-general asked me to go on.

"Again according to Darwin, who wrote a book that changed the course of all humanity [*Editor's note:* The Origin of Species, *1859, in which he first posited that human beings evolved from a type of ape*], those who manage to arouse passions are repeating something that has been going on since the days we lived in caves, where rituals for courting a partner were fundamental for the survival and evolution of the human species. Now, what difference is there between the evolution of the human race and that of the branch of a bank? None. Both obey the same laws—only the fittest survive and evolve."

At this point, I was obliged to admit that I'd developed this idea thanks to the spontaneous collaboration of one of my employees, Sherine Khalil.

"Sherine, who likes to be known as Athena, brought into the workplace a new kind of emotion—passion. Yes, passion, something we never normally consider when discussing loans or spreadsheets. My employees started using music as a stimulus for dealing more efficiently with their clients."

Another executive interrupted, saying that this was an old idea: supermarkets did the same thing, using piped-in music to encourage their customers to buy more.

"I'm not saying that we used music in the workplace. People simply started living differently because Sherine, or Athena if you prefer, taught them to dance *before* facing their daily tasks. I don't know precisely what mechanism this awakens in people; as a manager, I'm only responsible for the results, not for the process. I myself didn't participate in the dancing, but I understand that, through dance, they all felt more connected with what they were doing.

"We were born and brought up with the maxim that 'time is money.' We know exactly what money is, but what does the word *time* mean? The day is made up of twenty-four hours and an infinite number of moments. We need to be aware of each of those moments and to make the most of them regardless of whether we're busy doing something or merely contemplating life. If we slow down, everything lasts much longer. Of course, that means that washing the dishes might last longer, as might totting up the debits and credits on a balance sheet or checking promissory notes, but why not use that time to think about pleasant things and to feel glad simply to be alive?"

The director-general was looking at me in surprise. I was sure he wanted me to explain in detail what I'd learned, but some of those present were beginning to grow restless.

"I understand exactly what you mean," he said. "I understand too that your employees worked with more enthusiasm because they were able to enjoy one moment in the day when they came into full contact with themselves. And I'd like to compliment you on being flexible enough to allow such unorthodox practices, which are, it must be said, producing excellent results. However, speaking of time, this is a conference, and you have only five minutes to conclude your presentation. Could you possibly try to list the main points which would allow us to apply these principles in other branches?"

He was right. This was fine for the employees, but it could

prove fatal to my career, and so I decided to summarize the points Sherine and I had written together.

"Basing ourselves on personal observations, Sherine Khalil and I developed certain points, which I would be delighted to discuss with anyone who's interested. Here are the main ones:

"1. We all have an unknown ability, which will probably remain unknown forever. And yet that ability can become our ally. Since it's impossible to measure that ability or give it an economic value, it's never taken seriously, but I'm speaking here to other human beings and I'm sure you understand what I mean, at least in theory.

"2. At my branch, employees have learned how to tap into that ability through a dance based on a rhythm that comes, I believe, from the desert regions of Asia. However, its place of origin is irrelevant, as long as people can express through their bodies what their souls are trying to say. I realize that the word *soul* might be misunderstood, so I suggest we use the word *intuition* instead. And if that word is equally hard to swallow, then let's use the term *primary emotions*, which sounds more scientific, although, in fact, it has rather less meaning than the other two words.

"3. Before going to work, instead of encouraging my employees to do keep-fit or aerobics, I get them to dance for at least an hour. This stimulates the body and the mind; they start the day demanding a certain degree

of creativity from themselves and channel that accu-
mulated energy into their work at the bank.

"4. Customers and employees live in the same world: reality is nothing but a series of electrical stimuli to the
brain. What we think we 'see' is a pulse of energy to a
completely dark part of the brain. However, if we get
on the same wavelength as other people, we can try
to change that reality. In some way that I don't understand joy is infectious, as is enthusiasm and love.
Or indeed sadness, depression, or hatred—things
that can be picked up 'intuitively' by customers and
other employees. In order to improve performance,
we have to create mechanisms that keep these positive stimuli alive."

"How very esoteric," commented a woman who managed
investment funds at a branch in Canada.

I slightly lost confidence. I had failed to convince anyone.
Nevertheless, I pretended to ignore her remark and, using all my
creativity, sought to give my paper a practical conclusion:

"The bank should earmark a fund to do research into how
this infectious state of mind works, and thus noticeably increase
our profits."

This seemed a reasonably satisfactory ending, and so I
preferred not to use the two minutes remaining to me. When
I finished the seminar, at the end of an exhausting day, the
director-general asked me to have supper with him, and he did
so in front of all our other colleagues, as if he were trying to

show that he supported everything I'd said. I had never before had an opportunity to dine with the director-general, and so I tried to make the most of it. I started talking about performance, about spreadsheets, difficulties on the stock exchange, and possible new markets. He interrupted me; he was more interested in knowing more of what I'd learned from Athena.

In the end, to my surprise, he turned the conversation to more personal matters.

"I understood what you meant when, during your paper, you talked about time. At New Year, when I was still enjoying the holiday season, I decided to go and sit in the garden for a while. I picked up the newspaper from the mailbox, but it contained nothing of any importance, only the things that journalists had decided we should know, feel involved in, and have an opinion about.

"I thought of phoning someone at work, but that would be ridiculous, since they would all be with their families. I had lunch with my wife, children, and grandchildren, took a nap, and when I woke up, I made a few notes, then realized that it was still only two o'clock in the afternoon. I had another three days of not working, and however much I love being with my family, I started to feel useless.

"The following day, taking advantage of this free time, I went to have my stomach checked out, and, fortunately, the tests revealed nothing seriously wrong. I went to the dentist, who said there was nothing wrong with my teeth either. I again had lunch with my wife, children, and grandchildren, took another nap, again woke up at two in the afternoon, and realized that I had absolutely nothing on which to focus my attention.

"I felt uneasy: Shouldn't I be doing something? Well, if I wanted to invent work, that wouldn't take much effort. We all have projects to develop, lightbulbs to change, leaves to sweep, books to put away, computer files to organize, etc. But how about just facing up to the void? It was then that I remembered something that seemed to me of great importance: I needed to walk to the letter-box—which is less than a mile from my house in the country—and post one of the Christmas cards lying forgotten on my desk.

"And I was surprised: Why did I need to send that card today? Was it really so hard just to stay where I was, doing nothing?

"A series of thoughts crossed my mind: friends who worry about things that haven't yet happened; acquaintances who manage to fill every minute of their lives with tasks that seem to me absurd; senseless conversations; long telephone calls in which nothing of any importance is ever said. I've seen my directors inventing work in order to justify their jobs; employees who feel afraid because they've been given nothing important to do that day, which might mean that they're no longer useful. My wife, who torments herself because our son has got divorced, my son who torments himself because our grandson, his son, got bad marks at school, our grandson, who is terrified because he's making his parents sad—even though we all know that marks aren't that important.

"I had a long, hard struggle with myself not to get up from my desk. Gradually, though, the anxiety gave way to contemplation, and I started listening to my soul—or intuition or primary emotions, or whatever you choose to believe in. Whatever you call it, that part of me had been longing to speak to me, but I had always been too busy.

"In that case, it wasn't a dance, but the complete absence of noise and movement, the silence, that brought me into contact with myself. And, believe it or not, I learned a great deal about the problems bothering me, even though all those problems had dissolved completely while I was sitting there. I didn't see God, but I had a clearer understanding of what decisions to make."

Before paying the bill, he suggested that I send the employee in question to Dubai, where the bank was opening a new branch, and where the risks were considerable. As a good manager, he knew that I had learned all I needed to learn, and now it was merely a question of providing continuity. My employee could make a useful contribution somewhere else. He didn't know this, but he was helping me to keep the promise I'd made.

When I returned to London, I immediately told Athena about this invitation, and she accepted at once. She told me that she spoke fluent Arabic (I knew this already because of her father), although, since we would mainly be doing deals with foreigners, not Arabs, this would not be essential. I thanked her for her help, but she showed no curiosity about my talk at the conference and merely asked when she should pack her bags.

I still don't know whether the story of the boyfriend in Scotland Yard was a fantasy or not. If it were true, I think Athena's murderer would already have been arrested, because I don't believe anything the newspapers wrote about the crime. I can understand financial engineering, I can even allow myself the

luxury of saying that dancing helps my employees to work better, but I will never comprehend how it is that the best police
force in the world catches some murderers but not others. Not
that it makes much difference now.

Nabil Alaihi, age unknown, Bedouin

It made me very happy to know that Athena had kept a photo
of me in a place of honor in her apartment, but I don't really
think what I taught her had any real use. She came here to the
desert, leading a three-year-old boy by the hand. She opened her
bag, took out a cassette tape player, and sat down outside my
tent. I know that people from the city usually give my name to
foreigners who want to experience some local cooking, and so I
told her at once that it was too early for supper.

"I came for another reason," she said. "Your nephew Hamid
is a client at the bank where I work and he told me that you're
a wise man."

"Hamid is a rather foolish youth who may well say that I'm a
wise man, but who never follows my advice. Mohammed, the
Prophet, may the blessings of God be upon him, *he* was a wise man."

I pointed to her car.

"You shouldn't drive alone in a place you don't know, and
you shouldn't come here without a guide."

Instead of replying, she turned on the tape player. Then all I
could see was this young woman dancing on the dunes and her

son watching her in joyous amazement; and the sound seemed to fill the whole desert. When she finished, she asked if I had enjoyed it.

I said that I had. There is a sect in our religion that uses dance as a way of getting closer to Allah—blessed be his name. [*Editor's note: The sect in question is Sufism.*]

"Well," said the woman, who introduced herself as Athena, "ever since I was a child, I've felt that I should grow closer to God, but life always took me farther away from him. Music is one way I've discovered of getting close, but it isn't enough. Whenever I dance, I see a light, and that light is now asking me to go further. But I can't continue learning on my own; I need someone to teach me."

"Anything will do," I told her. "Because Allah, the merciful, is always near. Lead a decent life, and that will be enough."

But the woman appeared unconvinced. I said that I was busy, that I needed to prepare supper for the few tourists who might appear. She told me that she'd wait for as long as was necessary.

"And the child?"

"Don't worry about him."

While I was making my usual preparations, I observed the woman and her son. They could have been the same age; they ran about the desert, laughed, threw sand at each other, and rolled down the dunes. The guide arrived with three German tourists, who ate and asked for beer, and I had to explain that my religion forbade me to drink or to serve alcoholic drinks. I invited the woman and her son to join us for supper, and in that unexpected female presence, one of the Germans became quite animated. He said that he was thinking of buying some land, that he had a large fortune saved up and believed in the future of the region.

"Great," she replied. "I believe in the region too."

"It would be good to have supper somewhere, so that we could talk about the possibility of—"

"No," she said, holding a card out to him, "but if you like, you can get in touch with my bank."

When the tourists left, we sat down outside the tent. The child soon fell asleep on her lap. I fetched blankets for us all, and we sat looking up at the starry sky. Finally, she broke the silence.

"Why did Hamid say that you were a wise man?"

"Perhaps so that I'll be more patient with him. There was a time when I tried to teach him my art, but Hamid seemed more interested in earning money. He's probably convinced by now that he's wiser than I am: he has an apartment and a boat, while here I am in the middle of the desert, making meals for the occasional tourist. He doesn't understand that I'm satisfied with what I do."

"He understands perfectly, and he always speaks of you with great respect. And what do you mean by your 'art'?"

"I watched you dancing today—well, I do the same thing, except that it's the letters, not my body, that dance."

She looked surprised.

"My way of approaching Allah—may his name be praised— has been through calligraphy, and the search for the perfect meaning of each word. A single letter requires us to distill in it all the energy it contains, as if we were carving out its meaning. When sacred texts are written, they contain the soul of the man who served as an instrument to spread them throughout the world. And that doesn't apply only to sacred texts, but to every mark we place on paper. Because the hand that draws each line reflects the soul of the person making that line."

"Would you teach me what you know?"

"First, I don't think anyone as full of energy as you would have the patience for this. Besides, it's not part of your world, where everything is printed without, if you'll allow me to say so, much thought being given to what is being published."

"I'd like to try."

And so, for more than six months, that woman—whom I'd judged to be too restless and exuberant to be able to sit still for a moment—came to visit me every Friday. Her son would go to one corner of the tent, take up paper and brushes, and he too would devote himself to revealing in his paintings whatever the heavens determined.

When I saw the immense effort it took her to keep still and to maintain the correct posture, I said: "Don't you think you'd be better off finding something else to do?" She replied: "No, I need this, I need to calm my soul, and I still haven't learned everything you can teach me. The light of the Vertex told me that I should continue." I never asked her what the Vertex was, nor was I interested.

The first lesson, and perhaps the most difficult, was: "Patience!"

Writing wasn't just the expression of a thought but also a way of reflecting on the meaning of each word. Together we be-

gan work on texts written by an Arab poet, because I do not feel
that the Koran is suitable for someone brought up in another
faith. I dictated each letter, and that way she could concentrate
on what she was doing, instead of immediately wanting to know
the meaning of each word or phrase or line.

"Once, someone told me that music had been created by
God, and that rapid movement was necessary for people to get
in touch with themselves," said Athena on one of those after-
noons we spent together. "For years, I felt that this was true,
and now I'm being forced to do the most difficult thing in the
world—slow down. Why is patience so important?"

"Because it makes us pay attention."

"But I can dance obeying only my soul, which forces me to
concentrate on something greater than myself, and brings me
into contact with God—if I can use that word. Dance has already helped me to change many things in my life, including my
work. Isn't the soul more important?"

"Of course it is, but if your soul could communicate with
your brain, you would be able to change even more things."

We continued our work together. I knew that, at some point,
I would have to tell her something that she might not be ready to
hear, and so I tried to make use of every minute to prepare her
spirit. I explained that before the word comes the thought. And
before the thought, there is the divine spark that placed it there.
Everything, absolutely everything on this earth makes sense, and
even the smallest things are worthy of our consideration.

"I've educated my body so that it can manifest every sensation in my soul," she said.

"Now you must educate only your fingers, so that they can manifest every sensation in your body. That will concentrate your body's strength."

"Are you a teacher?"

"What is a teacher? I'll tell you: it isn't someone who teaches something, but someone who inspires the student to give of her best in order to discover what she already knows."

I sensed that, despite her youth, Athena had already experienced this. Writing reveals the personality, and I could see that she was aware of being loved, not just by her son, but also by her family and possibly by a man. I saw too that she had mysterious gifts, but I tried never to let her know that I knew this, since these gifts could bring about not only an encounter with God, but also her perdition.

I taught her not only calligraphy techniques. I also tried to pass on to her the philosophy of the calligraphers.

"The brush with which you are making these lines is just an instrument. It has no consciousness, it follows the desires of the person holding it. And in that it is very like what we call 'life.' Many people in this world are merely playing a role, unaware that there is an Invisible Hand guiding them. At this moment, in your hands, in the brush tracing each letter, lie all the intentions of your soul. Try to understand the importance of this."

"I do understand, and I see that it's important to maintain a certain elegance. You tell me to sit in a particular position, to venerate the materials I'm going to use, and only to begin when I have done so."

Naturally, if she respected the brush that she used, she would realize that in order to learn to write she must cultivate serenity and elegance. And serenity comes from the heart.

"Elegance isn't a superficial thing, it's the way mankind has found to honor life and work. That's why, when you feel uncomfortable in that position, you mustn't think that it's false or artificial: it's real and true precisely because it's difficult. That position means that both the paper and the brush feel proud of the effort you're making. The paper ceases to be a flat, colorless surface and takes on the depth of the things placed on it. Elegance is the correct posture if the writing is to be perfect. It's the same with life: when all superfluous things have been discarded, we discover simplicity and concentration. The simpler and more sober the posture, the more beautiful it will be, even though, at first, it may seem uncomfortable."

Occasionally, she would talk about her work. She said she was enjoying what she was doing and that she had just received a job offer from a powerful emir. He had gone to the bank to see the manager, who was a friend of his (emirs never go to banks to withdraw money, they have staff who can do that for them), and while he was talking to Athena, he mentioned that he was looking for someone to take charge of selling land, and wondered if she would be interested.

Who would want to buy land in the middle of the desert or in a far-flung port? I decided to say nothing, and looking back, I'm glad I stayed silent.

Only once did she mention the man she loved, although whenever she was there when tourists arrived, one of the men would always start flirting with her. Normally Athena simply ignored them, but one day a man suggested that he knew her boyfriend. She turned pale and immediately shot a glance at her son, who, fortunately, wasn't listening to the conversation.

"How do you know him?"

"I'm joking," said the man. "I just wanted to find out if you were unattached."

She didn't say anything, but I understood from this exchange that the man in her life was not the father of her son.

One day, she arrived earlier than usual. She said that she'd left her job at the bank and started selling real estate, and would now have more free time. I explained that I couldn't start her class any earlier because I had various things to do.

"I can combine two things: movement and stillness; joy and concentration."

She went over to the car to fetch her cassette tape player, and from then on, Athena would dance in the desert before the start of our class while the little boy ran round her, laughing. When she sat down to practice calligraphy, her hand was steadier than usual.

"There are two kinds of letters," I explained. "The first is precise but lacks soul. In this case, although the calligrapher may have mastered the technique, he has focused solely on the craft, which is why it hasn't evolved, but become repetitive; he hasn't grown at all, and one day he'll give up the practice of writing, because he feels it is mere routine.

"The second kind is done with great technique but with soul as well. For that to happen, the intention of the writer must be in harmony with the word. In this case, the saddest verses cease to be clothed in tragedy and are transformed into simple facts encountered along the way."

"What do you do with your drawings?" asked the boy in perfect Arabic. He might not understand our conversation, but he was eager to share in his mother's work.

"I sell them."

"Can I sell my drawings?"

"You *should* sell your drawings. One day, you'll become rich that way and be able to help your mother."

He was pleased by my comment and went back to what he was doing, painting a colorful butterfly.

"And what shall I do with my texts?" asked Athena.

"You know the effort it took to sit in the correct position, to quiet your soul, keep your intentions clear, and respect each letter of each word. Meanwhile, keep practicing. After a great deal of practice, we no longer think about all the necessary movements we must make; they become part of our existence. Before reaching that stage, however, you must practice and repeat. And if that's not enough, you must practice and repeat some more.

"Look at a skilled blacksmith working steel. To the untrained eye, he's merely repeating the same hammer blows, but anyone trained in the art of calligraphy knows that each time the blacksmith lifts the hammer and brings it down, the intensity of the blow is different. The hand repeats the same gesture, but as it approaches the metal, it understands that it must touch it with more or less force. It's the same thing with repetition: it may seem the same, but it's always different. The moment will come when you no longer need to think about what you're doing. You become the letter, the ink, the paper, the word."

This moment arrived almost a year later. By then, Athena was already known in Dubai and recommended my tent as a place for her customers to dine, and through them I learned that her career was going very well: she was selling pieces of desert! One night, the emir in person arrived, preceded by a great retinue. I was terrified; I wasn't prepared for that, but he reassured me and thanked me for what I was doing for his employee.

"She's an excellent person and attributes her qualities to what she's learning from you. I'm thinking of giving her a share in the company. It might be a good idea to send my other sales staff to learn calligraphy, especially now that Athena is about to take a month's holiday."

"It wouldn't help," I replied. "Calligraphy is just one of the ways which Allah—blessed be his name—places before us. It teaches objectivity and patience, respect and elegance, but we can learn all that—"

"Through dance," said Athena, who was standing nearby.

"Or through selling land," I added.

When they had all left, and the little boy had lain down in one corner of the tent, his eyes heavy with sleep, I brought out the calligraphy materials and asked her to write something. In the middle of the word, I took the brush from her hand. It was time to say what had to be said. I suggested that we go for a little walk in the desert.

"You have learned what you needed to learn," I said. "Your calligraphy is getting more and more individual and spontaneous. It's no longer a mere repetition of beauty, but a personal, creative gesture. You have understood what all great painters understand: in order to forget the rules, you must know them and respect them.

"You no longer need the tools that helped you learn. You no longer need paper, ink, or brush, because the path is more important than whatever made you set off along it. Once you told me that the person who taught you to dance used to imagine the music playing in his head, and even so, he was able to repeat the necessary rhythms."

"He was."

"If all the words were joined together, they wouldn't make sense, or, at the very least, they'd be extremely hard to decipher. The spaces are crucial."

She nodded.

"And although you have mastered the words, you haven't yet mastered the blank spaces. When you're concentrating, your hand is perfect, but when it jumps from one word to the next, it gets lost."

"How do you know that?"

"Am I right?"

"Absolutely. Before I focus on the next word, for a fraction of a second I lose myself. Things I don't want to think about take over."

"And you know exactly what those things are."

Athena knew, but she said nothing until we went back to the tent and she could cradle her sleeping son in her arms. Her eyes were full of tears, although she was trying hard to control herself.

"The emir said that you were going on holiday."

She opened the car door, put the key in the ignition, and started the engine. For a few moments, only the noise of the engine troubled the silence of the desert.

"I know what you mean," she said at last. "When I write, when I dance, I'm guided by the Hand that created everything. When I look at Viorel sleeping, I know that he knows he's the fruit of my love for his father, even though I haven't seen his father for more than a year. But I ..."

She fell silent again. Her silence was the blank space between the words.

"... but I don't know the hand that first rocked me in the cradle. The hand that wrote me in the book of the world."

I merely nodded.

"Do you think that matters?"

"Not necessarily. But in your case, until you touch that hand, your, shall we say, calligraphy will not improve."

"I don't see why I should bother to look for someone who never took the trouble to love me."

She closed the car door, smiled, and drove off. Despite her last words, I knew what her next step would be.

SAMIRA R. KHALIL, ATHENA'S MOTHER

It was as if all her professional success, her ability to earn money, her joy at having found a new love, her contentment when she played with her son—my grandson—had all been relegated to second place. I was quite simply terrified when Sherine told me that she'd decided to go in search of her birth mother.

At first, of course, I took consolation in the thought that the adoption center would no longer exist, the paperwork would all have been lost, any officials she encountered would prove implacable, the recent collapse of the Romanian government would make travel impossible, and the womb that bore her would long since have vanished. This, however, provided only a momentary consolation: my daughter was capable of anything and would overcome seemingly impossible obstacles.

Up until then, the subject had been taboo in the family. Sherine knew she was adopted, because the psychiatrist in Beirut had advised me to tell her as soon as she was old enough to understand. But she had never shown any desire to know where she had come from. Her home had been Beirut, when it *was* still our home.

The adopted son of a friend of mine had committed suicide at the age of sixteen when he acquired a biological sister, and so we had never attempted to have more children of our own, and we did everything we could to make her feel that she was the sole reason for our joys and sadnesses, our love and our hopes. And yet it seemed that none of this counted. Dear God, how ungrateful children can be!

Knowing my daughter as I did, I realized that there was no point in arguing with her about this. My husband and I didn't sleep for a whole week, and every morning, every evening, we were bombarded with the same question: "Whereabouts in Romania was I born?" To make matters worse, Viorel kept crying, as if he understood what was going on.

I decided to consult a psychiatrist again. I asked why a young woman who had everything in life should always be so dissatisfied.

"We all want to know where we came from," he said. "On the philosophical level that's the fundamental question for all human beings. In your daughter's case, I think it's perfectly reasonable that she should want to go in search of her roots. Wouldn't you be curious to know?"

"No, I wouldn't. On the contrary, I'd think it dangerous to go in search of someone who had denied and rejected me when I was still too helpless to survive on my own."

But the psychiatrist insisted: "Rather than getting into a confrontation with her, try to help. Perhaps when she sees that it's no longer a problem for you, she'll give up. The year she spent far from her friends must have created a sense of emotional need, which she's now trying to make up for by provoking you like this. She simply wants to be sure that she's loved."

It would have been better if Sherine had gone to the psychiatrist herself, then she would have understood the reasons for her behavior.

"Show that you're confident and don't see this as a threat. And if, in the end, she really does go ahead with it, simply give her the information she needs. As I understand it, she's always been a difficult child. Perhaps she'll emerge from this search a stronger person."

I asked if the psychiatrist had any children. He didn't, and I knew then that he wasn't the right person to advise me.

That night, when we were sitting in front of the TV, Sherine returned to the subject.

"What are you watching?"

"The news."

"What for?"

"To find out what's going on in Lebanon," replied my husband.

I saw the trap, but it was too late. Sherine immediately pounced on this opening.

"You see, you're curious to know what's going on in the country where you were born. You're settled in England, you have friends, Dad earns plenty of money, you've got security, and yet you still buy Lebanese newspapers. You channel-hop until you find a bit of news to do with Beirut. You imagine the future as if it were the past, not realizing that the war will never end. What I mean is that if you're not in touch with your roots, you feel as if you've lost touch with the world. Is it so very hard then for you to understand what I'm feeling?"

"You're our daughter."

"And proud to be. And I'll always be your daughter. Please don't doubt my love or my gratitude for everything you've done for me. All I'm asking is to be given the chance to visit the place where I was born and perhaps ask my birth mother why she abandoned me or perhaps, when I look into her eyes, simply say nothing. If I don't at least try and do that, I'll feel like a coward and I won't ever understand the blank spaces."

"The blank spaces?"

"I learned calligraphy while I was in Dubai. I dance when-ever I can, but music only exists because the pauses exist, and sentences only exist because the blank spaces exist. When I'm doing something, I feel complete, but no one can keep active twenty-four hours a day. As soon as I stop, I feel there's some-thing lacking. You've often said to me that I'm a naturally rest-less person, but I didn't choose to be that way. I'd like to sit here quietly, watching television, but I can't. My brain won't stop. Sometimes I think I'm going mad. I need always to be dancing, writing, selling land, taking care of Viorel, or reading whatever I find to read. Do you think that's normal?"

"Perhaps it's just your temperament," said my husband.

The conversation ended there, as it always ended, with Vio-rel crying, Sherine retreating into silence, and with me convinced that children never acknowledge what their parents have done for them. However, over breakfast the next day, it was my hus-band who brought the subject up again.

"A while ago, while you were in the Middle East, I looked into the possibility of going home to Beirut. I went to the street where we used to live. The house is no longer there, but despite the foreign occupation and the constant incursions, they are slowly rebuilding the country. I felt a sense of euphoria. Perhaps it was the moment to start all over again. And it was precisely that expression, 'start all over again,' that brought me back to re-ality. The time has passed when I could allow myself that luxury. Nowadays, I just want to go on doing what I'm doing, and I don't need any new adventures.

"I sought out the people I used to enjoy a drink with after work. Most of them have left, and those who have stayed complain all the time about a constant feeling of insecurity. I walked past some of my old haunts, and I felt like a stranger, as if nothing there belonged to me anymore. The worst of it was that my dream of one day returning gradually disappeared when I found myself back in the city where I was born. Even so, I needed to make that visit. The songs of exile are still there in my heart, but I know now that I'll never again live in Lebanon. In a way, the days I spent in Beirut helped me to a better understanding of the place where I live now, and to value each second that I spend in London."

"What are you trying to tell me, Dad?"

"That you're right. Perhaps it really would be best to understand those blank spaces. We can look after Viorel while you're away."

He went to the bedroom and returned with the yellow file containing the adoption papers. He gave them to Sherine, kissed her, and said it was time he went to work.

HERON RYAN, JOURNALIST

For a whole morning in 1990, all I could see from the sixth-floor window of the hotel was the main government building. A flag had just been placed on the roof, marking the exact spot where the megalomaniacal dictator had fled in a helicopter only to find death a few hours later at the hands of those he had oppressed for twenty-two years.

In his plan to create a capital that would rival Washington, Ceausescu had ordered all the old houses to be razed to the ground. Indeed, Bucharest had the dubious honor of being described as the city that had suffered the worst destruction outside of a war or a natural disaster.

The day I arrived, I attempted to go for a short walk with my interpreter, but in the streets I saw only poverty, bewilderment, and a sense that there was no future, no past, and no present: the people were living in a kind of limbo, with little idea of what was happening in their country or in the rest of the world. When I went back ten years later and saw the whole country rising up out of the ashes, I realized human beings can overcome any difficulty, and that the Romanian people were a fine example of just that.

But on that other gray morning, in the gray foyer of a gloomy hotel, all I was concerned about was whether my interpreter would manage to get a car and enough petrol so that I could carry out some final research for the BBC documentary I was working on. He was taking a very long time, and I was beginning to have my doubts. Would I have to go back to England having failed to achieve my goal? I'd already invested a significant amount of money in contracts with historians, in the script, in filming interviews, but before the BBC would sign the final contract, they insisted on me visiting Dracula's castle to see what state it was in. The trip was costing more than I expected.

I tried phoning my girlfriend but was told I'd have to wait nearly an hour to get a line. My interpreter might arrive at any moment with the car and there was no time to lose, and so I decided not to risk waiting.

I asked around to see if I could buy an English newspaper, but there were none to be had. To take my mind off my anxiety, I started looking, as discreetly as I could, at the people around me drinking tea, possibly oblivious to everything that had happened the year before—popular uprisings, the cold-blooded murder of civilians in Timisoara, shoot-outs in the streets between the people and the dreaded secret service as the latter tried desperately to hold on to the power fast slipping from their grasp. I noticed a group of three Americans, an interesting-looking woman who was, however, glued to the fashion magazine she was reading, and some men sitting round a table, talking loudly in a language I couldn't identify.

I was just about to get up yet again and go over to the entrance to see if my interpreter was anywhere to be seen, when she came in. She must have been a little more than twenty years old. She sat down, ordered some breakfast, and I noticed that she spoke English. None of the other men present appeared to notice her arrival, but the other woman interrupted her reading.

Perhaps because of my anxiety or because of the place, which was beginning to depress me, I plucked up my courage and went over to her.

"Excuse me, I don't usually do this. I always think breakfast is the most private meal of the day."

She smiled, told me her name, and I immediately felt wary. It had been too easy—she might be a prostitute. Her English, however, was perfect, and she was very discreetly dressed. I decided not to ask any questions and began talking at length about myself, noticing as I did so that the woman at the next table had put down her magazine and was listening to our conversation.

"I'm an independent producer working for the BBC in London, and, at the moment, I'm trying to find a way to get to Transylvania ..."

I noticed the light in her eyes change.

"... so that I can finish the documentary I'm making about the myth of the vampire."

I waited. This subject always aroused people's curiosity, but she lost interest as soon as I mentioned the reason for my visit.

"You'll just have to take the bus," she said. "Although I doubt you'll find what you're looking for. If you want to know more about Dracula, read the book. The author never even visited Romania."

"What about you, do you know Transylvania?"

"I don't know."

That was not an answer, perhaps it was because English—despite her British accent—was not her mother tongue.

"But I'm going there too," she went on. "On the bus, of course."

Judging by her clothes, she was not an adventuress who sets off round the world visiting exotic places. The idea that she might be a prostitute returned; perhaps she was trying to get closer to me.

"Would you like a lift?"

"I've already bought my ticket."

I insisted, thinking that her first refusal was just part of the game. She refused again, saying that she needed to make that journey alone. I asked where she was from, and there was a long pause before she replied.

"Like I said, from Transylvania."

"That isn't quite what you said. But if that's so, perhaps you could help me with finding locations for the film and . . ."

My unconscious mind was telling me to explore the territory a little more, because although the idea that she might be a prostitute was still buzzing around in my head, I very, *very* much wanted her to come with me. She politely refused my offer. The other woman joined in the conversation at this point, as if to protect the younger woman, and I felt then that I was in the way and decided to leave.

My interpreter arrived shortly afterward, out of breath, saying that he'd made all the necessary arrangements, but that (as expected) it was going to cost a lot of money. I went up to my room, grabbed my suitcase, which I'd packed earlier, got into the Russian wreck of a car, drove down the long, almost deserted avenues, and realized that I had with me my small camera, my belongings, my anxieties, a couple of bottles of mineral water, some sandwiches, and the image of someone that stubbornly refused to leave my head.

In the days that followed, as I was trying to piece together a script on the historical figure of Dracula, and interviewing both locals and intellectuals on the subject of the vampire myth (with, as foreseen, little success), I gradually became aware that I was no longer merely trying to make a documentary for British television. I wanted to meet that arrogant, unfriendly, self-sufficient young woman whom I'd seen in a café in a hotel in Bucharest, and who would, at that moment, be somewhere nearby. I knew absolutely nothing about her apart from her name, but like the vampire of the myth, she seemed to be sucking up all my energy.

In my world, and in the world of those I lived with, this was absurd, nonsensical, unacceptable.

Deidre O'Neill, known as Edda

"I don't know what you came here to do, but whatever it was, you must see it through to the end."

She looked at me, startled.

"Who are you?"

I started talking about the magazine I was reading, and after a while, the man sitting with her decided to get up and leave. Now I could tell her who I was.

"If you mean what do I do for a living, I qualified as a doctor some years ago, but I don't think that's the answer you want to hear."

I paused.

"Your next step, though, will be to try to find out, through clever questioning, exactly what I'm doing here, in a country that's only just emerging from years of terrible oppression."

"I'll be straightforward then. What did you come here to do?"

I could have said: I came for the funeral of my teacher, because I felt he deserved that homage. But it would be imprudent to touch on the subject. She may have shown no interest in vampires, but the word *teacher* would be sure to attract her attention. Since my oath will not allow me to lie, I replied with a half-truth.

"I wanted to see where a writer called Mircea Eliade lived. You've probably never heard of him, but Eliade, who spent a great part of his life in France and the USA, was a world authority on myths."

The young woman looked at her watch, feigning indifference. I went on:

"And I'm not talking about vampires, I'm talking about people who, let's say, are following the same path you're following."

She was about to take a sip of her coffee, but she stopped: "Are you from the government? Or are you someone my parents engaged to follow me?"

It was my turn then to feel uncertain as to whether to continue the conversation. Her response had been unnecessarily aggressive. But I could see her aura, her anxiety. She was very like me when I was her age: full of internal and external wounds that drove me to want to heal people on the physical plane and to help them find their path on the spiritual plane. I wanted to say, "Your wounds will help you, my dear," then pick up my magazine and leave.

If I had done that, Athena's path might have been completely different, and she would still be alive and living with the man she loved. She would have brought up her son and watched him grow, get married, and have lots of children. She would be rich, possibly the owner of a company selling real estate. She had all the necessary qualities to find success and happiness. She'd suffered enough to be able to use her scars to her advantage, and it was just a matter of time before she'd manage to control her anxiety and move on.

So what kept me sitting there, trying to keep the conversation going? The answer is very simple: curiosity. I couldn't understand what that brilliant light was doing there in the cold hotel foyer.

I continued: "Mircea Eliade wrote books with strange titles: *Occultism, Witchcraft and Cultural Fashions*, for example. Or *The Sacred and the Profane*. My teacher" —I inadvertently let the word slip, but she either wasn't listening or else pretended not to have noticed—"loved his work. And something tells me it's a subject you're interested in too."

She glanced at her watch again.

"I'm going to Sibiu," she said. "My bus leaves in an hour. I'm looking for my mother, if that's what you want to know. I work as a real estate agent in the Middle East, I have a son of nearly four, I'm divorced, and my parents live in London. My adoptive parents, of course, because I was abandoned as a baby."

She was clearly at a very advanced stage of perception and had identified with me, even though she wasn't aware of this yet.

"Yes, that's what I wanted to know."

"Did you have to come all this way just to do research into a writer? Aren't there any libraries where you live?"

"The fact is that Eliade only lived in Romania until he graduated from university. So if I really wanted to know more about his work, I should go to Paris, London, or to Chicago, where he died. However, what I'm doing isn't research in the normal sense of the word: I wanted to see the ground where he placed his feet. I wanted to feel what inspired him to write about things that affect my life and the lives of people I respect."

"Did he write about medicine too?"

I knew I had better not answer that. I saw that she'd picked up on the word *teacher* and assumed it must be related to my profession.

The young woman got to her feet. I felt she knew what I was talking about. I could see her light shining more intensely. I only achieve this state of perception when I'm close to someone very like myself.

"Would you mind coming with me to the bus station?" she asked.

Not at all. My plane didn't leave until later that night, and a whole, dull, endless day stretched out before me. At least I would have someone to talk to for a while.

She went upstairs, returned with her suitcases in her hand and a series of questions in her head. She began her interrogation as soon as we left the hotel.

"I may never see you again," she said, "but I feel that we have something in common. Since this may be the last opportunity we have in this incarnation to talk to each other, would you mind being direct in your answers?"

I nodded.

"Based on what you've read in all those books, do you believe that through dance we can enter a trancelike state that helps us to see a light? And that the light tells us nothing—only whether we're happy or sad?"

A good question!

"Of course, and that happens not only through dance, but also through anything that allows us to focus our attention and to separate body from spirit. Like yoga or prayer or Buddhist meditation."

"Or calligraphy."

"I hadn't thought of that, but it's possible. At such moments, when the body sets the soul free, the soul either rises up to heaven or descends into hell, depending on the person's state of mind. In both cases, it learns what it needs to learn: to destroy or to heal. But I'm no longer interested in individual paths; in my tradition, I need the help of— Are you listening to me?"

"No."

She had stopped in the middle of the street and was staring at a little girl who appeared to have been abandoned. She went to put her hand in her bag.

"Don't do that," I said. "Look across the street at that woman, the one with cruel eyes. She's put the girl there purely in order to—"

"I don't care."

She took out a few coins. I grabbed her hand.

"Let's buy her something to eat. That would be more useful."

I asked the little girl to go with us to a bar and bought her a sandwich. The little girl smiled and thanked me. The eyes of the woman across the street seemed to glitter with hatred, but for the first time, the gray eyes of the young woman walking at my side looked at me with respect.

"What were you saying?" she asked.

"It doesn't matter. Do you know what happened to you a few moments ago? You went into the same trance that your dancing provokes."

"No, you're wrong."

"I'm right. Something touched your unconscious mind. Perhaps you saw yourself as you would have been if you hadn't been adopted—begging in the street. At that moment, your brain stopped reacting. Your spirit left you and traveled down to hell to meet the demons from your past. Because of that, you didn't notice the woman across the street—you were in a trance, a disorganized, chaotic trance that was driving you to do something that was good in theory, but, in practice, pointless. As if you were—"

"In the blank space between the letters. In the moment when a note of music ends and the next has not yet begun."

"Exactly. And such a trance can be dangerous."

I almost said: "It's the kind of trance provoked by fear. It paralyzes the person, leaves them unable to react; the body doesn't respond, the soul is no longer there. You were terrified by everything that could have happened to you had fate not placed your parents in your path." But she had put her suitcases down on the ground and was standing in front of me.

"Who are you? Why are you saying all this?"

"As a doctor, I'm known as Deidre O'Neill. Pleased to meet you, and what's your name?"

"Athena. Although according to my passport I'm Sherine Khalil."

"Who gave you the name Athena?"

"No one important. But I didn't ask you for your name, I asked who you are and why you spoke to me. And why I felt the same need to talk to you. Was it just because we were the only two women in that café? I don't think so. And you're saying things to me that make sense of my life."

She picked up her bags again, and we continued walking toward the bus station.

"I have another name too—Edda. But it wasn't chosen by chance, nor do I believe it was chance that brought us together."

Before us was the entrance to the bus station, with various people going in and out—soldiers in uniform, farmers, pretty women dressed as if they were still living in the 1950s.

"If it wasn't chance, what was it?"

She had another half an hour before her bus left, and I could have said: "It was the Mother. Some chosen spirits emit a special light and are drawn to one another, and you—Sherine or Athena—are one of those spirits, but you need to work very hard to use that energy to your advantage."

I could have explained that she was following the classic path of the witch, who, through her individual persona, seeks contact with the upper and lower world but always ends up destroying her own life—she serves others, gives out energy, but receives nothing in return.

I could have explained that although all paths are different, there is always a point when people come together, celebrate together, discuss their difficulties, and prepare themselves for the Rebirth of the Mother. I could have said that contact with

the Divine Light is the greatest reality a human being can experience, and yet, in my tradition, that contact cannot be made
alone, because we've suffered centuries of persecution, and this
has taught us many things.

"Would you like to have a coffee while I wait for the bus?"

No, I did not. I would only end up saying things that might,
at that stage, be misinterpreted.

"Certain people have been very important in my life," she
went on. "My landlord, for example, or the calligrapher I met
in the desert near Dubai. Who knows, you might have things
to say to me that I can share with them, and repay them for all
they've taught me."

So she had already had teachers in her life—excellent! Her
spirit was ripe. All she needed was to continue her training, otherwise she would end up losing all she had achieved. But was I
the right person?

I asked the Mother to inspire me, to tell me what to do. I got
no answer, which did not surprise me. She always behaves like
that when it's up to me to take responsibility for a decision.

I gave Athena my business card and asked her for hers. She
gave me an address in Dubai, a country I would have been unable to find on the map.

I decided to try making a joke, to test her out a little more.
"Isn't it a bit of a coincidence that three English people should
meet in a café in Bucharest?"

"Well, from your card I see that you're Scottish. The man
I met apparently works in England, but I don't know any-

thing else about him." She took a deep breath. "And I'm ... Romanian."

I gave an excuse and said that I had to rush back to the hotel and pack my bags.

Now she knew where to find me. If it was written that we would meet again, we would. The important thing is to allow fate to intervene in our lives and to decide what is best for everyone.

VOSHO "BUSHALO," SIXTY-FIVE,
RESTAURANT OWNER

These Europeans come here thinking they know everything, thinking they deserve the very best treatment, that they have the right to bombard us with questions that we're obliged to answer. On the other hand, they think that by giving us some tricksy name, like "travelers" or "Roma," they can put right the many wrongs they've done us in the past.

Why can't they just call us gypsies and put an end to all the stories that make us look as if we were cursed in the eyes of the world? They accuse us of being the fruit of the illicit union between a woman and the Devil himself. They say that one of us forged the nails that fixed Christ to the cross, that mothers should be careful when our caravans come near, because we steal children and enslave them.

And because of this there have been frequent massacres throughout history; in the Middle Ages we were hunted as witches; for centuries our testimony wasn't even accepted in the

German courts. I was born before the Nazi wind swept through Europe and I saw my father marched off to a concentration camp in Poland, with a humiliating black triangle sewn to his clothes. Of the five-hundred-thousand gypsies sent for slave labor, only five-thousand survived to tell the tale.

And no one, absolutely no one, wants to hear about this.

Right up until last year, our culture, religion, and language were banned in this godforsaken part of the world, where most of the tribes decided to settle. If you asked anyone in the city what they thought of gypsies, their immediate response would be: "They're all thieves." However hard we try to lead normal lives by ceasing our eternal wanderings and living in places where we're easily identifiable, the racism continues. Our children are forced to sit at the back of the class, and not a week goes by without someone insulting them.

Then people complain that we don't give straight answers, that we try to disguise ourselves, that we never openly admit our origins. Why would we do that? Everyone knows what a gypsy looks like, and everyone knows how to "protect" themselves from our "curses."

When a stuck-up, intellectual young woman appears, smiling and claiming to be part of our culture and our race, I'm immediately on my guard. She might have been sent by the Securitate, the secret police who work for that mad dictator—the Conducator, the Genius of the Carpathians, the Leader. They say he was put on trial and shot, but I don't believe it. His son may have disappeared from the scene for the moment, but he's still a powerful figure in these parts.

The young woman insists; she smiles, as if she were saying something highly amusing, and tells me that her mother is a gypsy and that she'd like to find her. She knows her full name. How could she obtain such information without the help of the Securitate?

It's best not to get on the wrong side of people who have government contacts. I tell her that I know nothing, that I'm just a gypsy who's decided to lead an honest life, but she won't listen: she wants to find her mother. I know who her mother is, and I know too that more than twenty years ago, she had a child she gave up to an orphanage that she never heard from again. We had to take her mother in because a blacksmith who thought he was the master of the universe insisted on it. But who can guarantee that this intellectual young woman standing before me really is Liliana's daughter? Before trying to find out who her mother is, she should at least respect some of our customs and not turn up dressed in red if it's not her wedding day. She ought to wear longer skirts as well, so as not to arouse men's lust. And she should be more respectful.

If I speak of her now in the present tense, it's because for those who travel, time does not exist, only space. We came from far away, some say from India, others from Egypt, but the fact is that we carry the past with us as if it has all just happened. And the persecutions continue.

The young woman is trying to be nice and to show that she knows about our culture, when that doesn't matter at all. After all, she *should* know about our traditions.

"In town I was told that you're a Rom Baro, a tribal leader. Before I came here, I learned a lot about our history—"

"Not 'our,' please. It's *my* history, the history of *my* wife, *my* children, *my* tribe. You're a European. You were never stoned in the street as I was when I was five years old."

"I think the situation is getting better."

"The situation is always getting better, then it immediately gets worse."

But she keeps smiling. She orders a whiskey. One of our women would never do that.

If she'd come in here just to have a drink or look for company, I'd treat her like any other customer. I've learned to be friendly, attentive, discreet, because my business depends on that. When my customers want to know more about the gypsies, I offer them a few curious facts, tell them to listen to the group who'll be playing later on, make a few remarks about our culture, and then they leave with the impression that they know everything about us.

But this young woman isn't just another tourist: she says she belongs to our race.

She again shows me the certificate she got from the government. I can believe that the government kills, steals, and lies, but it wouldn't risk handing out false certificates, and so she really must be Liliana's daughter, because the certificate gives her full name and address. I learned from the television that the Genius of the Carpathians, the Father of the People, our Conductor, the one who left us to starve while he exported all our food, the one who lived in palaces and used gold-plated cutlery while the people were dying of starvation, that same man and his wretched wife used to get the Securitate to trawl the orphanages, selecting babies to be trained as state assassins.

They only ever took boys, though, never girls. Perhaps she really is Liliana's daughter.

I look at the certificate once more and wonder whether or not I should tell her where her mother is. Liliana deserves to meet this intellectual, claiming to be "one of us." Liliana deserves to look this woman in the eye. I think she suffered enough when she betrayed her people, slept with a *gadje* [*Editor's note: foreigner*], and shamed her parents. Perhaps the moment has come to end her hell, for her to see that her daughter survived, got rich, and might even be able to help her out of the poverty she lives in.

Perhaps this young woman will pay me for this information; perhaps it'll be of some advantage to our tribe, because we're living in confusing times. Everyone's saying that the Genius of the Carpathians is dead, and they even show photos of his execution, but who knows, he could come back tomorrow, and it'll all turn out to have been a clever trick on his part to find out who really was on his side and who was prepared to betray him.

The musicians will start playing soon, so I'd better talk business.

"I know where you can find this woman. I can take you to her." I adopt a friendlier tone of voice. "But I think that information is worth something."

"I was prepared for that," she says, holding out a much larger sum of money than I was going to ask for.

"That's not even enough for the taxi fare."

"I'll pay you the same amount again when I reach my destination."

And I sense that, for the first time, she feels uncertain. She suddenly seems afraid of what she's about to do. I grab the money she's placed on the counter.

"I'll take you to see Liliana tomorrow."

Her hands are trembling. She orders another whiskey, but suddenly a man comes into the bar, sees her, blushes scarlet, and comes straight over to her. I gather that they only met yesterday, and yet here they are, talking as if they were old friends. His eyes are full of desire. She's perfectly aware of this and encourages him. The man orders a bottle of wine, and the two sit down at a table, and it's as if she's forgotten all about her mother.

However, I want the other half of that money. When I serve them their drinks, I tell her I'll be at her hotel at ten o'clock in the morning.

Heron Ryan, journalist

Immediately after the first glass of wine, she told me, unprompted, that she had a boyfriend who worked for Scotland Yard. It was a lie, of course. She must have read the look in my eyes, and this was her way of keeping me at a distance.

I told her that I had a girlfriend, which made us even.

Ten minutes after the music had started, she stood up. We had said very little—she asked no questions about my research into vampires, and we exchanged only generalities: our impressions of the city, complaints about the state of the roads. But what I saw next—or, rather, what everyone in the restaurant saw—was a goddess revealing herself in all her glory, a priestess invoking angels and demons.

Her eyes were closed, and she seemed no longer to be conscious of who she was or where she was or why she was there; it was as if she were floating and simultaneously summoning up her past, revealing her present, and predicting the future. She mingled eroticism with chastity, pornography with revelation, worship of God and nature, all at the same time.

People stopped eating and started watching what was happening. She was no longer following the music, the musicians were trying to keep up with her steps, and that restaurant in the basement of an old building in the city of Sibiu was transformed into an Egyptian temple, where the worshippers of Isis used to gather for their fertility rites. The smell of roast meat and wine was transmuted into an incense that drew us all into the same trancelike state, into the same experience of leaving this world and entering an unknown dimension.

The string and wind instruments had given up, only the percussion played on. Athena was dancing as if she were no longer there, with sweat running down her face, her bare feet beating on the wooden floor. A woman got up and very gently tied a scarf around her neck and breasts, because her blouse kept threatening to slip off her shoulders. Athena, however, appeared not to notice; she was inhabiting other spheres, experiencing the frontiers of worlds that almost touch ours but never reveal themselves.

The other people in the restaurant started clapping in time to the music, and Athena was dancing ever faster, feeding on that energy, spinning round and round, balancing in the void, snatching up everything that we, poor mortals, wanted to offer to the supreme divinity.

And suddenly she stopped. Everyone stopped, including the percussionists. Her eyes were still closed, but tears were now rolling down her cheeks. She raised her arms in the air and cried, "When I die, bury me standing, because I've spent all my life on my knees!"

No one said anything. She opened her eyes, as if waking from a deep sleep, and walked back to the table as if nothing had happened. The band started up again, and couples took to the floor in an attempt to enjoy themselves, but the atmosphere in the place had changed completely. People soon paid their bills and started to leave the restaurant.

"Is everything all right?" I asked when I saw that she'd recovered from the physical effort of dancing.

"I feel afraid. I discovered how to reach a place I don't want to go to."

"Do you want me to go with you?"

She shook her head.

In the days that followed, I completed my research for the documentary, sent my interpreter back to Bucharest with the hired car, and then stayed on in Sibiu simply because I wanted to meet her again. All my life I've always been guided by logic and I know that love is something that can be built rather than simply discovered, but I sensed that if I never saw her again, I would be leaving a very important part of my life in Transylvania, even though I might only realize this later on. I fought against the monotony of those endless hours; more than once, I went to the bus station to find out the times of buses to Bucharest; I spent more than my tiny budget as an independent filmmaker allowed on phone calls to the BBC and to my girlfriend. I explained that I didn't yet have all the material I needed, that there were still a few things lacking, that I might need another day or possibly a week; I said that the Romanians were being very difficult and got upset if anyone associated their beautiful Transylvania with the hideous story of Dracula. I finally managed to convince the producers, and they let me stay on longer than I really needed to.

We were staying in the only hotel in the city, and one day she saw me in the foyer and seemed suddenly to remember our first encounter. This time, she invited me out, and I tried to contain my joy. Perhaps I *was* important in her life.

Later on, I learned that the words she had spoken at the end of her dance were an ancient gypsy saying.

LILIANA, SEAMSTRESS, AGE
AND SURNAME UNKNOWN

I speak in the present tense because for us time does not exist, only space. And because it seems like only yesterday.

The one tribal custom I did not follow was that of having my man by my side when Athena was born. The midwives came to me even though they knew I had slept with a *gadje*, a foreigner.

They loosened my hair, cut the umbilical cord, tied various knots, and handed it to me. At that point, tradition demands that the child be wrapped in some item of the father's clothing; he had left a scarf, which reminded me of his smell and which I sometimes pressed to my nose so as to feel him close to me, but now that perfume would vanish forever.

I wrapped the baby in the scarf and placed her on the floor so that she would receive energy from the earth. I stayed there with her, not knowing what to feel or think; my decision had been made.

The midwives told me to choose a name and not to tell anyone what it was—it could only be pronounced once the child was baptized. They gave me the consecrated oil and the amulets I must hang around her neck for the two weeks following her birth. One of them told me not to worry, the whole tribe was responsible for my child, and although I would be the butt of much criticism, this would soon pass. They also advised me not to go out between dusk and dawn because the *tsinvari* [*Editor's note: evil spirits*] might attack us and take possession of us, and from then on our lives would be a tragedy.

A week later, as soon as the sun rose, I went to an adoption center in Sibiu and placed her on the doorstep, hoping that some charitable person would take her in. As I was doing so, a nurse caught me and dragged me inside. She insulted me in every way she could and said that they were used to such behavior, but that there was always someone watching and I couldn't escape so easily from the responsibility of bringing a child into the world.

"Although, of course, what else would one expect from a gypsy! Abandoning your own child like that!"

I was forced to fill in a form with all my details, and since I didn't know how to write, she said again, more than once: "Yes, well, what can you expect from a gypsy. And don't try to trick us by giving false information. If you do, it could land you in jail." Out of pure fear, I told them the truth.

I looked at my child one last time, and all I could think was: Child without a name, may you find love, much love in your life.

Afterward, I walked in the forest for hours. I remembered many nights during my pregnancy when I had both loved and hated the child herself and the man who had put her inside me.

Like all women, I'd dreamed of one day meeting an enchanted prince, who would marry me, give me lots of children, and shower attentions on my family. Like many women, I fell in love with a man who could give me none of those things, but with whom I shared some unforgettable moments, moments my child would never understand, for she would always be stigmatized in our tribe as a *gadje* and a fatherless child. I could bear that, but I didn't want her to suffer as I had suffered ever since I first realized I was pregnant. I wept and tore at my own skin, thinking that the pain of the scratches would perhaps stop me thinking about a return to ordinary life, to face the shame I had brought on the tribe. Someone would take care of the child, and I would always cherish the hope of seeing her again one day, when she had grown up.

Unable to stop crying, I sat down on the ground and put my arms around the trunk of a tree. However, as soon as my tears and the blood from my wounds touched the trunk of the tree, a strange calm took hold of me. I seemed to hear a voice telling me not to worry, saying that my blood and my tears had purified the path of the child and lessened my suffering. Ever since then, whenever I despair, I remember that voice and feel calm again.

That's why I wasn't surprised when I saw her arrive with our tribe's Rom Baro, who asked me for a coffee and a drink, then smiled slyly and left. The voice told me that she would come back, and now here she is, in front of me. She's pretty. She looks like her father. I don't know what feelings she has for me; perhaps she hates me because I abandoned her. I don't need to explain why I did what I did; no one would ever understand.

We sit for an age without saying anything to each other, just looking—not smiling, not crying, nothing. A surge of love rises up from the depths of my soul, but I don't know if she's interested in what I feel.

"Are you hungry? Would you like something to eat?"

Instinct. Instinct above all else. She nods. We go into the small room in which I live, and which is living room, bedroom, kitchen, and sewing workshop. She looks around, shocked, but I pretend not to notice. I go over to the stove and return with two bowls of thick meat and vegetable broth. I've prepared some strong coffee too, and just as I'm about to add sugar, she speaks for the first time.

"No sugar for me, thank you. I didn't know you spoke English."

I almost say that I learned it from her father, but I bite my tongue. We eat in silence, and as time passes, everything starts to feel familiar to me: here I am with my daughter; she went off into the world and now she's back; she followed paths different from mine and has come home. I know this is an illusion, but life has given me so many moments of harsh reality that it does no harm to dream a little.

"Who's that saint?" she asks, pointing to a painting on the wall.

"St. Sarah, the patron saint of gypsies. I've always wanted to visit her church in France, but I can't leave the country. I'd never get a passport or permission ..."

I'm about to say: "And even if I did, I wouldn't have enough money," but I stop myself in time. She might think I was asking her for something.

"... and besides, I have too much work to do."

Silence falls again. She finishes her soup, lights a cigarette, and her eyes give nothing away, no emotion.

"Did you think you would ever see me again?"

I say that I did, and that I'd heard yesterday, from the Rom Baro's wife, that she'd visited his restaurant.

"A storm is coming. Wouldn't you like to sleep a little?"

"I can't hear anything. The wind isn't blowing any harder or softer than before. I'd rather talk."

"Believe me, I have all the time in the world. I have the rest of my life to spend by your side."

"Don't say that."

"... but you're tired," I go on, pretending not to have heard her remark. I can see the storm approaching. Like all storms, it brings destruction, but at the same time, it soaks the fields, and the wisdom of the heavens falls with the rain. Like all storms, it will pass. The more violent it is, the more quickly it will pass.

I have, thank God, learned to weather storms.

And as if all the Holy Marys of the Sea were listening to me, the first drops of rain begin to fall on the tin roof. The young woman finishes her cigarette. I take her hand and lead her to my bed. She lies down and closes her eyes.

I don't know how long she slept. I watched her without thinking anything, and the voice I'd heard once in the forest was telling me that all was well, that I needn't worry, that the ways in which fate changes people are always favorable if we only know how to decipher them. I don't know who saved her from the orphanage and brought her up and made her into the independent woman she appears to be. I offered up a prayer to that family who had allowed my daughter to survive and achieve a better life. In the middle of the prayer, I felt jealousy, despair, regret, and I stopped talking to St. Sarah. Had it really been so important to bring her back? There lay everything I'd lost and could never recover.

But there too was the physical manifestation of my love. I knew nothing and yet everything was revealed to me: I remembered the times I'd considered suicide and, later, abortion, when I'd imagined leaving that part of the world and setting off on foot to wherever my strength would take me; I remembered my blood and tears on the tree trunk, the dialogue with nature that had intensified from that moment on and has never left me since, although few people in my tribe have any inkling of this. My protector, whom I met while I was wandering in the forest, understood, but he had just died.

"The light is unstable, the wind blows it out, the lightning ignites it, it is never simply there, shining like the sun, but it is worth fighting for," he used to say.

He was the only person who accepted me and persuaded the tribe that I could once again form part of their world. He was the only one with the moral authority to ensure that I wasn't expelled.

And, alas, the only one who would never meet my daughter. I wept for him while she lay sleeping on my bed, she who must be used to all the world's comforts. Thousands of questions filled my head—who were her adoptive parents, where did she live, had she been to university, was there someone she loved, what were her plans? But I wasn't the one who had traveled the world in search of her. On the contrary, I wasn't there to ask questions, but to answer them.

She opened her eyes. I wanted to touch her hair, to give her the affection I'd kept locked inside all these years, but I wasn't sure how she would react and thought it best to do nothing.

"You came here to find out why …"

"No, I don't want to know why a mother would abandon her daughter. There is no reason for anyone to do that."

Her words wound my heart, but I don't know how to respond.

"Who am I? What blood runs in my veins? Yesterday, when I found out where you were, I was absolutely terrified. Where do I start? I suppose, like all gypsies, you can read the future in the cards."

"No, that's not true. We only do that with *gadje* as a way of earning a living. We never read cards or hands or try to predict the future within our own tribe. And you …"

"I'm part of the tribe. Even though the woman who brought me into the world sent me far away."

"Yes."

"So what am I doing here? Now that I've seen your face I can go back to London. My holidays are nearly over."

"Do you want to know about your father?"

"No, I haven't the slightest interest in him."

And suddenly I realized that I could help her. It was as if someone else's voice came out of my mouth. "Try to understand the blood that flows in my veins and in your heart."

That was my teacher speaking through me. She closed her eyes again and slept for nearly twelve hours.

The following day, I took her to the outskirts of Sibiu where there's a kind of museum of the different kinds of houses found in the region. For the first time, I'd had the pleasure of preparing her breakfast. She was more rested, less tense, and she asked me questions about gypsy culture, but never about me. She told me a little of her life. I learned that I was a grandmother! She didn't mention her husband or her adoptive parents. She said she sold land in a country far from there and that she would soon return to her work.

I explained that I could show her how to make amulets to ward off evil, but she didn't seem interested. However, when I spoke to her about the healing properties of herbs, she asked me to teach her how to recognize them. In the park where we were walking, I tried to pass on to her all the knowledge I possessed, although I was sure she'd forget everything as soon as she returned to her home country, which by then I knew was England.

"We don't possess the earth, the earth possesses us. We used to travel constantly, and everything around us was ours: the plants, the water, the landscapes through which our caravans passed. Our laws were nature's laws: the strong survived, and we, the weak, the eternal exiles, learned to hide our strength and to use it only when necessary. We don't believe that God made the universe. We believe that God is the universe and that we are contained in him, and he in us. Although ..."

I stopped, then decided to go on, because it was a way of paying homage to my protector.

"... in my opinion, we should call 'him' 'goddess' or 'Mother.' Not like the woman who gives her daughter up to an orphanage, but like the Woman in all of us, who protects us when we are in danger. She will always be with us while we perform our daily tasks with love and joy, understanding that nothing is suffering, that everything is a way of praising Creation."

Athena—now I knew her name—looked across at one of the houses in the park.

"What's that? A church?"

The hours I'd spent by her side had allowed me to recover my strength. I asked if she was trying to change the subject. She thought for a moment before replying.

"No, I want to go on listening to what you have to tell me, although, according to everything I read before I came here, what you're saying isn't part of the gypsy tradition."

"My protector taught me these things. He knew things the gypsies don't know and he made the tribe take me back. And as I learned from him, I gradually became aware of the power of the Mother, I, who had rejected the blessing of being a mother."

I pointed at a small bush. "If one day your son has a fever, place him next to a young plant like this and shake its leaves. The fever will pass over into the plant. If ever you feel anxious, do the same thing."

"I'd rather you told me more about your protector."

"He taught me that in the beginning Creation was so lonely that it created someone else to talk to. Those two creatures, in an act of love, made a third person, and from then on, they multiplied by thousands and millions. You asked about the church we just saw: I don't know when it was built and I'm not interested. My temple is the park, the sky, the water in the lake, and the stream that feeds it. My people are those who share my ideas and not those I'm bound to by bonds of blood. My ritual is being with those people and celebrating everything around me. When are you thinking of going home?"

"Possibly tomorrow. I don't want to inconvenience you."

Another wound to my heart, but I could say nothing.

"No, please, stay as long as you like. I only asked because I'd like to celebrate your arrival with the others. If you agree, I can do this tonight."

She says nothing, and I understand this as a yes. Back home, I give her more food, and she explains that she needs to go to her hotel in Sibiu to fetch some clothes. By the time she returns, I have everything organized. We go to a hill to the south of the town; we sit around a fire that has just been lit; we play instruments, we sing, we dance, we tell stories. She watches but doesn't take part, although the Rom Baro told me that she was a fine dancer. For the first time in many years, I feel happy, because I've had the chance to prepare a ritual for my daughter and to celebrate with her the miracle of the two of us being together, alive and healthy and immersed in the love of the Great Mother.

Afterward, she says that she'll sleep at the hotel that night. I ask her if this is good-bye, but she says it isn't. She'll come back tomorrow.

For a whole week, my daughter and I share together the adoration of the Universe. One night, she brought a friend, making it quite clear that he was neither her boyfriend nor the father of her child. The man, who must have been ten years older than her, asked who we were worshipping in our rituals. I explained that worshipping someone means—according to my protector—placing that person outside of our world. We are not worshipping anyone or anything, we are simply communing with Creation.

"But do you pray?"

"Myself, I pray to St. Sarah, but here we are part of everything and we celebrate rather than pray."

I felt that Athena was proud of my answer, but I was really only repeating my protector's words.

"And why do this in a group, when we can all celebrate the Universe on our own?"

"Because the others are me. And I am the others."

Athena looked at me then, and I felt it was my turn to wound her heart.

"I'm leaving tomorrow," she said.

"Before you do, come and say good-bye to your mother."

That was the first time, in all those days, I had used the word. My voice didn't tremble, my gaze was steady, and I knew that, despite everything, standing before me was the blood of my blood, the fruit of my womb. At that moment, I was behaving like a little girl who has just found out that the world isn't full of ghosts and curses as grown-ups have taught us. It's full of love, regardless of how that love is manifested, a love that forgives our mistakes and redeems our sins.

She gave me a long embrace. Then she adjusted the veil I wear to cover my hair; I may not have had a husband, but according to gypsy tradition, I had to wear a veil because I was no longer a virgin. What would tomorrow bring me, along with the departure of the being I've always both loved and feared from a distance? I was everyone, and everyone was me and my solitude.

The following day, Athena arrived bearing a bunch of flowers. She tidied my room, told me that I should wear glasses because my eyes were getting worn out from all that sewing. She asked if the friends I celebrated with experienced any problems with the tribe, and I told her that they didn't, that my protector had been a very respected man, had taught us many things, and had followers all over the world. I explained that he'd died shortly before she arrived.

"One day, a cat brushed against him. To us, that means death, and we were all very worried. But although there is a ritual that can lift such a curse, my protector said it was time for him to leave, that he needed to travel to those other worlds that he knew existed, to be reborn as a child, and to rest for a while in the arms of the Mother. His funeral took place in a forest nearby. It was a very simple affair, but people came from all over the world."

"Among those people, was there a woman of about thirty-five, with dark hair?"

"I can't be sure, but possibly. Why do you ask?"

"I met someone at a hotel in Bucharest who said that she'd come to attend the funeral of a friend. I think she said something about 'her teacher.'"

She asked me to tell her more about the gypsies, but there wasn't much she didn't already know, mainly because, apart from customs and traditions, we know little of our own history. I suggested that she go to France one day and take, on my behalf, a shawl to present to the image of St. Sarah in the little French village of Saintes-Maries-de-la-Mer.

"I came here because there was something missing in my life," she said. "I needed to fill up my blank spaces, and I thought just seeing your face would be enough. But it wasn't. I also needed to understand that … I was loved."

"You *are* loved."

I said nothing else for a long time. I'd finally put into words what I'd wanted to say ever since I let her go. So that she would not become too emotional, I went on:

"I'd like to ask you something."

"Ask me anything you like."

"I want to ask your forgiveness."

She bit her lip.

"I've always been a very restless person. I work hard, spend too much time looking after my son, I dance like a mad thing, I learned calligraphy, I go to courses on selling, I read one book after another. But that's all a way of avoiding those moments when nothing is happening, because those blank spaces give me a feeling of absolute emptiness, in which not a single crumb of love exists. My parents have always done everything they could for me, and I do nothing but disappoint them. But here, during the time we've spent together, celebrating nature and the Great Mother, I've realized that those empty spaces were starting to get filled up. They were transformed into pauses—the moment when the man lifts his hand from the drum before bringing it down again to strike it hard. I think I can leave now. I'm not saying that I'll go in peace, because my life needs to follow the rhythm I'm accustomed to. But I won't leave feeling bitter. Do all gypsies believe in the Great Mother?"

"If you were to ask them, none of them would say yes. They've adopted the beliefs and customs of the places where they've settled, and the only thing that unites us in religious terms is the worship of St. Sarah and making a pilgrimage, at least once in our lifetime, to visit her tomb in Saintes-Maries-de-la-Mer. Some tribes call her Kali Sarah, Black Sarah. Or the Virgin of the Gypsies, as she's known in Lourdes."

"I have to go," Athena said after a while. "The friend you met the other day is leaving with me."

"He seems like a nice man."

"You're talking like a mother."

"I am your mother."

"And I'm your daughter."

She embraced me, this time with tears in her eyes. I stroked her hair as I held her in my arms, as I'd always dreamed I would, ever since the day when fate—or my fear—separated us. I asked her to take good care of herself, and she told me that she had learned a lot.

"You'll learn a lot more too because although nowadays we're all trapped in houses, cities, and jobs, there still flows in your blood the time of caravans and journeyings and the teachings that the Great Mother placed in our path so that we could survive. Learn, but always learn with other people by your side. Don't be alone in the search, because if you take a wrong step, you'll have no one there to help put you right."

She was still crying, still clinging to me, almost begging me to let her stay. I pleaded with my protector not to let me shed one tear, because I wanted the best for Athena, and her destiny was to go forward. Here in Transylvania, apart from my love, she would find nothing else. And although I believe that love is enough to justify a whole existence, I was quite sure that I couldn't ask her to sacrifice her future in order to stay by my side.

Athena planted a kiss on my forehead and left without saying good-bye, perhaps thinking she would return one day. Every Christmas, she sent me enough money to spend the whole year without having to sew, but I never went to the bank to cash her checks, even though everyone in the tribe thought I was behaving like a foolish woman.

Six months ago, she stopped sending money. She must have

realized that I need my sewing to fill up what she called the "blank spaces."

I would love to see her again, but I know she'll never come back. She's probably a big executive now, married to the man she loves. And I probably have lots of grandchildren, which means that my blood will remain on this earth, and my mistakes will be forgiven.

SAMIRA R. KHALIL, HOUSEWIFE

As soon as Sherine arrived home, whooping with joy and clutching a rather startled Viorel to her, I knew that everything had gone much better than I'd imagined. I felt that God had heard my prayers, and that now she no longer had anything more to learn about herself, she would finally adapt to normal life, bring up her child, remarry, and forget all about the strange restlessness that left her simultaneously euphoric and depressed.

"I love you, Mum."

It was my turn to put my arms around her and hold her to me. During all the nights she'd been away, I had, I confess, been terrified by the thought that she might send someone to fetch Viorel, and then they would never come back.

After she'd eaten, had a bath, told us about the meeting with her birth mother, and described the Transylvanian countryside (I could barely remember it, since all I was interested in, at the time, was finding an orphanage), I asked her when she was going back to Dubai.

"Next week, but first I have to go to Scotland to see someone."

A man!

"A woman," she said at once, perhaps in response to my knowing smile. "I feel that I have a mission. While we were celebrating life and nature, I discovered things I didn't even know existed. What I thought could be found only through dance is everywhere. And it has the face of a woman. I saw in the ..."

I felt frightened. Her mission, I told her, was to bring up her son, do well at her job, earn more money, remarry, and respect God as we know him.

But Sherine wasn't listening.

"It was one night when we were sitting round the fire, drinking, telling funny stories, and listening to music. Apart from in the restaurant, I hadn't felt the need to dance all the time I was there, as if I were storing up energy for something different. Suddenly I felt as if everything around me were alive and pulsating, as if the Creation and I were one and the same thing. I wept with joy when the flames of the fire seemed to take on the form of a woman's face, full of compassion, smiling at me."

I shuddered. It was probably gypsy witchcraft. And at the same time, the image came back to me of the little girl at school, who said she'd seen "a woman in white."

"Don't get caught up in things like that, they're the Devil's work. We've always set you a good example, so why can't you lead a normal life?"

I'd obviously been too hasty when I thought the journey in search of her birth mother had done her good. However, instead of reacting aggressively, as she usually did, she smiled and went on.

"What *is* normal? Why is Dad always laden down with work, when we have money enough to support three generations? He's an honest man and he deserves the money he earns, but he always says, with a certain pride, that he's got far too much work. Why? What for?"

"He's a man who lives a dignified, hardworking life."

"When I lived at home, the first thing he'd ask me when he got back every evening was how my homework was going, and he'd give me a few examples illustrating how important his work was to the world. Then he'd turn on the TV, make a few comments about the political situation in Lebanon, and read some technical book before going to sleep. But he was always busy. And it was the same thing with you. I was the best-dressed girl at school; you took me to parties; you kept the house spick-and-span; you were always kind and loving and brought me up impeccably. But what happens now that you're getting older? What are you going to do with your life now that I've grown up and am independent?"

"We're going to travel the world and enjoy a well-earned rest."

"But why don't you do that now, while your health is still good?"

I'd asked myself the same question, but I felt that my husband needed his work, not because of the money, but out of a need to feel useful, to prove that an exile also honors his commitments. Whenever he took a holiday and stayed in town, he always found some excuse to slip into the office, to talk to his colleagues and make some decision that could easily have waited. I tried to make him go to the theater, to the cinema, to museums, and he'd do as I asked, but I always had the feeling that it bored him. His only interest was the company, work, business.

For the first time, I talked to her as if she were a friend and not my daughter, but I chose my words carefully and spoke in a way that she could understand.

"Are you saying that your father is also trying to fill in what you call the 'blank spaces'?"

"The day he retires, although I really don't think that day will ever come, he'll fall into a deep depression. I'm sure of it. What to do with that hard-won freedom? Everyone will congratulate him on a brilliant career, on the legacy he leaves behind him because of the integrity with which he ran his company, but no one will have time for him anymore—life flows on, and everyone is caught up in that flow. Dad will feel like he is an exile again, but this time he won't have a country where he can seek refuge."

"Have you got a better idea?"

"Only one: I don't want the same thing to happen to me. I'm too restless, and please don't take this the wrong way, because I'm not blaming you and Dad at all for the example you set me, but I need to change, and change fast."

DEIDRE O'NEILL, KNOWN AS EDDA

She's sitting in the pitch-black.

The boy, of course, left the room at once—the night is the kingdom of terror, of monsters from the past, of the days when we wandered like gypsies, like my former teacher—may the Mother have mercy on his soul, and may he be loved and cherished until it is time for him to return.

Athena hasn't known what to do since I switched off the light. She asks about her son, and I tell her not to worry, to leave everything to me. I go out, put the TV on, find a cartoon channel, and turn off the sound; the child sits there hypnotized—problem solved. I wonder how it must have been in the past, because the women who came to perform the same ritual Athena is about to take part in would have brought their children, and in those days there was no TV. What did teachers do then?

Fortunately, I don't have to worry about that.

What the boy is experiencing in front of the television—a gateway into a different reality—is the same state I am going to induce in Athena. Everything is at once so simple and so complicated! It's simple because all it takes is a change of attitude: I'm not going to look for happiness anymore. From now on, I'm independent; I see life through my eyes and not through other people's. I'm going in search of the adventure of being alive.

And it's complicated: Why am I not looking for happiness when everyone has taught me that happiness is the only goal worth pursuing? Why am I going to risk taking a path that no one else is taking?

After all, what *is* happiness?

Love, they tell me. But love doesn't bring and never has brought happiness. On the contrary, it's a constant state of anxiety, a battlefield; it's sleepless nights, asking ourselves all the time if we're doing the right thing. Real love is composed of ecstasy and agony.

All right then, peace. Peace? If we look at the Mother, she's never at peace. The winter does battle with the summer, the sun and the moon never meet, the tiger chases the man, who's afraid of the dog, who chases the cat, who chases the mouse, who frightens the man.

Money brings happiness. Fine. In that case, everyone who earns enough to have a high standard of living would be able to stop working. But then they're more troubled than ever, as if they were afraid of losing everything. Money attracts money, that's true. Poverty might bring unhappiness, but money won't necessarily bring happiness.

I spent a lot of my life looking for happiness; now what I want is joy. Joy is like sex—it begins and ends. I want pleasure. I want to be contented, but happiness? I no longer fall into that trap.

When I'm with a group of people and I want to provoke them by asking that most important of questions—Are you happy? —they all reply: "Yes, I am."

Then I ask: "But don't you want more? Don't you want to keep on growing?" And they all reply: "Of course."

Then I say: "So you're not happy." And they change the subject.

I must go back to the room where Athena is sitting. It's dark. She hears my footsteps; a match is struck and a candle lit.

"We're surrounded by Universal Desire. It's not happiness, it's desire. And desires are never satisfied, because once they are, they cease to be desires."

"Where's my son?"

"Your son is fine; he's watching TV. I just want you to look at the candle; don't speak, don't say anything. Just believe."

"Believe what?"

"I asked you not to say anything. Simply believe—don't doubt anything. You're alive, and this candle is the only point in your universe. Believe in that. Let go of the idea that the path will lead you to your goal. The truth is that with each step we take, we arrive. Repeat that to yourself every morning: 'I've arrived.' That way you'll find it much easier to stay in touch with each second of your day."

I paused.

"The candle flame is illuminating your world. Ask the candle: 'Who am I?'"

I paused again, then went on. "I can imagine your answer. I'm so-and-so. I've had these experiences. I have a son. I work in Dubai. Now ask the candle again: 'Who am I not?'"

Again I waited and again I went on. "You probably said: I'm not a contented person. I'm not a typical mother concerned only with her son and her husband, with having a house and a garden and a place to spend the summer holidays. Is that so? You can speak now."

"Yes, it is."

"Good, we're on the right path. You, like me, are a dissatisfied person. Your 'reality' does not coincide with the 'reality' of other people. And you're afraid that your son will follow the same path as you, is that correct?"

"Yes."

"Nevertheless, you know you cannot stop. You struggle, but

you can't control your doubts. Look hard at the candle. At the moment, the candle is your universe. It fixes your attention; it lights up the room around you a little. Breathe deeply, hold the air in your lungs as long as possible, and then breathe out. Repeat this five times."

She obeyed.

"This exercise should have calmed your soul. Now remember what I said: believe. Believe in your abilities; believe that you have already arrived where you wanted to arrive. At a particular moment in your life, as you told me over tea this afternoon, you said that you'd changed the behavior of the people in the bank where you worked because you'd taught them to dance. That isn't true. You changed everything because, through dance, you changed their reality. You believed in the story of the Vertex, which, although I've never heard of it before, seems to me an interesting one. You like dancing and you believed in what you were doing. You can't believe in something you don't like, can you?"

Athena shook her head, keeping her eyes fixed on the candle flame.

"Faith is not Desire. Faith is Will. Desires are things that need to be satisfied, whereas Will is a force. Will changes the space around us, as you did with your work at the bank. But for that you also need Desire. Please, concentrate on the candle!

"Your son left the room and went to watch TV because he's afraid of the dark. But why? We can project anything onto the darkness, and we usually project our own ghosts. That's true for children and for adults. Slowly raise your right arm."

She raised her arm. I asked her to do the same with her left arm. I looked at her breasts, far prettier than mine.

"Now slowly lower them again. Close your eyes and breathe deeply. I'm going to turn on the light. Right, that's the end of the ritual. Let's go into the living room."

She got up with some difficulty. Her legs had gone numb because of the position I'd told her to adopt.

Viorel had fallen asleep. I turned off the TV, and we went into the kitchen.

"What was the point of all that?" she asked.

"Merely to remove you from everyday reality. I could have asked you to concentrate on anything, but I like the darkness and the candle flame. But you want to know what I'm up to, isn't that right?"

Athena remarked that she'd traveled for nearly five hours on the train with her son on her lap, when she should have been packing her bags to go back to work. She could have sat looking at a candle in her own room without any need to come to Scotland at all.

"Yes, there was a need," I replied. "You needed to know that you're not alone, that other people are in contact with the same thing as you. Just knowing that allows you to believe."

"To believe what?"

"That you're on the right path. And as I said before, arriving with each step you take."

"What path? I thought that by going to find my mother in Romania, I would, at last, find the peace of mind I so need, but I haven't. What path are you talking about?"

"I haven't the slightest idea. You'll only discover that when you start to teach. When you go back to Dubai, find a student."

"Do you mean teach dance or calligraphy?"

"Those are things you know about already. You need to teach what you don't know, what the Mother wants to reveal through you."

She looked at me as if I had gone mad.

"It's true," I said. "Why else do you think I asked you to breathe deeply and to raise your arms? So that you'd believe that I knew more than you. But it isn't true. It was just a way of taking you out of the world you're accustomed to. I didn't ask you to thank the Mother, to say how wonderful she is or that you saw her face shining in the flames of a fire. I asked only that absurd and pointless gesture of raising your arms and focusing your attention on a candle. That's enough—trying, whenever possible, to do something that is out of kilter with the reality around us.

"When you start creating rituals for your student to carry out, you'll be receiving guidance. That's where the apprenticeship begins, or so my protector told me. If you want to heed my words, fine, but if you don't and you carry on with your life as it is at the moment, you'll end up bumping up against a wall called 'dissatisfaction.'"

I rang for a taxi, and we talked a little about fashion and men, and then Athena left. I was sure she would listen to me, mainly because she was the kind of person who never refuses a challenge.

"Teach people to be different. That's all!" I shouted after her as the taxi moved off.

That is joy. Happiness would be feeling satisfied with everything she already had—a lover, a son, a job. And Athena, like
me, wasn't born for that kind of life.

HERON RYAN, JOURNALIST

I couldn't admit I was in love, of course; I already had a girlfriend who loved me and shared with me both my troubles and
my joys.

The various encounters and events that had taken place in
Sibiu were part of a journey, and it wasn't the first time this kind
of thing had happened while I was away from home. When we
step out of our normal world and leave behind us all the usual
barriers and prejudices, we tend to become more adventurous.

When I returned to England, the first thing I did was to
tell the producers that making a documentary about the historical figure of Dracula was nonsense, and that one book by a
mad Irishman had created a truly terrible image of Transylvania,
which was, in fact, one of the loveliest places on the planet. Obviously the producers were none too pleased, but at that point, I
didn't care what they thought. I left television and went to work
for one of the world's most prestigious newspapers.

That was when I began to realize that I wanted to meet
Athena again.

I phoned her and we arranged to go for a walk together before she went back to Dubai. She suggested showing me around
London.

We got on the first bus that stopped, without asking where it was going, then we chose a female passenger at random and decided that we would get off wherever she did. She got off at Temple and so did we. We passed a beggar who asked us for money, but we didn't give him any and walked on, listening to the insults he hurled after us, accepting that this was merely his way of communicating with us.

We saw someone vandalizing a telephone booth, and I wanted to call the police, but Athena stopped me; perhaps that person had just broken up with the love of his life and needed to vent his feelings. Or, who knows, perhaps he had no one to talk to and couldn't stand to see others humiliating him by using that phone to discuss business deals or love.

She told me to close my eyes and to describe exactly the clothes we were both wearing; to my surprise, I got nearly every detail wrong.

She asked me what was on my desk at work and said that some of the papers were only there because I was too lazy to deal with them.

"Have you ever considered that those bits of paper have a life and feelings, have requests to make and stories to tell? I don't think you're giving life the attention it deserves."

I promised that I'd go through them one by one when I returned to work the following day.

A foreign couple with a map asked Athena how to get to a particular tourist spot. She gave them very precise, but totally inaccurate, directions.

"Everything you told them was completely wrong!"

"It doesn't matter. They'll get lost, and that's the best way to discover interesting places. Try to fill your life again with a little fantasy; above our heads is a sky about which the whole of humanity—after thousands of years spent observing it—has given various apparently reasonable explanations. Forget everything you've ever learned about the stars and they'll once more be transformed into angels, or into children, or into whatever you want to believe at that moment. It won't make you more stupid—after all, it's only a game—but it could enrich your life."

The following day, when I went back to work, I treated each sheet of paper as if it were a message addressed to me personally and not to the organization I represent. At midday, I went to talk to the deputy editor and suggested writing an article about the Goddess worshipped by the gypsies. He thought it an excellent idea and I was commissioned to go to the celebrations in the gypsy Mecca, Saintes-Maries-de-la-Mer.

Incredible though it may seem, Athena showed no desire to go with me. She said that her boyfriend—that fictitious policeman, whom she was using to keep me at a distance—wouldn't be very happy if she went off traveling with another man.

"Didn't you promise your mother to take the saint a new shawl?"

"Yes, I did, but only if the town happened to be on my path, which it isn't. If I do ever pass by there, then I'll keep my promise."

She was returning to Dubai the following Sunday, but first she traveled up to Scotland with her son to see the woman we'd both met in Bucharest. I didn't remember anyone, but perhaps the "phantom woman in Scotland," like the "phantom boy-friend," was another excuse, and I decided not to insist. But I nevertheless felt jealous, as if she were telling me that she preferred being with other people.

I found my jealousy odd. And I decided that if I was asked to go to the Middle East to write an article about the property boom that someone on the business pages had mentioned, I would read everything I could on real estate, economics, politics, and oil, simply as a way of getting closer to Athena.

My visit to Saintes-Maries-de-la-Mer produced an excellent article. According to tradition, Sarah was a gypsy who happened to be living in the small seaside town when Jesus's aunt, Mary Salome, along with other refugees, arrived there, fleeing persecution by the Romans. Sarah helped them and, in the end, converted to Christianity.

During the celebrations, bones from the skeletons of the two women who are buried beneath the altar are taken out of a reliquary and raised up on high to bless the multitude of gypsies who arrive in their caravans from all over Europe with their bright clothes and their music. Then the image of Sarah, decked out in splendid robes, is brought from the place near the church where it's kept—for Sarah has never been canonized by the Vatican—and carried in procession to the sea through narrow streets strewn with rose petals. Four gypsies in traditional costume place the relics in a boat full of flowers and wade into the water, reenacting the arrival of the fugitives and their meeting with Sarah. From then on, it's all music, celebration, songs, and bull running.

A historian, Antoine Locadour, helped me flesh out the article with interesting facts about the Female Divinity. I sent Athena the two pages I'd written for the newspaper's travel section. All I received in return was a friendly reply, thanking me for sending her the article, but with no other comment.

At least I'd confirmed that her address in Dubai existed.

ANTOINE LOCADOUR, SEVENTY-FOUR,
HISTORIAN, ICP, FRANCE

It's easy to label Sarah as just one of the many black Virgins in the world. According to tradition, Sarah-la-Kali was of noble lineage and knew the secrets of the world. She is, I believe, one more manifestation of what people call the Great Mother, the Goddess of Creation.

And it doesn't surprise me in the least that more and more people are becoming interested in pagan traditions. Why? Because God the Father is associated with the rigor and discipline of worship, whereas the Mother Goddess shows the importance of love above and beyond all the usual prohibitions and taboos.

The phenomenon is hardly a new one. Whenever a religion tightens its rules, a significant number of people break away and go in search of more freedom in their search for spiritual contact. This happened during the Middle Ages when the Catholic Church did little more than impose taxes and build splendid monasteries and convents; the phenomenon known as "witchcraft" was a reaction to this, and even though it was suppressed because of its revolutionary nature, it left behind it roots and traditions that have managed to survive over the centuries.

According to pagan tradition, nature worship is more important than reverence for sacred books. The Goddess is in everything and everything is part of the Goddess. The world is merely an expression of her goodness. There are many philosophical systems—such as Taoism and Buddhism—that make no distinction between creator and creature. People no longer try to decipher the mystery of life but choose instead to be a part of it. There is no female figure in Taoism or Buddhism, but there too the central idea is that "everything is one."

In the worship of the Great Mother, what we call "sin," usually a transgression of certain arbitrary moral codes, ceases to exist. Sex and customs in general are freer because they are part of nature and cannot be considered to be the fruits of evil.

The new paganism shows that man is capable of living without an institutionalized religion, while still continuing the spiritual search in order to justify his existence. If God is Mother, then we need only gather together with other people and adore her through rituals intended to satisfy the female soul, rituals involving dance, fire, water, air, earth, songs, music, flowers, and beauty.

This has been a growing trend over the last few years. We may be witnessing a very important moment in the history of the world, when the Spirit finally merges with the Material, and the two are united and transformed. At the same time, I imagine that there will be a very violent reaction from organized religious institutions, which are beginning to lose their followers. There will be a rise in fundamentalism.

As a historian, I'm content to collate all the data and analyze this confrontation between the freedom to worship and the duty to obey, between the God who controls the world and the Goddess who is part of the world, between people who join together in groups where celebration is a spontaneous affair and those who close ranks and learn only what they should and should not do.

I'd like to be optimistic and believe that human beings have at last found their path to the spiritual world, but the signs are not very positive. As so often in the past, a new conservative backlash could once more stifle the cult of the Mother.

ANDREA MCCAIN, THEATER ACTRESS

It's very difficult to be impartial and to tell a story that began in admiration and ended in rancor, but I'm going to try, yes, I'm really going to try and describe the Athena I met for the first time in an apartment in Victoria Street.

She'd just got back from Dubai with plenty of money and a desire to share everything she knew about the mysteries of magic. This time, she'd spent only four months in the Middle East: she sold some land for the construction of two supermarkets, earned a huge commission, and decided that she'd earned enough money to support herself and her son for the next three years, and that she could always resume work later on if she wanted. Now was the time to make the most of the present, to live what remained of her youth, and to teach others everything she had learned.

She received me somewhat unenthusiastically.

"What do you want?"

"I work in the theater and we're putting on a play about the female face of God. I heard from a journalist friend that you spent time in the Balkan mountains with some gypsies and would be prepared to tell me about your experiences there."

"You mean you only came here to learn about the Mother because of a play?"

"Why did you learn about her?"

Athena stopped, looked me up and down, and smiled.

"You're right. That's my first lesson as a teacher: teach those who want to learn. The reason doesn't matter."

"I'm sorry?"

"Nothing."

"The origins of the theater are sacred," I went on. "It began in Greece with hymns to Dionysus, the god of wine, rebirth, and fertility. But it's believed that even from very remote times, people performed a ritual in which they would pretend to be someone else as a way of communing with the sacred."

"Second lesson, thank you."

"I don't understand. I came here to learn, not to teach."

This woman was beginning to iritate me. Perhaps she was being ironic.

"My protector—"

"Your protector?"

"I'll explain another time. My protector said that I would only learn what I need to learn if I were provoked into it. And since my return from Dubai, you're the first person to demon-strate that to me. What she said makes sense."

I explained that, in researching the play, I'd gone from one teacher to the next but had never found their teachings to be in any way exceptional; despite this, however, I grew more and more interested in the matter as I went on. I also mentioned that these people had seemed confused and uncertain about what they wanted.

"For example."

Sex, for example. In some of the places I went to, sex was a complete no-no. In others, they not only advocated complete freedom, but even encouraged orgies. She asked for more details, and I couldn't tell if she was doing this in order to test me or because she had no idea what other people got up to.

Athena spoke before I could answer her question.

"When you dance, do you feel desire? Do you feel as if you were summoning up a greater energy? When you dance, are there moments when you cease to be yourself?"

I didn't know what to say. In nightclubs or at parties in friends' houses, sensuality was definitely part of how I felt when I danced. I would start by flirting and enjoying the desire in men's eyes, but as the night wore on, I seemed to get more in touch with myself, and it was no longer important to me whether I was or wasn't seducing someone.

Athena continued.

"If theater is ritual, then dance is too. Moreover, it's a very ancient way of getting close to a partner. It's as if the threads connecting us to the rest of the world were washed clean of preconceptions and fears. When you dance, you can enjoy the luxury of being you."

I started listening to her with more respect.

"Afterward, we go back to being who we were before—frightened people trying to be more important than we actually believe we are."

That was exactly how I felt. Or is it the same for everyone?

"Do you have a boyfriend?"

I remembered that in one of the places where I'd gone to learn about the Gaia tradition, a "druid" had asked me to make love in front of him. Ridiculous and frightening—how dare these people use the spiritual search to advance their own more sinister ends?

"Do you have a boyfriend?" she asked again.

"I do."

Athena said nothing else. She merely put her finger to her lips, indicating that I should remain silent.

And suddenly I realized that it was extremely difficult for me to remain silent in the presence of someone I'd only just met. The norm is to talk about something, anything—the weather, the traffic, the best restaurants to go to. We were sitting on the sofa in her completely white sitting room, with a CD player and a small shelf of CDs. There were no books anywhere, and no paintings on the walls. Given that she'd traveled to the Middle East, I'd expected to find objects and souvenirs from that part of the world.

But it was empty, and now there was this silence.

Her gray eyes were fixed on mine, but I held firm and didn't look away. Instinct perhaps. A way of saying that I'm not frightened, but facing the challenge head-on. Except that every-thing—the silence and the white room, the noise of the traffic outside in the street—began to seem unreal. How long were we going to stay there, saying nothing?

I started to track my own thoughts. Had I come there in search of material for my play or did I really want knowledge, wisdom, power? I couldn't put my finger on what it was that had led me to come and see ... what? A witch?

My adolescent dreams surfaced. Who wouldn't like to meet a real witch, learn how to perform magic, and gain the respect and fear of her friends? Who, as a young woman, hasn't been outraged by the centuries of repression suffered by women and felt that becoming a witch would be the best way of recovering her lost identity? I'd been through that phase myself; I was inde-pendent and did what I liked in the highly competitive world of the theater, but then why was I never content, why was I always testing out my curiosity?

We must have been about the same age ... or was I older? Did she too have a boyfriend?

Athena moved closer. We were now less than an arm's length from each other, and I started to feel afraid. Was she a lesbian?

I didn't look away, but I made a mental note of where the door was so that I could leave whenever I wished. No one had made me go to that house to meet someone I'd never seen before in my life and sit there wasting time, not saying anything and not learning anything either. What did she want?

That silence perhaps. My muscles began to grow tense. I was alone and helpless. I desperately needed to talk or to make my mind stop telling me that I was being threatened. How could she possibly know who I was? We are what we say!

Had she asked me anything about my life? She'd wanted to know if I had a boyfriend. I tried to say more about the theater, but couldn't. And what about the stories I'd heard about her gypsy ancestry, her stay in Transylvania, the land of vampires?

My thoughts wouldn't stop: How much would that consultation cost? I was terrified. I should have asked before. A fortune? And if I didn't pay, would she put a spell on me that would eventually destroy me?

I felt an impulse to get to my feet, thank her, and say that I hadn't come there just to sit in silence. If you go to a psychiatrist, you have to talk. If you go to a church, you listen to a sermon. If you go in search of magic, you find a teacher who wants to explain the world to you and who gives you a series of rituals to follow. But silence? Why did it make me feel so uncomfortable?

One question after another kept forming in my mind, and I couldn't stop thinking or trying to find a reason for the two of us to be sitting there, saying nothing. Suddenly, perhaps after five or ten long minutes of total immobility, she smiled.

I smiled too and relaxed.

"Try to be different. That's all."

"That's all? Is sitting in silence being different? I imagine that, at this very moment, there are thousands of people in London who are desperate for someone to talk to, and all you can say to me is that silence makes a difference?"

"Now that you're talking and reorganizing the universe, you'll end up convincing yourself that you're right and I'm wrong. But as you experienced for yourself—being silent *is* different."

"It's unpleasant. It doesn't teach you anything."

She seemed indifferent to my reaction.

"What theater are you working at?"

Finally, she was taking an interest in my life! I was being restored to my human condition, with a profession and everything! I invited her to come and see the play we were putting on—it was the only way I could find to avenge myself, by showing that I was capable of things that Athena was not. That silence had left a humiliating aftertaste.

She asked if she could bring her son, and I said no, it was for adults only.

"Well, I could always leave him with my mother. I haven't been to the theater in ages."

She didn't charge for the consultation. When I met up with the other members of the cast, I told them about my encounter with this mysterious creature. They were all mad keen to meet someone who, when she first met you, asked only that you sit in silence.

Athena arrived on the appointed day. She saw the play, came to my dressing room afterward to say hello, but didn't say whether she'd enjoyed herself or not. My colleagues suggested that I invite her to the bar where we usually went after the performance. There, instead of keeping quiet, she started answering a question that had been left unanswered at our first meeting.

"No one, not even the Mother, would ever want sex to take

place purely as a celebration. Love must always be present. Didn't you say that you'd met people like that? Well, be careful."

My friends had no idea what she was talking about, but they warmed to the subject and started bombarding her with questions. Something troubled me. Her answers were very academic, as if she didn't have much experience of what she was talking about. She spoke about the game of seduction, about fertility rites, and concluded with a Greek myth, probably because I'd mentioned during our first meeting that the theater had begun in Greece. She must have spent the whole week reading up on the subject.

"After millennia of male domination, we are returning to the cult of the Great Mother. The Greeks called her Gaia, and according to the myth, she was born out of Chaos, the void that existed before the universe. With her came Eros, the god of love, and then she gave birth to the Sea and the Sky."

"Who was the father?" asked one of my friends.

"No one. There's a technical term, parthenogenesis, which is a process of reproduction that does not require fertilization of the egg by a male. There's a mystical term too, one to which we're more accustomed: Immaculate Conception.

"From Gaia sprang all the gods who would later people the Elysian Fields of Greece, including our own dear Dionysus, your idol. But as man became established as the principal political power in the cities, Gaia was forgotten, and was replaced by Zeus, Ares, Apollo and company, all of whom were competent enough, but didn't have the same allure as the Mother who originated everything."

Then she questioned us about our work. The director asked if she'd like to give us some lessons.

"On what?"

"On what you know."

"To be perfectly honest, I learned all about the origins of theater this week. I learn everything as I need to learn it, that's what Edda told me to do."

So I was right!

"But I can share other things that life has taught me."

They all agreed. And no one asked who Edda was.

DEIDRE O'NEILL, KNOWN AS EDDA

I said to Athena: You don't have to keep coming here all the time just to ask silly questions. If a group has decided to take you on as a teacher, why not use that opportunity to turn yourself into a teacher?

Do what I always did.

Try to feel good about yourself even when you feel like the least worthy of creatures. Reject all those negative thoughts and let the Mother take possession of your body and soul; surrender yourself to dance or to silence or to ordinary, everyday activities—like taking your son to school, preparing supper, making sure the house is tidy. Everything is worship if your mind is focused on the present moment.

Don't try to convince anyone of anything. When you don't know something, ask or go away and find out. But when you do act, be like the silent, flowing river and open yourself to a greater energy. Believe—that's what I said at our first meeting—simply believe that you can.

At first, you'll be confused and insecure. Then you'll start to believe that everyone thinks they're being conned. It's not true. You have the knowledge, it's simply a matter of being aware. All the minds on the planet are so easily cast down—they fear illness, invasion, attack, death. Try to restore their lost joy to them.

Be clear.

Reprogram yourself every minute of each day with thoughts that make you grow. When you're feeling irritated or confused, try to laugh at yourself. Laugh out loud at this woman tormented by doubts and anxieties, convinced that her problems are the most important thing in the world. Laugh at the sheer absurdity of the situation, at the fact that despite being a manifestation of the Mother, you still believe God is a man who lays down the rules. Most of our problems stem from just that—from following rules.

Concentrate.

If you can find nothing on which to focus your mind, concentrate on your breathing. The Mother's river of light is flowing in through your nose. Listen to your heart beating, follow the thoughts you can't control, control your desire to get up at once and to do something "useful." Sit for a few minutes each day doing nothing, getting as much as you can out of that time.

When you're washing up, pray. Be thankful that there are plates to be washed; that means there was food, that you fed someone, that you've lavished care on one or more people, that you cooked and laid the table. Imagine the millions of people at this moment who have absolutely nothing to wash up and no one for whom to lay the table.

There are women who say: I'm not going to do the washing up, let the men do it. Fine, let the men do it if they want to, but that has nothing to do with equality. There's nothing wrong with doing simple things, although if I were to publish an article tomorrow saying everything I think, I'd be accused of working against the feminist cause. Nonsense! As if washing up or wearing a bra or having someone open or close a door could be humiliating to me as a woman. The fact is, I love it when a man opens the door for me. According to etiquette this means, "She needs me to do this because she's fragile," but in my soul is written: "I'm being treated like a goddess. I'm a queen." I'm not here to work for the feminist cause, because both men and women are a manifestation of the Mother, the Divine Unity. No one can be greater than that.

I'd love to see you giving classes on what you're learning. That's the main aim of life—revelation! You make yourself into a channel, you listen to yourself and are surprised at how capable you are. Remember your job at the bank? Perhaps you never properly understood that what happened there was a result of the energy flowing out of your body, your eyes, your hands.

You'll say: "No, it was the dance."

The dance was simply a ritual. What is a ritual? It means transforming something monotonous into something different, rhythmic, capable of channeling the Unity. That's why I say again: be different even when you're washing up. Move your hands so that they never repeat the same gesture twice, even though they maintain the rhythm.

If you find it helpful, try to visualize images—flowers, birds, trees in a forest. Don't imagine single objects, like the candle you focused on when you came here for the first time. Try to think of something collective. And do you know what you'll find? That you didn't choose your thought.

I'll give you an example: imagine a flock of birds flying. How many birds did you see? Eleven, nineteen, five? You have a vague idea, but you don't know the exact number. So where did that thought come from? Someone put it there. Someone who knows the exact number of birds, trees, stones, flowers. Someone who, in that fraction of a second, took charge of you and showed you her power.

You are what you believe yourself to be.

Don't be like those people who believe in "positive thinking" and tell themselves that they're loved and strong and capable. You don't need to do that, because you know it already. And when you doubt it—which happens, I think, quite often at this stage of evolution—do as I suggested. Instead of trying to prove that you're better than you think, just laugh. Laugh at your worries and insecurities. View your anxieties with humor. It will be difficult at first, but you'll gradually get used to it.

Now go back and meet all those people who think you know everything. Convince yourself that they're right, because we all know everything, it's merely a question of believing.

Believe.

As I said to you in Bucharest, the very first time we met,

groups are very important because they force us to progress. If you're alone, all you can do is laugh at yourself, but if you're with others, you'll laugh and then immediately act. Groups challenge us. Groups allow us to choose our affinities. Groups create a collective energy, and ecstasy comes more easily because everyone infects everyone else.

Groups can also destroy us, of course, but that's part of life and the human condition—living with other people. And anyone who's failed to develop an instinct for survival has understood nothing of what the Mother is saying.

You're lucky. A group has just asked you to teach them something, and that will make you a teacher.

HERON RYAN, JOURNALIST

Before the first meeting with the actors, Athena came to my house. Ever since I published the article on St. Sarah, she'd been convinced that I understood her world, which wasn't true at all. I simply wanted to attract her attention. I was trying to come round to the idea that there might be an invisible reality capable of interfering in our lives, but the only reason I did so was because of a love I didn't want to believe I felt but which was continuing to grow in a subtle, devastating way.

I was content with my universe and didn't want to change it at all, even though I was being propelled in that direction.

"I'm afraid," she said as soon as she arrived. "But I must go ahead and do what they're asking of me. I need to believe."

"You've had a lot of experiences in life. You learned from the gypsies, from the dervishes in the desert, from—"

"Well, that's not quite true. Besides, what does learning mean: accumulating knowledge or transforming your life?"

I suggested we go out that night for supper and to dance a little. She agreed to supper but rejected the dancing.

"Answer me," she said, looking around my apartment. "Is learning just putting things on a shelf or is it discarding whatever is no longer useful and then continuing on your way feeling lighter?"

On the shelves were all the books I'd invested so much money and time in buying, reading, and annotating. There were my personality, my education, my true teachers.

"How many books have you got? Over a thousand, I'd say. But most of them you'll probably never open again. You hang on to them because you don't believe."

"I don't believe?"

"No, you don't believe, full stop. Anyone who believes will go and read up about theater as I did when Andrea asked me about it, but after that, it's a question of letting the Mother speak through you and making discoveries as she speaks. And as you make those discoveries, you'll manage to fill in the blank spaces that all those writers left there on purpose to provoke the reader's imagination. And when you fill in the spaces, you'll start to believe in your own abilities.

"How many people would love to read those books but don't have the money to buy them? Meanwhile, you sit here surrounded by all this stagnant energy, purely to impress the friends who visit you. Or is it that you don't feel you've learned anything from them and need to consult them again?"

I thought she was being rather hard on me, and that intrigued me.

"So you don't think I need this library?"

"I think you need to read, but why hang on to all these books? Would it be asking too much if we were to leave here right now, and before going to the restaurant, distribute most of them to whomever we happened to pass in the street?"

"They wouldn't all fit in my car."

"We could hire a truck."

"But then we wouldn't get to the restaurant in time for supper. Besides, you came here because you were feeling insecure, not in order to tell me what I should do with my books. Without them I'd feel naked."

"Ignorant, you mean."

"*Uncultivated* would be the right word."

"So your culture isn't in your heart, it's on your bookshelves."

Enough was enough. I picked up the phone to reserve a table and told the restaurant that we'd be there in fifteen minutes. Athena was trying to avoid the problem that had brought her here. Her deep insecurity was making her go on the attack, rather than looking at herself. She needed a man by her side and, who knows, was perhaps sounding me out to see how far I'd go, using her feminine wiles to discover just what I'd be prepared to do for her.

Simply being in her presence seemed to justify my very existence. Was that what she wanted to hear? Fine, I'd tell her over supper. I'd be capable of doing almost anything, even leaving the woman I was living with, but I drew the line, of course, at giving away my books.

In the taxi, we returned to the subject of the theater group, although I was, at that moment, prepared to discuss something I never normally spoke about—love, a subject I found far more complicated than Marx, Jung, the British Labour Party, or the day-to-day problems at a newspaper office.

"You don't need to worry," I said, feeling a desire to hold her hand. "It'll be all right. Talk about calligraphy. Talk about dancing. Talk about the things you know."

"If I did that, I'd never discover what it is I don't know. When I'm there, I'll have to allow my mind to go still and let my heart begin to speak. But it's the first time I've done that, and I'm frightened."

"Would you like me to come with you?"

She accepted at once. We arrived at the restaurant, ordered some wine, and started to drink. I was drinking in order to get up the courage to say what I thought I was feeling, although it seemed absurd to me to be declaring my love to someone I hardly knew. And she was drinking because she was afraid of talking about what she didn't know.

After the second glass of wine, I realized how on edge she was. I tried to hold her hand, but she gently pulled away.

"I can't be afraid."

"Of course you can, Athena. I often feel afraid, and yet,

when I need to, I go ahead and face up to whatever it is I'm afraid of."

I was on edge too. I refilled our glasses. The waiter kept coming over to ask what we'd like to eat, and I kept telling him that we'd order later.

I was talking about whatever came into my head. Athena was listening politely, but she seemed far away, in some dark universe full of ghosts. At one point, she told me again about the woman in Scotland and what she'd said. I asked if it made sense to teach what you didn't know.

"Did anyone ever teach you how to love?" she replied.

Could she be reading my thoughts?

"And yet," she went on, "you're as capable of love as any other human being. How did you learn? You didn't, you simply believe. You believe, therefore you love."

"Athena …"

I hesitated, then managed to finish my sentence, although not at all as I had intended.

"… perhaps we should order some food."

I realized that I wasn't yet prepared to mention the things that were troubling my world. I called the waiter over and ordered some starters, then some more starters, a main dish, a pudding, and another bottle of wine. The more time I had, the better.

"You're acting strangely. Was it my comment about your books? You do what you like. It's not my job to change your world. I was obviously sticking my nose in where it wasn't wanted."

I had been thinking about that business of "changing the world" only a few seconds before.

"Athena, you're always telling me about … no, I need to talk about something that happened in that bar in Sibiu, with the gypsy music."

"In the restaurant, you mean?"

"Yes, in the restaurant. Today we were discussing books, the things that we accumulate and that take up space. Perhaps you're right. There's something I've been wanting to do ever since I saw you dancing that night. It weighs more and more heavily on my heart."

"I don't know what you mean."

"Of course you do. I'm talking about the love I'm discovering now and doing my best to destroy before it reveals itself. I'd like you to accept it. It's the little I have of myself, but it's not my own. It's not exclusively yours, because there's someone else in my life, but I would be happy if you could accept it anyway. An Arab poet from your country, Khalil Gibran, says: *'It is well to give when asked, but it is better to give unasked.'* If I don't say everything I need to say tonight, I'll merely be a spectator watching events unfold rather than the person actually experiencing them."

I took a deep breath. The wine had helped me to free myself.

She drained her glass, and I did the same. The waiter appeared with the food, making a few comments about the various dishes, explaining the ingredients and the way in which they had been cooked. Athena and I kept our eyes fixed on each other. Andrea had told me that this is what Athena had done when they met for the first time, and she was convinced it was simply a way of intimidating others.

The silence was terrifying. I imagined her getting up from the table and citing her famous, invisible boyfriend from Scotland Yard, or saying that she was very flattered, but she had to think about the class she was to give the next day.

"And is there anything you would withhold? Some day, all that you have shall be given. The trees give that they may live, for to withhold is to perish."

She was speaking quietly and carefully because of the wine she'd drunk, but her voice nevertheless silenced everything around us.

"And what greater merit shall there be than that which lies in the courage and the confidence, nay the charity, of receiving? You give but little when you give of your possessions. It is when you give of yourself that you truly give."

She said all this without smiling. I felt as if I were conversing with a sphinx.

"Words written by the same poet you were quoting. I learned them at school, but I don't need the book where he wrote those words. I've kept his words in my heart."

She drank a little more wine. I did the same. I couldn't bring myself to ask if she accepted my love or not, but I felt lighter.

"You may be right. I'll donate my books to a public library and only keep those I really will reread one day."

"Is that what you want to talk about now?"

"No. I just don't know how to continue the conversation."

"Shall we eat, then, and enjoy the food. Does that seem a good idea?"

No, it didn't seem like a good idea. I wanted to hear something different, but I was afraid to ask, and so I babbled on about libraries, books, and poets, regretting having ordered so many dishes. I was the one who wanted to escape now, because I didn't know how to continue.

In the end, she made me promise that I would be at the theater for her first class, and for me that was a signal. She needed me; she had accepted what I had unconsciously dreamed of offering her ever since I saw her dancing in a restaurant in Transylvania, but which I had only been capable of understanding that night.

Or, as Athena would have said, of believing.

ANDREA McCAIN, ACTRESS

Of course I'm to blame. If it hadn't been for me, Athena would never have come to the theater that morning, gathered us all together, asked us to lie down on the stage and begin a relaxation exercise involving breathing and bringing our awareness to each part of the body.

"Relax your thighs ..."

We all obeyed, as if we were before a goddess, someone who knew more than all of us, even though we'd done this kind of exercise hundreds of times before. We were all curious to know what would come after "... now relax your face and breathe deeply."

Did she really think she was teaching us anything new? We were expecting a lecture, a talk! But I must control myself. Let's get back to what happened then. We relaxed, and then came a silence that left us completely disoriented. When I discussed it with my colleagues afterward, we all agreed that we felt the exercise was over, that it was time to sit up and look around, except that no one did. We remained lying down, in a kind of enforced meditation, for fifteen interminable minutes.

Then she spoke again.

"You've had plenty of time to doubt me now. One or two of you looked impatient. But now I'm going to ask you just one thing: when I count to three, be different. I don't mean be another person, an animal, or a house. Try to forget everything you've learned in drama courses. I'm not asking you to be actors and to demonstrate your abilities. I'm asking you to cease being human and to transform yourselves into something you don't know."

We were all still lying on the floor with our eyes closed and so couldn't see how anyone else was reacting. Athena was playing on that uncertainty.

"I'm going to say a few words and you'll immediately associate certain images with those words. Remember that you're all full of the poison of preconceived ideas and that if I were to say *fate*, you would probably start imagining your lives in the future. If I were to say *red*, you would probably make some psychoanalytic interpretation. That isn't what I want. As I said, I want you to be different."

She couldn't explain what she really wanted. When no one complained, I felt sure they were simply being polite, but that when the "lecture" was over, they would never invite Athena back. They would even tell me that I'd been naive to have sought her out in the first place.

"The first word is *sacred*."

So as not to die of boredom, I decided to join in the game. I imagined my mother, my boyfriend, my future children, a brilliant career.

"Make a gesture that means *sacred*."

I folded my arms over my chest, as if I were embracing all my loved ones. I found out later that most people opened their arms to form a cross, and that one of the women opened her legs, as if she were making love.

"Relax again, and again forget about everything and keep your eyes closed. I'm not criticizing, but from what I saw, you seem to be giving form to what you consider to be sacred. That isn't what I want. When I give you the next word, don't try to define it as it manifests itself in the world. Open all the channels and allow the poison of reality to drain away. Be abstract, and then you will enter the world I'm guiding you toward."

That last phrase had real authority, and I felt the energy in the theater change. Now the voice knew where it wanted to take us. She was a teacher now, not a lecturer.

Earth, she said.

Suddenly I understood what she meant. It was no longer my imagination that mattered, but my body in contact with the soil. I was the earth.

"Make a gesture that represents *earth*."

I didn't move. I was the soil of that stage.

"Perfect," she said. "None of you moved. For the first time you all experienced the same feeling. Instead of describing something, you transformed yourself into an idea."

She fell silent again for what I imagined were five long minutes. The silence made us feel lost, unable to tell whether she simply had no idea how to continue, or if she was merely unfamiliar with our usual intense rhythm of working.

"I'm going to say a third word."

She paused.

"*Center.*"

I felt—and this was entirely unconscious—that all my vital energy went to my navel, where it glowed yellow. This frightened me. If someone touched it, I could die.

"Make a gesture for *center!*"

Her words sounded like a command. I immediately placed my hands on my belly to protect myself.

"Perfect," said Athena. "You can sit up now."

I opened my eyes and saw the extinguished stage lights up above me, distant and dull. I rubbed my face and got to my feet. I noticed that my colleagues looked surprised.

"Was that the lecture?" asked the director.

"You can call it a lecture if you like."

"Well, thank you for coming. Now, if you'll excuse us, we have to start rehearsals for the next play."

"But I haven't finished yet."

"Perhaps another time."

Everyone seemed confused by the director's reaction. After some initial doubts, I think we were enjoying the session—it was different, no pretending to be things or people, no visualizing apples or candles. No sitting in a circle holding hands, as if we were practicing some sacred ritual. It was simply something slightly absurd, and we wanted to know where it would take us.

Without a flicker of emotion, Athena bent down to pick up her bag. At that moment, we heard a voice from the stalls.

"Marvelous!"

Heron had come to join her. The director was afraid of him because Heron knew the theater critics on his newspaper and had close ties with the media generally.

"You stopped being individuals and turned into ideas. What a shame you're so busy, but don't worry, Athena, we'll find another group to work with and then I can see how your 'lecture' ends. I have contacts."

I was still thinking about the light traveling through my whole body to my navel. Who was that woman? Had my colleagues experienced the same thing?

"Just a moment," said the director, aware of the look of surprise on everyone's face. "I suppose we could postpone rehearsals today ..."

"No, you mustn't do that. Besides, I have to get back to the newspaper and write something about this woman. You carry on doing what you always do. I've just found an excellent story."

If Athena felt lost in that debate between the two men, she didn't show it. She climbed down from the stage and went off with Heron. We turned to the director and asked him why he'd reacted like that.

"With all due respect, Andrea, I thought the conversation in the bar about sex was far more interesting than the nonsense we've just been engaging in. Did you notice how she kept falling silent? She didn't know what to do next!"

"But I felt something strange," said one of the older actors.

"When she said *center*, it was as if all my vital energy were suddenly focused in my navel. I've never experienced that before."

"Did you? Are you sure?" asked an actress, and judging by her words, she'd experienced the same thing.

"She's a bit of a witch, that woman," said the director, interrupting the conversation. "Let's get back to work."

We started doing our usual stretching exercises, warm-ups, and meditation, all strictly by the book. Then after a few improvisations, we went straight into a read-through of the new script. Gradually, Athena's presence seemed to be dissolving, and everything was returning to what it was—a theater, a ritual created by the Greeks thousands of years ago, where we were used to pretending to be different people.

But that was pure playacting. Athena wasn't like that, and I was determined to see her again, especially after what the director had said about her.

HERON RYAN, JOURNALIST

Unbeknownst to Athena, I'd followed exactly the same steps as the actors, obeying everything she told us to do, except that I kept my eyes open so that I could follow what was happening onstage. The moment she said, "Make a gesture for *center*," I'd placed my hand on my navel, and to my surprise, I saw that everyone, including the director, had done the same. What was going on?

That afternoon, I had to write a dreary article about a visit-

ing head of state—a real drag. In order to amuse myself between phone calls, I decided to ask colleagues in the office what
gesture they would make if I said the word *center*. Most of them
made jokey comments about political parties. One pointed to
the center of the Earth. Another put his hand on his heart. But
no one, absolutely no one, thought of their navel as the center
of anything. In the end, though, I managed to speak to someone
who had some interesting information on the subject.

When I got home, Andrea had had a bath, laid the table, and
was waiting for me to start supper. She opened a bottle of very
expensive wine, filled two glasses, and offered me one.

"So how was supper last night?"

How long can a man live with a lie? I didn't want to lose
the woman standing there before me, who had stuck with me
through thick and thin, who was always by my side when I felt
my life had lost meaning and direction. I loved her, but in the
crazy world into which I was blindly plunging, my heart was far
away, trying to adapt to something it possibly knew but couldn't
accept: being large enough for two people.

Since I would never risk letting go of a certainty in favor of
a mere possibility, I tried to minimize the significance of what
had happened at the restaurant, mainly because nothing *had* happened, apart from an exchange of lines by a poet who had suffered greatly for love.

"Athena's a difficult person to get to know."

Andrea laughed.

"That's precisely why men must find her so fascinating. She
awakens that rapidly disappearing protective instinct of yours."

Best to change the subject. I've always been convinced that women have a supernatural ability to know what's going on in a man's soul. They're all witches.

"I've been looking into what happened at the theater today. You don't know this, but I had my eyes open throughout the exercises."

"You've always got your eyes open. I assume it's part of being a journalist. And you're going to talk about the moment when we all did exactly the same thing. We talked a lot about that in the bar after rehearsals."

"A historian told me about a Greek temple where they used to predict the future [*Editor's note: the temple of Apollo at Delphi*] and which housed a marble stone called 'the navel.' Stories from the time describe Delphi as the center of the planet. I went to the newspaper archives to make a few enquiries: in Petra, in Jordan, there's another 'conic navel,' symbolizing not just the center of the planet, but also of the entire universe. Both 'navels' try to show the axis through which the energy of the world travels, marking in a visible way something that is only there on the 'invisible' map. Jerusalem is also called the navel of the world, as is an island in the Pacific Ocean, and another place I've forgotten now, because I had never associated the two things."

"Like dance!"

"What?"

"Nothing."

"No, I know what you mean—belly dancing, the oldest form of dance recorded, in which everything revolves about the belly. I was trying to avoid the subject because I told you

that in Transylvania I saw Athena dance. She was dressed, of
course, but—"

"All the movement began with her navel and gradually spread
to the rest of the body."

She was right.

Best to change the subject again and talk about the theater,
about boring journalistic stuff, then drink a little wine and end
up in bed making love while, outside, the rain was starting to
fall. I noticed that, at the moment of orgasm, Andrea's body was
all focused on her belly. I'd seen this many times before, but had
never thought anything of it.

ANTOINE LOCADOUR, HISTORIAN

Heron started spending a fortune on phone calls to France, asking me to get all the information I could by the weekend, and
he kept going on about the navel, which seemed to me the least
interesting and least romantic thing in the world. But, then, the
English don't see things in the same way as the French, and so,
instead of asking questions, I tried to find out what science had
to say on the subject.

I soon realized that historical knowledge wasn't enough. I
could locate a monument here, a dolmen there, but the odd
thing was that the ancient cultures all seemed to agree on the
subject and even use the same word to define the places they
considered sacred. I'd never noticed this before and I started to
get interested. When I saw the number of coincidences, I went

in search of something that would complement them—human behavior and beliefs.

I immediately had to reject the first and most logical explanation, that we're nourished through the umbilical cord, which is why the navel is, for us, the center of life. A psychologist immediately pointed out that the theory made no sense at all: man's central idea is always to "cut" the umbilical cord and, from then on, the brain or the heart become the more important symbols.

When we're interested in something, everything around us appears to refer to it (the mystics call these phenonema "signs," the sceptics "coincidence," and psychologists "concentrated focus," although I've yet to find out what term historians should use). One night, my adolescent daughter came home with a navel piercing.

"Why did you do that?"

"Because I felt like it."

A perfectly natural and honest explanation, even for a historian who needs to find a reason for everything. When I went into her room, I saw a poster of her favorite female pop star. She had a bare midriff, and in that photo on the wall, her navel did look like the center of the world.

I phoned Heron and asked why he was so interested. For the first time, he told me about what had happened at the theater and how the people there had all responded to a command in the same spontaneous, unexpected manner. It was impossible to get any more information out of my daughter, and so I decided to consult some specialists.

No one seemed very interested until I found François Shepka, an Indian psychologist [*Editor's note: the scientist requested that his name and nationality be changed*], who was starting to revolutionize the therapies currently in use. According to him, the idea that traumas could be resolved by a return to childhood had never got anyone anywhere. Many problems that had been overcome in adult life resurfaced, and grown-ups started blaming their parents for failures and defeats. Shepka was at war with the various French psychoanalytic associations, and a conversation about absurd subjects, like the navel, seemed to relax him.

He warmed to the theme but didn't, at first, tackle it directly. He said that according to one of the most respected psychoanalysts in history, the Swiss analyst Carl Gustav Jung, we all drank from the same spring. It's called the "soul of the world." However much we try to be independent individuals, a part of our memory is the same. We all seek the ideal of beauty, dance, divinity, and music.

Society, meanwhile, tries to define how these ideals should be manifested in reality. Currently, for example, the ideal of beauty is to be thin, and yet thousands of years ago all the images of goddesses were fat. It's the same with happiness: there are a series of rules, and if you fail to follow them, your conscious mind will refuse to accept the idea that you're happy.

Jung used to divide individual progress into four stages. The first was the Persona—the mask we use every day, pretending to be who we are. We believe that the world depends on us, that we're wonderful parents and that our children don't understand us, that our bosses are unfair, that the dream of every human being is never to work and to travel constantly. Many people realize that there's something wrong with this story, but because they don't want to change anything, they quickly drive the thought from their head. A few do try to understand what is wrong and end up finding the Shadow.

The Shadow is our dark side, which dictates how we should act and behave. When we try to free ourselves from the Persona, we turn on a light inside us and we see the cobwebs, the cowardice, the meanness. The Shadow is there to stop our progress, and it usually succeeds, and we run back to what we were before we doubted. However, some do survive this encounter with their own cobwebs, saying: "Yes, I have a few faults, but I'm good enough, and I want to go forward."

At this moment, the Shadow disappears and we come into contact with the Soul.

By Soul, Jung didn't mean "soul" in the religious sense; he speaks of a return to the Soul of the World, the source of all knowledge. Instincts become sharper, emotions more radical, the interpretation of signs becomes more important than logic, perceptions of reality grow less rigid. We start to struggle with things to which we are unaccustomed and we start to react in ways that we ourselves find unexpected.

And we discover that if we can channel that continuous flow of energy, we can organize it around a very solid center, what Jung calls the Wise Old Man for men and the Great Mother for women.

Allowing this to manifest itself is dangerous. Generally speaking, anyone who reaches this stage has a tendency to consider themselves a saint, a tamer of spirits, a prophet. A great deal of maturity is required if someone is to come into contact with the energy of the Wise Old Man or the Great Mother.

"Jung went mad," said my friend, when he had explained the four stages described by the Swiss psychoanalyst. "When he got in touch with his Wise Old Man, he started saying that he was guided by a spirit called Philemon."

"And finally ..."

"... we come to the symbol of the navel. Not only people, but societies too fit these four stages. Western civilization has a Persona, the ideas that guide us. In its attempt to adapt to changes, it comes into contact with the Shadow, and we see mass demonstrations, in which the collective energy can be manipulated both for good and ill. Suddenly, for some reason, the Persona or the Shadow are no longer enough for human beings, and then comes the moment to make the leap, the unconscious connection with the Soul. New values begin to emerge."

"I've noticed that. I've noticed a resurgence in the cult of the female face of God."

"An excellent example. And at the end of this process, if those new values are to become established, the entire race comes into contact with the symbols, the coded language by which present-day generations communicate with their ancestral knowledge. One of those symbols of rebirth is the navel. In the navel of Vishnu, the Indian divinity responsible for creation and destruction, sits the god who will rule each cycle. Yogis consider the navel one of the chakras, one of the sacred points on the human body. Primitive tribes often used to build monuments in the place that they believed to be the navel of the world. In

South America, people who go into trances say that the true form of the human being is a luminous egg that connects with other people through filaments that emerge from the navel. The mandala, a design said to stimulate meditation, is a symbolic representation of this."

I passed all this information on to Heron in England before the agreed date. I told him that the woman who had succeeded in provoking the same absurd reaction in a group of people must have enormous power, and that I wouldn't be surprised if she wasn't some kind of paranormal. I suggested that he study her more closely.

I had never thought about the subject before, and I tried to forget it at once. However, my daughter said that I was behaving oddly, thinking only of myself, that I was, in short, navel gazing!

Deidre O'Neill, known as Edda

"It was a complete disaster. How could you have put the idea in my head that I could teach? Why humiliate me in front of other people? I should just forget you even exist. When I was taught to dance, I danced. When I was taught calligraphy, I practiced calligraphy. But demanding that I go so far beyond my limits was pure wickedness. That's why I caught the train up to Scotland, that's why I came here, so that you could see how much I hate you!"

She couldn't stop crying. Fortunately, she'd left the child with her parents, because she was talking rather too loudly and there was a faint whiff of wine on her breath. I asked her to come in. Making all that noise at my front door would do nothing to help my already somewhat tarnished reputation, with people putting it around that I received visits from both men and women and organized sex orgies in the name of Satan.

But she still stood there, shouting, "It's all your fault! You humiliated me!"

One window opened, and then another. Well, anyone working to change the axis of the world must be prepared for the fact that her neighbors won't always be happy. I went over to Athena and did exactly what she wanted me to do: I put my arms around her.

She continued weeping, her head resting on my shoulder. Very gently I helped her up the steps and into the house. I made some tea, the recipe for which I share with no one because it was taught to me by my protector. I placed it in front of her and she drank it down in one gulp. By doing so, she demonstrated that her trust in me was still intact.

"Why am I like this?" she asked.

I knew then that the effects of the alcohol had been neutralized.

"There are men who love me. I have a son who adores me and sees me as his model in life. I have adoptive parents whom I consider to be my real family and who would lay down their lives for me. I filled in all the blank spaces in my past when I went in search of my birth mother. I have enough money to spend the next three years doing nothing but enjoying life, and still I'm not content!"

"I feel miserable and guilty because God blessed me with tragedies that I've managed to overcome and with miracles to which I've done credit, but I'm never content. I always want more. The last thing I needed was to go to that theater and add a failure to my list of victories!"

"Do you think you did the wrong thing?"

She looked at me in surprise.

"Why do you ask that?"

I said nothing but awaited her answer.

"No, I did the right thing. I went there with a journalist friend, and I didn't have a clue what I was going to do, but suddenly things started to emerge as if out of the void. I felt the presence of the Great Mother by my side, guiding me, instructing me, filling my voice with a confidence I didn't really feel."

"So why are you complaining?"

"Because no one understood!"

"Is that important? Important enough to make you travel up to Scotland and insult me in front of everyone?"

"Of course it's important! If I can do absolutely anything and know I'm doing the right thing, how come I'm not at least loved and admired?"

So that was the problem. I took her hand and led her into the same room where, weeks before, she had sat contemplating a candle. I asked her to sit down and try to calm herself a little, although I was sure the tea was already taking effect. I went to my room, picked up a round mirror, and placed it before her.

"You have everything and you've fought for every inch of your territory. Now look at your tears. Look at your face and the bitterness etched on it. Look at the woman in the mirror, but don't laugh this time, try to understand her."

I allowed her time to follow my instructions. When I saw that she was, as I intended, going into a trance, I went on.

"What is the secret of life? We call it 'grace' or 'blessing.' Everyone struggles to be satisfied with what they have. Apart from me. Apart from you. Apart from a few people who will, alas, have to make a small sacrifice in the name of something greater.

"Our imagination is larger than the world around us; we go beyond our limits. This used to be called 'witchcraft,' but fortunately things have changed, otherwise we would both already have been burned at the stake. When they stopped burning women, science found an explanation for our behavior, normally referred to as 'female hysteria.' We don't get burned anymore, but it does cause problems, especially in the workplace. But don't worry, eventually they'll call it 'wisdom.' Keep looking into the mirror. Who can you see?"

"A woman."

"And what is there beyond that woman?"

She hesitated. I asked again and she said, "Another woman, more authentic and more intelligent than me. It's as if she were a soul that didn't belong to me, but which is nonetheless part of me."

"Exactly. Now I'm going to ask you to imagine one of the most important symbols in alchemy: a snake forming a circle and swallowing its own tail. Can you imagine that?"

She nodded.

"That's what life is like for people like you and me. We're constantly destroying and rebuilding ourselves. Everything in your life has followed the same pattern: from lost to found; from divorce to new love; from working in a bank to selling real estate in the desert. Only one thing remains intact—your son. He is the connecting thread, and you must respect that."

She started to cry again, but her tears were different this time.

"You came here because you saw a female face in the flames. That face is the face you can see now in the mirror, so try to honor it. Don't let yourself be weighed down by what other people think, because in a few years, in a few decades, or in a few centuries, that way of thinking will have changed. Live now what others will only live in the future.

"What do you want? You can't want to be happy, because that's too easy and too boring. You can't want only to love, because that's impossible. What do you want? You want to justify your life, to live it as intensely as possible. That is at once a trap and a source of ecstasy. Try to be alert to that danger and experience the joy and the adventure of being that woman who is beyond the image reflected in the mirror."

Her eyes closed, but I knew that my words had penetrated her soul and would stay there.

"If you want to take a risk and continue teaching, do so. If you don't want to, know that you've already gone further than most other people."

Her body began to relax. I held her in my arms until she fell asleep, her head on my breast.

I tried to whisper a few more things to her, because I'd been through the same stages, and I knew how difficult it was—just as my protector had told me it would be and as I myself had found out through painful experience. However, the fact that it was difficult didn't make the experience any less interesting.

What experience? Living as a human being and as a divinity. Moving from tension into relaxation. From relaxation into trance. From trance into a more intense contact with other people. From that contact back into tension and so on, like the serpent swallowing its own tail.

It was no easy matter, mainly because it requires unconditional love, which does not fear suffering, rejection, loss.

Whoever drinks this water once can never quench her thirst at other springs.

ANDREA MCCAIN, ACTRESS

"The other day you mentioned Gaia, who created herself and had a child without the help of a man. You said, quite rightly, that the Great Mother was eventually superseded by the male gods. But you forgot about Hera, a descendant of your favorite goddess. Hera is more important because she's more practical. She rules the skies and the earth, the seasons of the year and storms. According to the same Greeks you cited, the Milky Way that we see in the sky was created out of the milk that spurted forth from her breast. A beautiful breast, it must be said, because all-powerful Zeus changed himself into a bird purely in order to be able to have his way with her without being rejected."

We were walking through a large department store in Knights-bridge. I'd phoned her, saying that I'd like to talk, and she'd invited me to the winter sales. It would have been far more pleasant to have a cup of tea together or lunch in some quiet restaurant.

"Your son could get lost in this crowd."

"Don't worry about him. Go on with what you were telling me."

"Hera discovered the trick and forced Zeus to marry her. Immediately after the ceremony, however, the great king of Olympus returned to his playboy lifestyle, seducing any woman, mortal or immortal, who happened by. Hera, however, remained faithful. Rather than blame her husband, she blamed the women for their loose behavior."

"Isn't that what we all do?"

I didn't know what she meant, and so I carried on talking as if I hadn't heard what she'd said.

"Then she decided to give him a taste of his own medicine and find a god or a man to take to her bed. Look, couldn't we stop for a while and have a coffee?"

But Athena had just gone into a lingerie shop.

"Do you think this is pretty?" she asked, holding up a pro-vocative flesh-colored bra and panty set.

"Yes, very. Will anyone see it if you wear it?"

"Of course, or do you think I'm a saint? But go on with what you were saying about Hera."

"Zeus was horrified by her behavior, but Hera was leading an independent life and didn't give two hoots about her mar-riage. Have you really got a boyfriend?"

"Yes."

"I've never seen him."

She went over to the checkout, paid for the lingerie, and put it in her bag.

"Viorel's hungry, and I'm sure he's not the slightest bit interested in Greek myths, so hurry up and finish Hera's story."

"It has a rather silly ending. Zeus, afraid of losing his beloved, pretended that he was getting married again. When Hera found out, she saw that things had gone too far. Lovers were one thing, but divorce was unthinkable."

"Nothing new there, then."

"She decided to go to the ceremony and kick up a fuss, and it was only then that she realized Zeus was marrying a statue."

"What did Hera do?"

"She roared with laughter. That broke the ice between them, and she became once more the queen of the skies."

"Great. So if that ever happens to you …"

"What?"

"If your man gets himself another woman, don't forget to laugh."

"I'm not a goddess. I'd be much more vengeful. Anyway, why is it I've never seen your boyfriend?"

"Because he's always busy."

"Where did you meet him?"

"At the bank where I used to work. He had an account there. And now, if you don't mind, my son's waiting for me. You're right, if I don't keep my eye on him, he could get lost among all these people. By the way, we're having a meeting at my place next week. You're invited, of course."

"Yes, and I know who organized it."

Athena kissed me lightly on both cheeks and left. At least she'd got the message.

That afternoon, at the theater, the director made a point of telling me that he was annoyed because, he said, I'd arranged for a group of actors to go and visit "that woman." I explained that it hadn't been my idea. Heron had become obsessed with the subject of navels and had asked me if some of the other actors would be prepared to continue the interrupted "lecture."

"That said," I added, "it was my choice to ask them."

Of course it was, but the last thing I wanted was for him to go to Athena's house alone.

The actors had all arrived, but instead of another read-through of the new play, the director decided to change the program.

"Today we'll do another exercise in psychodrama." [*Editor's note: a therapeutic technique that involves people acting out their personal experiences.*]

There was no need. We all knew how the characters would behave in the situations described by the playwright.

"Can I suggest a subject?"

Everyone turned to look at me. The director seemed surprised.

"What's this, a revolt?"

"No, listen. We create a situation where a man, after great difficulty, manages to get a group of people together to celebrate an important ritual in the community, something, let's say, like the autumn harvest. Meanwhile, a strange woman arrives, and because of her beauty and the various rumors circulating—about her being a goddess in disguise, for example—the group the man has formed in order to keep alive the traditions in his village breaks up, and its members all go off to see the woman instead."

"But that's got nothing to do with the play we're rehearsing!" said one of the actresses.

The director, however, had understood what I was driving at.

"That's an excellent idea. Let's begin."

And turning to me, he said, "Andrea, you can be the new arrival. That way you can get a better understanding of the situation in the village. And I'll be the decent man trying to preserve the old ways. The group will be made up of couples who go to church, get together on Saturdays to do work in the community, and generally help one another."

We lay down on the floor, did some relaxation, and then began the exercise proper, which was really very simple. The main character (in this case, me) created various situations, and the others reacted to them.

When the relaxation was over, I transformed myself into Athena. In my fantasy, she roamed the world like Satan in search of subjects for her realm, but she disguised herself as Gaia, the goddess who knows everything and created everything. For fifteen minutes, the other actors paired up into "couples," got to know each other, and invented a common history involving children, farms, understanding, and friendship. When I felt this little universe was ready, I sat at one corner of the stage and began to speak about love.

"Here we are in this little village, and you think I'm a stranger, which is why you're interested in what I have to tell you. You've never traveled and don't know what goes on beyond the mountains, but I can tell you: there's no need to praise the earth. The earth will always be generous with this community. The important thing is to praise human beings. You say you'd love to travel, but you misuse the word *love*. Love is a relationship between people.

"Your one desire is for the harvest to be a good one, and that's why you've decided to love the earth. More nonsense: love isn't desire or knowledge or admiration. It's a challenge, it's an invisible fire. That's why, if you think I'm a stranger on this earth, you're wrong. Everything is familiar to me because I come in strength and in fire, and when I leave, no one will be the same. I bring true love, not the love they write about in books or in fairy tales."

The "husband" of one of the "couples" began looking at me. His "wife" became distraught.

During the rest of the exercise, the director—or, rather, the decent man—did all he could to explain the importance of maintaining traditions, praising the earth, and asking the earth to be as generous this year as it had been last year. I spoke only of love.

"He says the earth needs rituals, well, I can guarantee that if there's love enough among you, you'll have an abundant harvest, because love is the feeling that transforms everything. But what do I see? Friendship. Passion died out a long time ago, because you've all got used to one another. That's why the earth gives only what it gave last year, neither more nor less. And that's why, in the darkness of your souls, you silently complain that nothing in your lives changes. Why? Because you've always tried to control the force that transforms everything so that your lives can carry on without being faced by any major challenges."

The decent man explained, "Our community has survived because we've always respected the laws by which even love itself is guided. Anyone who falls in love without taking into account the common good will be condemned to live in constant fear of hurting his partner, of irritating his new love, of losing everything he built. A stranger with no ties and no history can say what she likes, but she doesn't know how hard it was to get where we are now. She doesn't know the sacrifices we made for our children. She doesn't know that we work tirelessly so that the earth will be generous with us, so that we will be at peace, and so that we can store away provisions for the future."

For an hour I defended the passion that devours everything, while the decent man spoke of the feeling that brings peace and tranquility. In the end, I was left talking to myself while the whole community gathered around him.

I'd played my role with great gusto and with a conviction I didn't even know I felt. Despite everything, though, the stranger left the village without having convinced anyone.

And that made me very, very happy.

HERON RYAN, JOURNALIST

An old friend of mine always says: "People learn twenty-five percent from their teacher, twenty-five percent from listening to themselves, twenty-five percent from their friends, and twenty-five percent from time." At that first meeting at Athena's apartment, where she was trying to conclude the class she had started at the theater, we all learned from … well, I'm not quite sure from what.

She was waiting for us, with her son, in her small living room. I noticed that the room was entirely painted in white and was completely empty apart from one item of furniture with a sound system on it, and a pile of CDs. I thought it odd that her son should be there, because he was sure to be bored by the class. I was assuming she would simply pick up from where we had stopped, giving us commands through single words. But she had other plans. She explained that she was going to play some music from Siberia and that we should all just listen.

Nothing more.

"I don't get anywhere meditating," she said. "I see people sitting there with their eyes closed, a smile on their lips or else grave-faced and arrogant, concentrating on absolutely nothing, convinced that they're in touch with God or with the Goddess. So instead, let's listen to some music together."

Again that feeling of unease, as if Athena didn't know exactly what she was doing. But nearly all the actors from the theater were there, including the director, who, according to Andrea, had come to spy on the enemy camp.

The music stopped.

"This time I want you to dance to a rhythm that has nothing whatever to do with the melody."

Athena put the music on again, with the volume right up, and started to dance, making no attempt to move gracefully. Only an older man, who took the role of the drunken king in our latest play, did as he was told. No one else moved. They all seemed slightly constrained. One woman looked at her watch— only ten minutes had passed.

Athena stopped and looked round.

"Why are you just standing there?"

"Well," said one of the actresses timidly, "it seems a bit ridiculous to be doing that. We've been trained in harmony, not its opposite."

"Just do as I say. Do you need an explanation? Right, I'll give you one. Changes only happen when we go totally against everything we're used to doing."

Turning to the "drunken king," she said, "Why did you agree to dance against the rhythm of the music?"

"Oh, I've never had any sense of rhythm anyway."

Everyone laughed, and the dark cloud hanging over us seemed to disperse.

"Right, I'm going to start again, and you can either follow me or leave. This time, I'm the one who decides when the class ends. One of the most aggressive things a human being can do is to go against what he or she believes is nice or pretty, and that's what we're going to do today. We're all going to dance badly."

It was just another experiment, and in order not to embarrass our hostess, everyone obediently danced badly. I struggled with myself, because one's natural tendency was to follow the rhythms of that marvelous, mysterious percussion. I felt as if I were insulting the musicians who were playing and the composer who created it. Every so often, my body tried to fight against that lack of harmony and I was forced to make myself behave as I'd been told to. The boy was dancing as well, laughing all the time, then at a certain point, he stopped and sat down on the sofa, as if exhausted by his efforts. The CD was switched off in midstream.

"Wait."

We all waited.

"I'm going to do something I've never done before."

She closed her eyes and held her head between her hands.

"I've never danced unrhythmically before ..."

So the experiment had been worse for her than for any of us.

"I don't feel well ..."

Both the director and I got to our feet. Andrea shot me a furious glance, but I still went over to Athena. Before I could reach her, however, she asked us to return to our places.

"Does anyone want to say anything?" Her voice sounded fragile, tremulous, and she had still not uncovered her face.

"I do."

It was Andrea.

"First, pick up my son and tell him that his mother's fine. But I need to stay like this for as long as necessary."

Viorel looked frightened. Andrea sat him on her lap and stroked him.

"What do you want to say?"

"Nothing. I've changed my mind."

"The boy made you change your mind, but carry on anyway."

Slowly Athena removed her hands and looked up. Her face was that of a stranger.

"No, I won't speak."

"All right. You," Athena said, pointing to the older actor. "Go to the doctor tomorrow. The fact that you can't sleep and have to keep getting up in the night to go to the toilet is serious. It's cancer of the prostate."

The man turned pale.

"And you"—she pointed at the director—"accept your sexual identity. Don't be afraid. Accept that you hate women and love men."

"Are you saying—"

"Don't interrupt me. I'm not saying this because of Athena. I'm merely referring to your sexuality. You love men, and there is, I believe, nothing wrong with that."

She wasn't saying that because of Athena? But she *was* Athena!

"And you." She pointed to me. "Come over here. Kneel down before me."

Afraid of what Andrea might do and embarrassed to have everyone's eyes on me, I nevertheless did as she asked.

"Bow your head. Let me touch the nape of your neck."

I felt the pressure of her fingers but nothing else. We remained like that for nearly a minute, and then she told me to get up and go back to my seat.

"You won't need to take sleeping pills anymore. From now on, sleep will return."

I glanced at Andrea. I thought she might say something, but she looked as amazed as I did.

One of the actresses, possibly the youngest, raised her hand.

"I'd like to say something, but I need to know who I'm speaking to."

"Hagia Sofia."

"I'd like to know if …"

She glanced round, ashamed, but the director nodded, asking her to continue.

"… if my mother is all right."

"She's by your side. Yesterday, when you left the house, she made you forget your handbag. You went back to find it and discovered that you'd locked yourself out and couldn't get in. You wasted a whole hour looking for a locksmith, when you could have kept the appointment you'd made, met the man who was waiting for you, and got the job you wanted. But if everything had happened as you planned that morning, in six months' time you would have died in a car accident. Forgetting your handbag yesterday changed your life."

The girl began to weep.

"Does anyone else want to ask anything?"

Another hand went up. It was the director.

"Does he love me?"

So it was true. The story about the girl's mother had stirred up a whirlwind of emotions in the room.

"You're asking the wrong question. What you need to know is are you in a position to give him the love he needs. And whatever happens or doesn't happen will be equally gratifying. Knowing that you are capable of love is enough. If it isn't him, it will be someone else. You've discovered a wellspring; simply allow it to flow and it will fill your world. Don't try to keep a safe distance so as to see what happens. Don't wait to be certain before you take a step. What you give, you will receive, although it might sometimes come from the place you least expect."

Those words applied to me too. Then Athena—or whoever she was—turned to Andrea.

"You!"

My blood froze.

"You must be prepared to lose the universe you created."

"What do you mean by 'universe'?"

"What you think you already have. You've imprisoned your world, but you know that you must liberate it. I know you understand what I mean, even though you don't want to hear it."

"I understand."

I was sure they were talking about me. Was this all a setup by Athena?

"It's finished," she said. "Bring the child to me."

Viorel didn't want to go; he was frightened by his mother's transformation. But Andrea took him gently by the hand and led him to her.

Athena—or Hagia Sofia, or Sherine, or whoever she was—did just as she had done with me, and pressed the back of the boy's neck with her fingers.

"Don't be frightened by the things you see, my child. Don't try to push them away because they'll go away anyway. Enjoy the company of the angels while you can. You're frightened now, but you're not as frightened as you might be because you know there are lots of people in the room. You stopped laughing and dancing when you saw me embracing your mother and asking to speak through her mouth. But you know I wouldn't be doing this if she hadn't given me her permission. I've always appeared before in the form of light, and I still am that light, but today I decided to speak."

The little boy put his arms around her.

"You can go now. Leave me alone with him."

One by one, we left the apartment, leaving the mother with her child. In the taxi home, I tried to talk to Andrea, but she said that we could talk about anything but what had just happened.

I said nothing. My soul filled with sadness. Losing Andrea was very hard. On the other hand, I felt an immense peace. The evening's events had wrought changes in us all, and that meant I wouldn't need to go through the pain of sitting down with a woman I loved very much and telling her that I was in love with someone else.

In this case, I chose silence. I got home, turned on the TV, and Andrea went to have a bath. I closed my eyes, and when I opened them, the room was full of light. It was morning, and I'd slept for ten hours. Beside me was a note, in which Andrea said that she hadn't wanted to wake me, that she'd gone straight to the theater, but had left me some coffee. The note was a romantic one, decorated in lipstick and a small cutout heart.

She had no intention of "letting go of her universe." She was going to fight. And my life would become a nightmare.

That evening she phoned, and her voice betrayed no particular emotion. She told me that the elderly actor had gone to see his doctor, who had examined him and found that he had an enlarged prostate. The next step was a blood test, where they had detected a significantly raised level of a type of protein called PSA. They took a sample for a biopsy, but the clinical picture indicated that there was a high chance he had a malignant tumor.

"The doctor said he was lucky, because even if their worst fears were proved right, they can still operate, and there's a ninety-nine percent chance of a cure."

DEIDRE O'NEILL, KNOWN AS EDDA

What do you mean, Hagia Sofia! It was her, Athena, but by touching the deepest part of the river that flows through her soul, she had come into contact with the Mother.

All she did was to see what was happening in another reality. The young actress's mother, now that she's dead, lives in a place outside of time and so was able to change the course of events, whereas we human beings can only know about the present. But that's no small thing: discovering a dormant illness before it gets worse, touching nervous systems and unblocking energies are within the reach of all of us.

Of course, many died at the stake, others were exiled, and many ended up hiding or suppressing the spark of the Great Mother in their souls. I never brought Athena into contact with the Power. She decided to do this, because the Mother had already given her various signs: she was a light while she danced, she changed into letters while she was learning calligraphy, she appeared to her in a fire and in a mirror. What my student didn't know was how to live with her, until, that is, she did something that provoked this whole chain of events.

Athena, who was always telling everyone to be different, was basically just like all other mortals. She had her own rhythm, a kind of cruise control. Was she more curious than most? Possibly. Had she managed to overcome her sense of being a victim? Definitely. Did she feel a need to share what she was learning with others, be they bank employees or actors? In some cases the answer was yes, but in others, I had to encourage her, because we are not meant for solitude, and we only know ourselves when we see ourselves in the eyes of others.

But that was as far as my interference went.

Maybe the Mother wanted to appear that night, and perhaps she whispered something in her ear: "Go against everything you've learned so far. You, who are a mistress of rhythm, allow the rhythm to pass through your body, but don't obey it." That was why Athena suggested the exercise. Her unconscious was already prepared to receive the Mother, but Athena herself was still dancing in time to the music, and so any external elements were unable to manifest themselves.

The same thing used to happen with me. The best way to meditate and enter into contact with the light was by knitting, something my mother had taught me when I was a child. I knew how to count the stitches, manipulate the needles, and create beautiful things through repetition and harmony. One day, my protector asked me to knit in a completely irrational way! I found this really distressing, because I'd learned how to knit with affection, patience, and dedication. Nevertheless, he insisted on me knitting really badly.

I knitted like this for two hours, thinking all the time that it was utterly ridiculous, absurd. My head ached, but I had to resist letting the needles guide my hands. Anyone can do things badly, so why was he asking this of me? Because he knew about my obsession with geometry and with perfection.

And suddenly it happened: I stopped moving the needles and felt a great emptiness, which was filled by a warm, loving, companionable presence. Everything around me was different, and I felt like saying things that I would never normally dare to say. I didn't lose consciousness; I knew I was still me, but, paradoxically, I wasn't the person I was used to being with.

So I can "see" what happened, even though I wasn't there—Athena's soul following the sound of the music while her body went in a totally contrary direction. After a time, her soul disconnected from her body, a space opened, and the Mother could finally enter.

Or, rather, a spark from the Mother appeared. Ancient, but apparently very young. Wise, but not omnipotent. Special, but not in the least arrogant. Her perceptions changed, and she began to see the same things she used to see when she was a child—the parallel universes that people this world. At such moments, we can see not only the physical body but people's emotions too. They say cats have this same power, and I believe them.

A kind of blanket lies between the physical and the spiritual world, a blanket that changes in color, intensity, and light; it's what mystics call "aura." From then on, everything is easy. The aura tells you what's going on. If I had been there, she would have seen a violet color with a few yellow splodges around my body. That means that I still have a long road ahead of me and that my mission on this earth has not yet been accomplished.

Mixed up with human auras are transparent forms, which people usually call "ghosts." That was the case with the young woman's mother, and only in such cases can someone's fate be altered. I'm almost certain that the young actress, even before she asked, knew that her mother was beside her, and the only real surprise to her was the story about the handbag.

Confronted by that rhythm-less dance, everyone was really intimidated. Why? Because we're used to doing things "as they should be done." No one likes to make the wrong moves, especially when we're aware that we're doing so. Even Athena. It can't have been easy for her to suggest doing something that went against everything she loved.

I'm glad that the Mother won the battle at that point. A man has been saved from cancer, another has accepted his sexuality, and a third has stopped taking sleeping pills. And all because Athena broke the rhythm, slamming on the brakes when the car was traveling at top speed and thus throwing everything into disarray.

To go back to my knitting: I used that method of knitting badly for quite some time until I managed to provoke the presence without any artificial means, now that I knew it and was used to it. The same thing happened with Athena. Once we know where the Doors of Perception are, it's really easy to open and close them, when we get used to our own "strange" behavior.

And it must be said that I knitted much faster and better after that, just as Athena danced with much more soul and rhythm once she had dared to break down those barriers.

Andrea McCain, actress

The story spread like wildfire. On the following Monday, when the theater was closed, Athena's apartment was packed. We had all brought friends. She did as she had on the previous evening; she made us dance without rhythm, as if she needed that collective energy in order to get in touch with Hagia Sofia. The boy was there again, and I decided to watch him. When he sat down on the sofa, the music stopped and the trance began.

As did the questions. The first three questions were, as you can imagine, about love—will he stay with me, does she love me, is he cheating on me. Athena said nothing. The fourth person to receive no answer asked again, more loudly this time, "So is he cheating on me or not?"

"I am Hagia Sofia, universal wisdom. I came into the world accompanied only by Love. I am the beginning of everything, and before I existed there was chaos. Therefore, if any of you wish to control the forces that prevailed in chaos, do not ask Hagia Sofia. For me, love fills everything. It cannot be desired because it is an end in itself. It cannot betray because it has nothing to do with possession. It cannot be held prisoner because it is a river and will overflow its banks. Anyone who tries to imprison love will cut off the spring that feeds it, and the trapped water will grow stagnant and rank."

Hagia looked around the group, most of whom were there for the first time, and she began to point out what she saw: the threat of disease, problems at work, frictions between parents and children, sexuality, potentialities that existed but were not being explored. I remember her turning to one woman in her thirties and saying, "Your father told you how things should be and how a woman should behave. You have always fought against your dreams, and 'I want' has never even shown its face. It was always drowned out by 'I must' or 'I hope' or 'I need,' but you're a wonderful singer. One year's experience could make a huge difference to your work."

"But I have a husband and a child."

"Athena has a child too. Your husband will be upset at first, but he'll come to accept it eventually. And you don't need to be Hagia Sofia to know that."

"Maybe I'm too old."

"You're refusing to accept who you are, but that is not my problem. I have said what needed to be said."

Gradually, everyone in that small room—unable to sit down because there wasn't enough space, sweating profusely even though the winter was nearly over, feeling ridiculous for having come to such an event—was called upon to receive Hagia Sofia's advice.

I was the last.

"Stay behind afterward if you want to stop being two and to be one instead."

This time, I didn't have her son on my lap. He watched everything that happened, and it seemed that the conversation they'd had after the first session had been enough for him to lose his fear.

I nodded. Unlike the previous session, when people had simply left when she'd asked to talk to her son alone, this time Hagia Sofia gave a sermon before ending the ritual.

"You are not here to receive definite answers. My mission is to provoke you. In the past, both governors and governed went to oracles who would foretell the future. The future, however, is unreliable because it is guided by decisions made in the here and now. Keep the bicycle moving, because if you stop pedaling, you will fall off.

"For those of you who came to meet Hagia Sofia wanting her merely to confirm what you hoped to be true, please, do not come back. Or else start dancing and make those around you dance too. Fate will be implacable with those who want to live in a universe that is dead and gone. The new world belongs to the Mother, who came with Love to separate the heavens from the waters. Anyone who believes they have failed will always fail. Anyone who has decided that they cannot behave any differently will be destroyed by routine. Anyone who has decided to block all changes will be transformed into dust. Cursed be those who do not dance and who prevent others from dancing!"

Her eyes glanced fire.

"You can go."

Everyone left, and I could see the look of confusion on most of their faces. They had come in search of comfort and had found only provocation. They had arrived wanting to be told how love can be controlled and had heard that the all-devouring flame will always burn everything. They wanted to be sure that their decisions were the right ones, that their husbands, wives, and bosses were pleased with them, but instead they were given only words of doubt.

Some people, though, were smiling. They had understood the importance of the dance and from that night on would doubtless allow their bodies and souls to drift—even though, as always happens, they would have to pay a price.

Only the boy, Hagia Sofia, Heron, and myself were left in the room.

"I asked you to stay here alone."

Without a word, Heron picked up his coat and left.

Hagia Sofia was looking at me. And, little by little, I watched her change back into Athena. The only way of describing that change is to compare it with the change that takes place in an angry child: we can see the anger in the child's eyes, but once distracted and once the anger has gone, the child is no longer the same child who, only moments before, was crying. The "being," if it can be called that, seemed to have vanished into the air as soon as its instrument lost concentration.

And now I was standing before an apparently exhausted woman.

"Make me some tea."

She was giving me an order! And she was no longer universal wisdom but merely someone my boyfriend was interested in or infatuated with. Where would this relationship take us?

But making a cup of tea wouldn't destroy my self-esteem. I went into the kitchen, boiled some water, added a few chamomile leaves, and returned to the living room. The child was asleep on her lap.

"You don't like me," she said.

I made no reply.

"I don't like you either," she went on. "You're pretty and elegant, a fine actress, and have a degree of culture and education which I, despite my family's wishes, do not. But you're also insecure, arrogant, and suspicious. As Hagia Sofia said, you are two, when you could be one."

"I didn't know you remembered what you said during the trance, because in that case, you are two people as well: Athena and Hagia Sofia."

"I may have two names, but I am only one—or else all the people in the world. And that is precisely what I want to talk about. Because I am one and everyone, the spark that emerges when I go into a trance gives me very precise instructions. I remain semiconscious throughout, of course, but I'm saying things that come from some unknown part of myself, as if I were suckling on the breast of the Mother, drinking the milk that flows through all our souls and carries knowledge around the earth. Last week, which was the first time I entered into contact with this new form, I received what seemed to me to be an absurd message: that I should teach you."

She paused.

"Obviously, this struck me as quite mad, because I don't like you at all."

She paused again, for longer this time.

"Today, though, the source repeated the same message, and so I'm giving you that choice."

"Why do you call it Hagia Sofia?"

"That was my idea. It's the name of a really beautiful mosque I saw in a book. You could, if you like, be my student. That's what brought you here on that first day. This whole new stage in my life, including the discovery of Hagia Sofia inside me, only happened because one day you came through that door and said: 'I work in the theater and we're putting on a play about the female face of God. I heard from a journalist friend that you've spent time in the Balkan mountains with some gypsies and would be prepared to tell me about your experiences there.'"

"Are you going to teach me everything you know?"

"No, everything I don't know. I'll learn through being in contact with you, as I said the first time we met, and as I say again now. Once I've learned what I need to learn, we'll go our separate ways."

"Can you teach someone you dislike?"

"I can love and respect someone I dislike. On the two occasions when I went into a trance, I saw your aura, and it was the most highly developed aura I've ever seen. You could make a difference in this world, if you accept my proposal."

"Will you teach me to see auras?"

"Until it happened to me the first time, I myself didn't know I was capable of doing so. If you're on the right path, you'll learn too."

I realized then that I too was capable of loving someone I disliked. I said yes.

"Then let us transform that acceptance into a ritual. A ritual throws us into an unknown world, but we know that we cannot treat the things of that world lightly. It isn't enough to say yes, you must put your life at risk, and without giving it much thought either. If you're the woman I think you are, you won't say: 'I need to think about it.' You'll say—"

"I'm ready. Let's move on to the ritual. Where did you learn the ritual, by the way?"

"I'm going to learn it now. I no longer need to remove myself from my normal rhythm in order to enter into contact with the spark from the Mother, because once that spark is installed inside you, it's easy to find again. I know which door I need to open, even though it's concealed among many other entrances and exits. All I need is a little silence."

Silence again!

We sat there, our eyes wide and staring, as if we were about to begin a fight to the death. Rituals! Before I even rang the bell of Athena's apartment for the first time, I had already taken part in various rituals, only to feel used and diminished afterward, standing outside a door I could see, but not open. Rituals!

All Athena did was drink a little of the tea I prepared for her.

"The ritual is over. I asked you to do something for me. You did, and I accepted it. Now it is your turn to ask me something."

I immediately thought of Heron, but it wasn't the right moment to talk about him.

"Take your clothes off."

She didn't ask me why. She looked at the child, checked that he was asleep, and immediately began to remove her sweater.

"No, really, you don't have to," I said. "I don't know why I asked that."

But she continued to undress, first her blouse, then her jeans, then her bra. I noticed her breasts, which were the most beautiful I'd ever seen. Finally she removed her knickers. And there she was, offering me her nakedness.

"Bless me," said Athena.

Bless my "teacher"? But I'd already taken the first step and couldn't stop now, so I dipped my fingers in the cup and sprinkled a little tea over her body.

"Just as this plant was transformed into tea, just as the water mingled with the plant, I bless you and ask the Great Mother that the spring from which this water came will never cease flowing, and that the earth from which this plant came will always be fertile and generous."

I was surprised at my own words. They had come neither from inside me nor outside. It was as if I'd always known them and had done this countless times before.

"You have been blessed. You can get dressed now."

But she didn't move, she merely smiled. What did she want? If Hagia Sofia was capable of seeing auras, she would know that I hadn't the slightest desire to have sex with another woman.

"One moment."

She picked up the boy, carried him to his room, and returned at once.

"You take your clothes off too."

Who was asking this? Hagia Sofia, who spoke of my potential and for whom I was the perfect disciple? Or Athena, whom I hardly knew, and who seemed capable of anything, a woman whom life had taught to go beyond her limits and to satisfy any curiosity?

We had started a kind of confrontation from which there was no retreat. I got undressed with the same nonchalance, the same smile, and the same look in my eyes.

She took my hand, and we sat down on the sofa.

During the next half hour, both Athena and Hagia Sofia were present; they wanted to know what my next steps would be. As they asked me this question, I saw that everything really was written there before me, and that the doors had only been closed before because I hadn't realized that I was the one person in the world with the authority to open them.

HERON RYAN, JOURNALIST

The deputy editor hands me a video and we go into the projection room to watch it.

The video was made on the morning of April 26, 1986, and shows normal life in a normal town. A man is sitting, drinking a cup of coffee. A mother is taking her baby for a walk. People in a hurry are going to work. A few people are waiting at a bus stop. A man on a bench in a square is reading a newspaper.

But there's a problem with the video. There are various horizontal lines on the screen, as if the tracking button needed to be adjusted. I get up to do this but the deputy editor stops me.

"That's just the way it is. Keep watching."

Images of the small provincial town continue to appear, showing nothing of interest apart from these scenes from ordinary everyday life.

"It's possible that some people may know that there's been an accident two kilometers from there," says my boss. "It's possible that they know there have been thirty deaths—a large number, but not enough to change the routine of the town's inhabitants."

Now the film shows school buses parking. They will stay there for many days. The images are getting worse and worse.

"It isn't the tracking, it's radiation. The video was made by the KGB. On the night of April 26, at twenty-three minutes past one in the morning, the worst ever man-made disaster occurred at Chernobyl, in the Ukraine. When a nuclear reactor exploded, the people in the area were exposed to ninety times more radiation than that given out by the bomb dropped on Hiroshima. The whole region should have been evacuated at once, but no one said anything—after all, the government doesn't make mistakes. Only a week later, on page thirty-two of the local newspaper, a five-line article appeared, mentioning the deaths of workers, but giving no further explanation. Meanwhile, Workers Day was celebrated throughout the former Soviet Union, and in Kiev, the Ukrainian capital, people paraded down the street unaware of the invisible death in the air."

And he concludes, "I want you to go and see what Chernobyl

is like now. You've just been promoted to special correspondent. You'll get a twenty percent increase in your salary and be able to suggest the kind of article you think we should be publishing."

I should be jumping for joy, but instead I'm gripped by a feeling of intense sadness, which I have to hide. It's impossible to argue with him, to say that there are two women in my life at the moment, that I don't want to leave London, that my life and my mental equilibrium are at stake. I ask when I should leave. As soon as possible, he says, because there are rumors that other countries are significantly increasing their production of nuclear energy.

I manage to negotiate an honorable way out, saying that, first, I need to talk to experts and really get a grip on the subject, and that I'll set off once I've collected the necessary material.

He agrees, shakes my hand, and congratulates me. I don't have time to talk to Andrea, because when I get home, she's still at the theater. I fall asleep at once and again wake up to find a note saying that she's gone to work and that coffee is on the table.

I go to the office, try to ingratiate myself with the boss who has "improved my life," and phone various experts on radiation and energy. I discover that, in total, nine million people worldwide were directly affected by the disaster, including three to four million children. The initial thirty deaths became, according to the expert John Gofmans, 475,000 cases of fatal cancers and an equal number of nonfatal cancers.

A total of two thousand towns and villages were simply wiped off the map. According to the Health Ministry in Belarus, the incidence of cancer of the thyroid will increase considerably between 2005 and 2010, as a consequence of continuing high levels of radioactivity. Another specialist explains that in addition to the nine million people directly exposed to radiation, more than sixty-five million in many countries around the world were indirectly affected by consuming contaminated foodstuffs.

It's a serious matter, which deserves to be treated with respect. At the end of the day, I go back to the deputy editor and suggest that I travel to Chernobyl for the actual anniversary of the accident, and meanwhile do more research, talk to more experts, and find out how the British government responded to the tragedy. He agrees.

I phone Athena. After all, she claims to be going out with someone from Scotland Yard and now is the time to ask her a favor, given that Chernobyl is no longer classified as secret and the Soviet Union no longer exists. She promises that she'll talk to her "boyfriend" but says she can't guarantee she'll get the answers I want.

She also says that she's leaving for Scotland the following day and will only be back in time for the next group meeting.

"What group?"

The group, she says. So that's become a regular thing, has it? What I want to know is when we can meet to talk and clear up various loose ends.

But she's already hung up. I go home, watch the news, have supper alone, and later go out again to pick Andrea up from the theater. I get there in time to see the end of the play, and to my surprise, the person onstage seems totally unlike the person I've been living with for nearly two years; there's something magical about her every gesture; monologues and dialogues are spoken with an unaccustomed intensity. I am seeing a stranger, a woman I would like to have by my side, then I realize that she *is* by my side and is in no way a stranger to me.

"How did your chat with Athena go?" I ask on the way home.

"Fine. How was work?"

She was the one to change the subject. I tell her about my promotion and about Chernobyl, but she doesn't seem interested. I start to think that I'm losing the love I have without having yet won the love I hope to win. However, as soon as we reach our apartment, she suggests we take a bath together, and before I know it, we're in bed. First, she puts on that percussion music at full volume (she explains that she managed to get hold of a copy) and tells me not to worry about the neighbors—people worry too much about them, she says, and never live their own lives.

What happens from then on is something that goes beyond my understanding. Has this woman making positively savage love with me finally discovered her sexuality, and was this taught to her or provoked in her by that other woman? While she was clinging to me with a violence I've never known before, she kept saying, "Today I'm your man, and you're my woman."

We carried on like this for almost an hour, and I experienced things I'd never dared experience before. At certain moments, I felt ashamed, wanted to ask her to stop, but she seemed to be in complete control of the situation, and so I surrendered, because I had no choice. In fact, I felt really curious.

I was exhausted afterward, but Andrea seemed reenergized.

"Before you go to sleep, I want you to know something," she said. "If you go forward, sex will offer you the chance to make love with gods and goddesses. That's what you experienced today. I want you to go to sleep knowing that I awoke the Mother that was in you."

I wanted to ask if she'd learned this from Athena, but my courage failed.

"Tell me that you liked being a woman for a night."

"I did. I don't know if I would always like it, but it was something that simultaneously frightened me and gave me great joy."

"Tell me that you've always wanted to experience what you've just experienced."

It's one thing to allow oneself to be carried away by the situation, but quite another to comment coolly on the matter. I said nothing, although I was sure that she knew my answer.

"Well," Andrea went on, "all of this was inside me and I had no idea. As was the person behind the mask that fell away while I was onstage today. Did you notice anything different?"

"Of course. You were radiating a special light."

"Charisma—the divine force that manifests itself in men and women. The supernatural power we don't need to show to anyone because everyone can see it, even usually insensitive people. But it only happens when we're naked, when we die to the world and are reborn to ourselves. Last night, I died. Tonight, when I walked onstage and saw that I was doing exactly what I had chosen to do, I was reborn from my ashes. I was always trying to be who I am but could never manage it. I was always trying to impress other people, have intelligent conversations, please my parents, and at the same time, I used every available means to do the things I would really like to do. I've always forged my path with blood, tears, and willpower, but last night, I realized that I was going about it the wrong way. My dream doesn't require that of me. I have only to surrender myself to it, and if I find I'm suffering, grit my teeth, because the suffering will pass."

"Why are you telling me this?"

"Let me finish. In that journey where suffering seemed to be the only rule, I struggled for things for which there was no point struggling. Like love, for example. People either feel it or they don't, and there isn't a force in the world that can make them feel it. We can pretend that we love each other. We can get used to each other. We can live a whole lifetime of friendship and complicity, we can bring up children, have sex every night, reach orgasm, and still feel that there's a terrible emptiness about it all, that something important is missing. In the name of all I've learned about relationships between men and women, I've been trying to fight against things that weren't really worth the struggle. And that includes you.

"Today, while we were making love, while I was giving all I have, and I could see that you too were giving of your best, I realized that your best no longer interests me. I will sleep beside you tonight, but tomorrow I'll leave. The theater is my ritual, and there I can express and develop whatever I want to express and develop."

I started to regret everything—going to Transylvania and meeting a woman who might be destroying my life, arranging that first meeting of the "group," confessing my love in that restaurant. At that moment, I hated Athena.

"I know what you're thinking," said Andrea. "That your friend Athena has brainwashed me, but that isn't true."

"I'm a man, even though tonight in bed I behaved like a woman. I'm a species in danger of extinction because I don't see many men around. Few people would risk what I have risked."

"I'm sure you're right, and that's why I admire you, but aren't you going to ask me who I am, what I want, and what I desire?"

I asked.

"I want everything. I want savagery and tenderness. I want to upset the neighbors and placate them too. I don't want a woman in my bed, I want men, real men, like you, for example. Whether they love me or are merely using me, it doesn't matter. My love is greater than that. I want to love freely, and I want to allow the people around me to do the same.

"What I talked about to Athena were the simple ways of awakening repressed energy, like making love, for example, or walking down the street saying: 'I'm here and now.' Nothing very special, no secret ritual. The only thing that made our meeting slightly different was that we were both naked. From now on, she and I will meet every Monday, and if I have any comments to make, I will do so after that session. I have no desire to be her friend. Just as, when she feels the need to share something, she goes up to Scotland to talk with that Edda woman, who, it seems, you know as well, although you've never mentioned her."

"I can't even remember meeting her!"

I sensed that Andrea was gradually calming down. I prepared two cups of coffee, and we drank them together. She recovered her smile and asked about my promotion. She said she was worried about those Monday meetings, because she'd learned only that morning that friends of friends were inviting other people, and Athena's apartment was a very small place. I made an enormous effort to pretend that everything that had happened that evening was just a fit of nerves or premenstrual tension or jealousy on her part.

I put my arms around her, and she snuggled into my shoulder. And despite my own exhaustion, I waited until she fell asleep. That night, I dreamed of nothing. I had no feelings of foreboding.

And the following morning, when I woke up, I saw that her clothes were gone, the key was on the table, and there was no letter of farewell.

DEIDRE O'NEILL, KNOWN AS EDDA

People read a lot of stories about witches, fairies, paranormals, and children possessed by evil spirits. They go to films showing rituals featuring pentagrams, swords, and invocations. That's fine, people need to give free rein to their imagination and to go through certain stages. Anyone who gets through those stages without being deceived will eventually get in touch with the Tradition.

The real Tradition is this: the teacher never tells the disciple what he or she should do. They are merely traveling companions, sharing the same uncomfortable feeling of "estrangement" when confronted by ever-changing perceptions, broadening horizons, closing doors, rivers that sometimes seem to block their path and which, in fact, should never be crossed, but followed.

There is only one difference between teacher and disciple: the former is slightly less afraid than the latter. Then, when they sit down at a table or in front of a fire to talk, the more experienced person might say: "Why don't you do that?" But he or she never says: "Go there and you'll arrive where I did," because every path and every destination are unique to the individual.

The true teacher gives the disciple the courage to throw his or her world off balance, even though the disciple is afraid of things already encountered and more afraid still of what might be around the next corner.

I was a young, enthusiastic doctor who, filled by a desire to help my fellow human beings, traveled to the interior of Romania on an exchange program run by the British government. I set off with my luggage full of medicines and my head full of preconceptions. I had clear ideas about how people should behave, about what we need to be happy, about the dreams we should keep alive inside us, about how human relations should evolve. I arrived in Bucharest during that crazed, bloody dictatorship and went to Transylvania to assist with a mass vaccination program for the local population.

I didn't realize that I was merely one more piece on a very complicated chessboard, where invisible hands were manipulat-

ing my idealism, and that ulterior motives lay behind everything
I believed was being done for humanitarian purposes: stabilizing
the government run by the dictator's son, allowing Britain to sell
arms in a market dominated by the Soviets.

All my good intentions collapsed when I saw that there was
barely enough vaccine to go round; that there were other diseases
sweeping the region; that however often I wrote asking for more
resources, they never came. I was told not to concern myself
with anything beyond what I'd been asked to do.

I felt powerless and angry. I'd seen poverty from close up and
would have been able to do something about it if only someone
would give me some money, but they weren't interested in results. Our government just wanted a few articles in the press so
that they could say to their political parties or to their electorate
that they'd dispatched groups to various places in the world on a
humanitarian mission. Their intentions were good—apart from
selling arms, of course.

I was in despair. What kind of world was this? One night,
I set off into the icy forest, cursing God, who was unfair to
everything and everyone. I was sitting beneath an oak tree when
my protector approached me. He said I could die of cold, and I
replied that I was a doctor and knew the body's limits, and that
as soon as I felt I was getting near those limits, I would go back
to the camp. I asked him what he was doing there.

"I'm speaking to a woman who can hear me, in a world in
which all the men have gone deaf."

I thought he meant me, but the woman he was referring
to was the forest itself. When I saw this man wandering about

among the trees, making gestures and saying things I couldn't understand, a kind of peace settled on my heart. I was not, after all, the only person in the world left talking to myself. When I got up to return to the camp, he came over to me again.

"I know who you are," he said. "People in the village say that you're a very decent person, always good-humored and prepared to help others, but I see something else: rage and frustration."

He might have been a government spy, but I decided to tell him everything I was feeling, even though I ran the risk of being arrested. We walked together to the field hospital where I was working; I took him to the dormitory, which was empty at the time (my colleagues were all having fun at the annual festival being held in the town), and I asked if he'd like a drink. He produced a bottle from his pocket.

"*Palinka*," he said, meaning the traditional drink of Romania, with an incredibly high alcohol content. "On me."

We drank together, and I didn't even notice that I was getting steadily drunk. I only realized the state I was in when I tried to go to the toilet, tripped over something, and fell flat.

"Don't move," said the man. "Look at what is there before your eyes."

A line of ants.

"They all think they're very wise. They have memory, intelligence, organizational powers, a spirit of sacrifice. They look for food in summer, store it away for the winter, and now they are setting forth again, in this icy spring, to work. If the world was destroyed by an atomic bomb tomorrow, the ants would survive."

"How do you know all this?"

"I studied biology."

"Why the hell don't you work to improve the living conditions of your own people? What are you doing in the middle of the forest, talking to the trees?"

"In the first place, I wasn't alone; apart from the trees, you were listening to me too. But to answer your question, I left biology to work as a blacksmith."

I struggled to my feet. My head was still spinning, but I was thinking clearly enough to understand the poor man's situation. Despite a university education, he had been unable to find work. I told him that the same thing happened in my country too.

"No, that's not what I meant. I left biology because I wanted to work as a blacksmith. Even as a child, I was fascinated by those men hammering steel, making a strange kind of music, sending out sparks all around, plunging the red-hot metal into water, and creating clouds of steam. I was unhappy as a biologist, because my dream was to make rigid metal take on soft shapes. Then, one day, a protector appeared."

"A protector?"

"Let's say that, on seeing those ants doing exactly what they're programmed to do, you were to exclaim: 'How fantastic!' The guards are genetically prepared to sacrifice themselves for the queen, the workers carry leaves ten times their own weight, the engineers make tunnels that can resist storms and floods. They enter into mortal combat with their enemies, they suffer for the community, and they never ask: 'Why are we doing this?' People try to imitate the perfect society of the ants, and as a biologist,

I was playing my part until someone came along with this question: 'Are you happy doing what you're doing?' 'Of course I am,' I said. 'I'm being useful to my own people.' 'And that's enough?'

"I didn't know whether it was enough or not, but I said that he seemed to me to be both arrogant and egotistical. He replied: 'Possibly. But all you will achieve is to repeat what has been done since man was man—keeping things organized.'

" 'But the world has progressed,' I said. He asked if I knew any history. Of course I did. He asked another question: 'Thousands of years ago, weren't we capable of building enormous structures like the pyramids? Weren't we capable of worshiping gods, weaving, making fire, finding lovers and wives, sending written messages? Of course we were. But although we've succeeded in replacing slaves with wage slaves, all the advances we've made have been in the field of science. Human beings are still asking the same questions as their ancestors. In short, they haven't evolved at all.' At that point, I understood that the person asking me these questions was someone sent from heaven, an angel, a protector."

"Why do you call him a protector?"

"Because he told me that there were two traditions, one that makes us repeat the same thing for centuries at a time, and another that opens the door into the unknown. However, the second tradition is difficult, uncomfortable, and dangerous, and if it attracted too many followers, it would end up destroying the society which, following the example of the ants, took so long to build. And so the second tradition went underground and has only managed to survive over so many centuries because its followers created a secret language of signs."

"Did you ask more questions?"

"Of course I did, because, although I'd denied it, he knew I was dissatisfied with what I was doing. My protector said: 'I'm afraid of taking steps that are not on the map, but by taking those steps despite my fears, I have a much more interesting life.' I asked more about the Tradition, and he said something like: 'As long as God is merely man, we'll always have enough food to eat and somewhere to live. When the Mother finally regains her freedom, we might have to sleep rough and live on love, or we might be able to balance emotion and work.' My protector then asked: 'If you weren't a biologist, what would you be?' I said: 'A blacksmith, but they don't earn enough money.' And he replied: 'Well, when you grow tired of being what you're not, go and have fun and celebrate life, hammering metal into shape. In time, you'll discover that it will give you more than pleasure, it will give you meaning.' 'How do I follow this tradition you spoke of?' I asked. 'As I said, through symbols,' he replied. 'Start doing what you want to do, and everything else will be revealed to you. Believe that God is the Mother and looks after her children and never lets anything bad happen to them. I did that and I survived. I discovered that there were other people who did the same but who are considered to be mad, irresponsible, superstitious. Since time immemorial, they've sought their inspiration in nature. We build pyramids, but we also develop symbols.'

"Having said that, he left, and I never saw him again. I only know, from that moment on, symbols did begin to appear because my eyes had been opened by that conversation. Hard though it was, one evening I told my family that, although I had everything a man could dream of having, I was unhappy, and that I had, in fact, been born to be a blacksmith. My wife protested, saying: 'You were born a gypsy and had to face endless humiliations to get where you are, and yet you want to go back?' My son, however, was thrilled, because he too liked to watch the blacksmiths in our village and hated the laboratories in the big cities.

"I started dividing my time between biological research and working as a blacksmith's apprentice. I was always tired, but I was much happier. One day I left my job and set up my own blacksmith's business, which went completely wrong from the start. Just when I was starting to believe in life, things got markedly worse. One day I was working away and I saw that there before me was a symbol.

"The unworked steel arrives in my workshop and I have to transform it into parts for cars, agricultural machinery, kitchen utensils. Do you know how that's done? First, I heat the metal until it's red-hot, then I beat it mercilessly with my heaviest hammer until the metal takes on the form I need. Then I plunge it into a bucket of cold water and the whole workshop is filled with the roar of steam while the metal sizzles and crackles in response to the sudden change in temperature. I have to keep repeating that process until the object I'm making is perfect: once is not enough."

The blacksmith paused for a long time, lit a cigarette, then went on.

"Sometimes the steel I get simply can't withstand such treatment. The heat, the hammer blows, the cold water cause it to crack. And I know that I'll never be able to make it into a good plowshare or an engine shaft. Then I throw it on the pile of scrap metal at the entrance to my forge."

Another long pause, then the blacksmith concluded: "I know that God is putting me through the fire of afflictions. I've accepted the blows that life has dealt me, and sometimes I feel as cold and indifferent as the water that inflicts such pain on the steel. But my one prayer is this: 'Please, God, my Mother, don't give up until I've taken on the shape that you wish for me. Do this by whatever means you think best, for as long as you like, but never ever throw me on the scrap heap of souls.'"

I may have been drunk when I finished my conversation with that man, but I knew that my life had changed. There was a tradition behind everything we learn, and I needed to go in search of people who, consciously or unconsciously, were able to make manifest the female side of God. Instead of cursing my government and all the political shenanigans, I decided to do what I really wanted to do: heal people. I wasn't interested in anything else.

Since I didn't have the necessary resources, I approached the local men and women, and they guided me to the world of medicinal herbs. I discovered that there was a popular tradition that went back hundreds of years and was passed from generation to generation through experience rather than through technical knowledge. With their help, I was able to do far more than

I would otherwise have been able to do, because I wasn't there merely to fulfill a university task or to help my government to sell arms, or, unwittingly, to spread party political propaganda. I was there because healing people made me happy.

This brought me closer to nature, to the oral tradition, and to plants. Back in Britain, I decided to talk to other doctors and I asked them: "Do you always know exactly which medicines to prescribe or are you sometimes guided by intuition?" Almost all of them, once they had dropped their guard, admitted that they were often guided by a voice and that when they ignored the advice of the voice, they ended up giving the wrong treatment. Obviously they make use of all the available technology, but they know that there is a corner, a dark corner, where lies the real meaning of the cure, and the best decision to make.

My protector threw my world off balance—even though he was only a gypsy blacksmith. I used to go at least once a year to his village, and we would talk about how, when we dare to see things differently, life opens up to our eyes. On one of those visits, I met other disciples of his, and together we discussed our fears and our conquests. My protector said: "I too get scared, but it's at such moments that I discover a wisdom that is beyond me, and I go forward."

Now I earn a lot of money working as a GP in Edinburgh, and I would earn even more if I went to work in London, but I prefer to make the most of life and to take time out. I do what I like: I combine the healing processes of the ancients, the Arcane Tradition, with the most modern techniques of present-day medicine, the Hippocratic Tradition. I'm writing a paper on the subject, and many people in the "scientific" community, when they see my text published in a specialist journal, will dare to take the steps which, deep down, they've always wanted to take.

I don't believe that the mind is the source of all ills; there are real diseases too. I think antibiotics and antivirals were great advances for humanity. I don't believe that a patient of mine with appendicitis can be cured by meditation alone; what he needs is some good emergency surgery. So I take each step with courage and fear, combining technique and inspiration. And I'm careful who I say these things to, because I might get dubbed a witch doctor, and then many lives that I could have saved would be lost.

When I'm not sure, I ask the Great Mother for help. She has never yet failed to answer me. But she has always counseled me to be discreet. She probably gave the same advice to Athena on more than one occasion, but Athena was too fascinated by the world she was just starting to discover, and she didn't listen.

A London newspaper, August 24, 1991

THE WITCH OF PORTOBELLO

London (© Jeremy Lutton)—"That's another reason why I don't believe in God. I mean, look at the behavior of people who do believe!" This was the reaction of Robert Wilson, one of the traders in Portobello Road.

This road, known around the world for its antique shops and its Saturday flea market, was transformed last night into a battlefield, requiring the intervention of at least fifty police officers from the Royal Borough of Kensington and Chelsea to restore order. By the end of the fracas, five people had been injured, although none seriously. The reason behind this pitched battle, which lasted nearly two hours, was a demonstration organized by the Rev. Ian Buck to protest about what he called "the Satanic cult at the heart of England."

According to Rev. Buck, a group of suspicious individuals have been keeping the neighborhood awake every Monday night for the last six months, Monday being their chosen night for invoking the Devil. The ceremonies are led by a Lebanese woman, Sherine H. Khalil, who calls herself Athena, after the goddess of wisdom.

About two hundred people began meeting in a former East India Company warehouse, but the numbers increased over time, and in recent weeks, an equally large crowd has been gathering outside, hoping to gain entry and take part in the ceremony. When his various verbal complaints, petitions, and letters to the local newspapers achieved nothing, the Rev. Buck decided to mobilize the community, calling on his parishioners to gather outside the warehouse by 1900 hours yesterday to stop the "devil worshipers" from getting in.

"As soon as we received the first complaint, we sent someone to inspect the place, but no drugs were found nor evidence of any other kind of illicit activity," said an official who preferred not to be identified because an inquiry has just been set up to investigate what happened. "They aren't contravening the noise nuisance laws because they turn off the music at ten o'clock prompt, so there's really nothing more we can do. Britain, after all, allows freedom of worship."

The Rev. Buck has another version of events.

"The fact is that this witch of Portobello, this mistress of charlatanism, has contacts with people high up in the government, which explains why the police—paid for by taxpayers' money to maintain order and decency—refuse to do anything. We're living in an age in which everything is allowed, and democracy is being devoured and destroyed by that limitless freedom."

The vicar says that he was suspicious of the group right from the start. They had rented a crumbling old building and spent whole days trying to renovate it, "which is clear evidence that they belong to some sect and have undergone some kind of brainwashing, because no one in today's world works for free." When asked if his parishioners ever did any charitable work in the community, the Rev. Buck replied: "Yes, but we do it in the name of Jesus."

Yesterday evening, when she arrived at the warehouse to meet her waiting followers, Sherine Khalil, her son, and some of her friends were prevented from entering by the Rev. Buck's parishioners, who were carrying placards and using megaphones to call on the rest of the neighborhood to join them. This verbal aggression immediately degenerated into fighting, and soon it was impossible to control either side.

"They say they're fighting in the name of Jesus, but what they really want is for people to continue to ignore the teachings of Christ, according to which 'we are all gods,'" said the well-known actress Andrea McCain, one of Sherine Khalil's, or Athena's, followers. Ms. McCain received a cut above her right eye, which was treated at once, and she left the area before your reporter could find out more about her links with the sect.

Once order was restored, Mrs. Khalil was anxious to reassure her eight-year-old son, but she did tell us that all that takes place in the warehouse is some collective dancing, followed by the invocation of a being known as Hagia Sofia, of whom people are free to ask questions. The celebration ends with a kind of sermon and a group prayer to the Great Mother. The officer charged with investigating the original complaints confirmed this.

As far as we could ascertain, the group has no name and is not registered as a charity. According to the lawyer Sheldon Williams, this is not necessary. "We live in a free country, and people can gather together in an enclosed space for non-profit-making activities, as long as these do not break any laws such as incitement to racism or the consumption of narcotics."

Mrs. Khalil emphatically rejected any suggestion that she should stop the meetings because of the disturbances.

"We gather together to offer mutual encouragement," she said, "because it's very hard to face social pressures alone. I demand that your newspaper denounce the religious discrimination to which we've been subjected over the centuries. Whenever we do something that is not in accord with state-instituted and state-approved religions, there is always an attempt to crush us, as happened today. Before, we would have faced martyrdom, prison, being burned at the stake, or sent into exile, but now we are in a position to respond, and force will be answered with force, just as compassion will be repaid with compassion."

When faced with the Rev. Buck's accusations, she accused him of "manipulating his parishioners and using intolerance and lies as an excuse for violence."

According to the sociologist Arthaud Lenox, phenomena like this will become increasingly common in the future, possibly involving more serious clashes between established religions. "Now that the Marxist utopia has shown itself incapable of channeling society's ideals, the world is ripe for a religious revival, born of civilization's natural fear of significant dates. However, I believe that when the year 2000 does arrive and the world survives intact, common sense will prevail and religions will revert to being a refuge for the weak, who are always in search of guidance."

This view is contested by Dom Evaristo Piazza, the Vatican's auxiliary bishop in the United Kingdom. "What we are seeing is not the spiritual awakening that we all long for, but a wave of what Americans call New Ageism, a kind of breeding ground in which everything is permitted, where dogmas are not respected, and the most absurd ideas from the past return to lay waste to the human mind. Unscrupulous people like this young woman are trying to instill their false ideas in weak, suggestible minds, with the one aim of making money and gaining personal power."

The German historian Franz Herbert, currently working at the Goethe Institute in London, has a different idea. "The established religions no longer ask fundamental questions about our identity and our reason for living. Instead, they concentrate purely on a series of dogmas and rules concerned only with fitting in with a particular social and political organization. People in search of real spirituality are, therefore, setting off in new directions, and that inevitably means a return to the past and to primitive religions, before those religions were contaminated by the structures of power."

At the police station where the incident was recorded, Sergeant William Morton stated that should Sherine Khalil's group decide to hold their meeting on the following Monday and feel that they are under threat, then they must apply in writing for police protection and thus avoid a repetition of last night's events.

(With additional information from Andrew Fish. Photos by Mark Guillhem.)

HERON RYAN, JOURNALIST

I read the report on the plane, when I was flying back from the Ukraine, feeling full of doubts. I still hadn't managed to ascertain whether the Chernobyl disaster had been as big as it was said to have been, or whether it had been used by the major oil producers to inhibit the use of other sources of energy.

Anyway, I was horrified by what I read in the article. The photos showed broken windows, a furious Reverend Buck, and—there lay the danger—a beautiful woman with fiery eyes and her son in her arms. I saw at once what could happen, both good and bad. I went straight from the airport to Portobello, convinced that both my predictions would become reality.

On the positive side, the following Monday's meeting was one of the most successful events in the area's history: many local people came, some curious to see the "being" mentioned in the article, others bearing placards defending freedom of religion and freedom of speech. The venue would only hold two hundred people, and so the rest of the crowd were all crammed together on the pavement outside, hoping for at least a glimpse of the woman who appeared to be the priestess of the oppressed.

When she arrived, she was received with applause, handwritten notes, and requests for help; some people threw flowers, and one lady of uncertain age asked her to keep on fighting for women's freedom and for the right to worship the Mother. The parishioners from the week before must have been intimidated by the crowd and so failed to turn up, despite the threats they had made during the previous days. There were no aggressive comments, and the ceremony passed off as normal, with dancing, the appearance of Hagia Sofia (by then, I knew that she was simply another facet of Athena herself), and a final celebration (this had been added recently, when the group moved to the warehouse, lent by one of its original members), and that was that.

During her sermon, Athena spoke as if possessed by someone else.

"We all have a duty to love and to allow love to manifest itself in the way it thinks best. We cannot and must not be frightened when the powers of darkness want to make themselves heard, those same powers that introduced the word *sin* merely to control our hearts and minds. Jesus Christ, whom we all know, turned to the woman taken in adultery and said: 'Has no man condemned thee? Neither do I condemn thee.' He healed people on the Sabbath, he allowed a prostitute to wash his feet, he promised a thief that he would enjoy the delights of Paradise, he ate forbidden foods, and he said that we should concern ourselves only with today, because the lilies in the field toil not, neither do they spin, but are arrayed in glory.

"What is sin? It is a sin to prevent Love from showing itself. And the Mother is Love. We are entering a new world in which we can choose to follow our own steps, not those that society forces us to take. If necessary, we will confront the forces of darkness again, as we did last week. But no one will silence our voice or our heart."

I was witnessing the transformation of a woman into an icon. She spoke with great conviction, with dignity and with faith in what she was saying. I hoped that things really were like that, that we truly were entering a new world, and that I would live to see it.

She left the warehouse to as much acclaim as she had entered

it, and when she saw me in the crowd, she called me over and
said that she'd missed me. She was happy and confident, sure
that she was doing the right thing.

This was the positive side of the newspaper article, and
things might have ended there. I wanted my analysis of events
to be wrong, but three days later, my prediction was confirmed.
The negative side emerged in full force.

Employing the services of one of the most highly regarded
and conservative law practices in Britain, whose senior part-
ners—unlike Athena—really did have contacts in all spheres of
the government, and basing his case on published statements
made by Athena, the Reverend Buck called a news conference
to say that he was suing for defamation, calumny, and moral
damages.

The deputy editor called me in. He knew I was friendly with
the central figure in that scandal and suggested that we publish
an exclusive interview. My first reaction was of disgust: How
could I use my friendship to sell newspapers?

However, after we had talked further, I started to think that
it might be a good idea. She would have the chance to present
her side of the story; indeed, she could use the interview to
promote all the things for which she was now openly fighting.
I left the deputy editor's office with the plan we had drawn up
together: a series of articles on new trends in society and on
radical changes that were taking place in the search for religious
belief. In one of those articles, I would publish Athena's point
of view.

That same afternoon, I went to her house, taking advantage

of the fact that the invitation had come from her when we met outside the warehouse. The neighbors told me that, the day before, court officials had attempted to serve a summons on her but failed.

I phoned later on, without success. I tried again as night was falling, but no one answered. From then on, I phoned every half an hour, growing more anxious with each call. Ever since Hagia Sofia had cured my insomnia, tiredness drove me to bed at eleven o'clock, but this time anxiety kept me awake.

I found her mother's number in the phone book, but it was late, and if Athena wasn't there, then I would only cause the whole family to worry. What to do? I turned on the TV to see if anything had happened—nothing special, London continued as before, with its marvels and its perils.

I decided to try one last time. The phone rang three times, and someone answered. I recognized Andrea's voice at once.

"What do you want?" she asked.

"Athena asked me to get in touch. Is everything all right?"

"Everything's all right and not all right, depending on your way of looking at things. But I think you might be able to help."

"Where is she?"

She hung up without saying any more.

DEIDRE O'NEILL, KNOWN AS EDDA

Athena stayed in a hotel near my house. News from London regarding local events, especially minor conflicts in the suburbs, never reaches Scotland. We're not much interested in how the English sort out their little problems. We have our own flag, our own football team, and soon we will have our own parliament.

I let Athena rest for a whole day. The following morning, instead of going into the little temple and performing the rituals I know, I decided to take her and her son to a wood near Edinburgh. There, while the boy played and ran about among the trees, she told me in detail what was going on.

When she'd finished, I said, "It's daylight, the sky is cloudy, and human beings believe that beyond the clouds lives an all-powerful God, guiding the fate of men. Meanwhile, look at your son, look at your feet, listen to the sounds around you: down here is the Mother, so much closer, bringing joy to children and energy to those who walk over her body. Why do people prefer to believe in something far away and forget what is there before their eyes, a true manifestation of the miracle?"

"I know the answer. Because up there someone is guiding us and giving his orders, hidden behind the clouds, unquestionable in his wisdom. Down here we have physical contact with a magical reality, and the freedom to choose where our steps will go."

"Exactly. But do you think that is what people want? Do they want the freedom to choose their own steps?"

"Yes, I think they do. The earth I'm standing on now has laid out many strange paths for me, from a village in Transylvania to a city in the Middle East, from there to another city on an island, and then to the desert and back to Transylvania. From a suburban bank to a real estate company in the Persian Gulf. From a dance group to a bedouin. And whenever my feet drove me onward, I said yes instead of saying no."

"What did you gain from all that?"

"Today I can see people's auras. I can awaken the Mother in my soul. My life now has meaning, and I know what I'm fighting for. But why do you ask? You too gained the most important power of all—the gift of healing. Andrea can now prophesy and converse with spirits. I've followed her spiritual development every step of the way."

"What else have you gained?"

"The joy of being alive. I know that I'm here, and that everything is a miracle, a revelation."

The little boy fell over and grazed his knee. Instinctively, Athena ran to him, wiped the wound clean, told him not to worry, and the boy continued running about in the forest. I used that as a signal.

"What just happened to your little boy, happened to me. And it's happening to you too, isn't it?"

"Yes, but I don't think I stumbled and fell. I think I'm being tested again, and that my next step will be revealed to me."

At such moments, a teacher must say nothing, only bless the disciple. Because however much the teacher may want to save her disciple from suffering, the paths are mapped out and the disciple's feet are eager to follow them. I suggested we go back to the wood that night, just the two of us. She asked where she could leave her son, and I said that I would take care of that.

I had a neighbor who owed me a favor and who would be delighted to look after Viorel.

As evening fell, we returned to that same place, and on the way, we spoke of things that had nothing to do with the ritual we were about to perform. Athena had seen me using a new kind of depilatory wax and was intrigued to know what advantages it had over the old methods. We talked animatedly about vanity, fashion, the cheapest places to buy clothes, female behavior, feminism, hairstyles. At one point she said something along the lines of: "But if the soul is ageless, I don't know why we should be so worried about all this," then realized that it was all right just to relax and talk about superficial subjects. More than that, such conversations were really fun, and how we look is something that's still very important in women's lives (it is in men's lives too, but in a different way, and they're not as open about it as we are).

As we approached the place I'd chosen—or, rather, which the wood was choosing for me—I started to feel the presence of the Mother. In my case, this presence manifests itself in a certain, mysterious inner joy that always touches me and almost moves me to tears. It was the moment to stop and change the subject.

"Collect some wood for kindling," I said.

"But it's dark."

"There's enough light from the full moon even if it's obscured by clouds. Train your eyes: they were made to see more than you think."

She began doing as I asked, occasionally cursing because she'd scratched herself on a thorn. Almost half an hour passed, and during that time, we didn't talk. I felt the excitement of knowing that the Mother was close by, the euphoria of being there with that woman who still seemed little more than a child and who trusted me and was keeping me company in the search that sometimes seemed too mad for the human mind.

Athena was still at the stage of answering questions, just as she'd responded to mine that afternoon. I had been like that once, until I allowed myself to be transported completely into the kingdom of mystery, where it was simply a matter of contemplating, celebrating, worshiping, praising, and allowing the gift to manifest itself.

I was watching Athena collecting firewood and I saw the girl I once was, in search of veiled secrets and secret powers. Life had taught me something completely different: the powers were not secret and the secrets had been revealed a long time ago. When I saw that she had gathered enough firewood, I indicated that she should stop.

I myself looked for some larger branches and put them on top of the kindling. So it was in life. In order for the more substantial pieces of wood to catch fire, the kindling must burn first. In order for us to liberate the energy of our strength, our weakness must first have a chance to reveal itself.

In order for us to understand the powers we carry within us and the secrets that have already been revealed, it was first necessary to allow the surface—expectations, fears, appearances—to be burned away. We were entering the peace now settling upon the forest, with the gentle wind, the moonlight behind the clouds, the noises of the animals that sally forth at night to hunt, thus fulfilling the cycle of birth and death of the Mother, and without ever being criticized for following their instincts and their nature.

I lit the fire.

Neither of us felt like saying anything. For what seemed like an eternity, we merely contemplated the dance of the fire, knowing that hundreds of thousands of people, all over the world, would also be sitting by their fireside, regardless of whether they had modern heating systems in their house or not; they did this because they were sitting before a symbol.

It took a great effort to emerge from that trance, which, although it meant nothing specific to me, and did not make me see gods, auras, or ghosts, nonetheless left me in the state of grace I needed to be in. I focused once more on the present, on the young woman by my side, on the ritual I needed to perform.

"How is your student?" I asked.

"Difficult, but if she wasn't, I might not learn what I need to learn."

"And what powers is she developing?"

"She speaks with beings in the parallel world."

"As you converse with Hagia Sofia?"

"No, as you well know, Hagia Sofia is the Mother manifesting herself in me. She speaks with invisible beings."

I knew this, but I wanted to be sure. Athena was more silent than usual. I don't know if she had discussed the events in London with Andrea, but that didn't matter. I got up, opened the bag I had with me, took out a handful of specially chosen herbs, and threw them into the flames.

"The wood has started to speak," said Athena, as if this were something perfectly normal, and that was good, it meant that miracles were now becoming part of her life.

"What is it saying?"

"Nothing at the moment, only noises."

Minutes later, she heard a song coming from the fire.

"Oh, it's wonderful!"

There spoke the little girl, not the wife or mother.

"Stay just as you are. Don't try to concentrate or follow my steps or understand what I'm saying. Relax and feel good. That is sometimes all we can hope for from life."

I knelt down, picked up a red-hot piece of wood, and drew a circle around her, leaving a small opening through which I could enter. I could hear the same music as Athena, and I danced around her, invoking the union of the male fire with the earth, which received it now with arms and legs spread wide, the fire that purified everything, transforming into energy the strength contained in the firewood, in those branches, in those beings, both human and invisible. I danced for as long as the melody from the fire lasted, and I made protective gestures to the child who was sitting, smiling, inside the circle.

When the flames had burned down, I took a little ash and sprinkled it on Athena's head. Then with my feet I erased the circle I'd drawn around her.

"Thank you," she said. "I felt very loved, wanted, protected."

"In difficult moments, remember that feeling."

"Now that I've found my path, there will be no more difficult moments. After all, I have a mission to fulfill, don't I?"

"Yes, we all have a mission to fulfill."

She started to feel uncertain.

"And what about the difficult moments?" she asked.

"That isn't an intelligent thing to ask. Remember what you said just now: you are loved, wanted, protected."

"I'll do my best."

Her eyes filled with tears. Athena had understood my answer.

Samira R. Khalil, housewife

My own grandson! What has my grandson got to do with all this? What kind of world are we living in? Are we still in the Middle Ages, engaging in witch hunts?

I ran to him. He had a bloody nose, but he didn't seem to care about my distress and pushed me away.

"I know how to defend myself, and I did."

I may never have produced a child in my own womb, but I know the hearts of children. I was far more worried about Athena than I was about Viorel. This was just one of many fights he would have to face in his life, and there was a flicker of pride in his swollen eyes.

"Some children at school said that Mum was a devil worshiper!"

Sherine arrived shortly afterward, soon enough to see the boy's bloodied face and to kick up a fuss. She wanted to go straight to the school and talk to the head teacher, but first I put my arms around her. I let her cry out all her tears and all her frustrations, and the best thing I could do then was to keep silent and try to convey my love for her through that silence.

When she had calmed down a little, I explained carefully that she could come back home and live with us, that we would take care of everything. When her father read about the case being brought against her, he had immediately spoken to some lawyers. We would do everything we could to get her out of this situation regardless of comments from the neighbors, ironic looks from acquaintances, and the false solidarity of friends.

Nothing in the world was more important than my daughter's happiness, even though I'd never understood why she always had to choose the most difficult and painful of paths. But a mother doesn't have to understand anything, she simply has to love and protect. And feel proud. Knowing that we could give her almost everything, she nevertheless set off early in search of her independence. She'd had her stumbles and her failures, but she insisted on facing any storms alone. She went looking for her mother, aware of the risks she was running, and in the end, that encounter brought her closer to us. I knew she had never once heeded my advice—get a degree, get married, put up with the problems of living with someone without complaint, don't try to go beyond the limits set by society. And what had been the result?

By following my daughter's story, I became a better person. Obviously I didn't understand about the Mother Goddess or Athena's need always to surround herself with strangers, or her inability to be content with all that she'd achieved after so much work. But deep down, even though it may be rather late in the day for such ideas, I wish I could have been like her.

I was about to get up and prepare something to eat, but she stopped me.

"I want to stay here for a while with your arms around me. That's all I need. Viorel, go and watch TV. I want to talk to your grandmother."

The boy obeyed.

"I must have caused you a lot of suffering."

"Not at all. On the contrary, you and your son are the source of all our joy and our reason for living."

"But I haven't exactly—"

"I'm glad it's been the way it has. I can say it now: there were moments when I hated you, when I bitterly regretted not having followed the advice of that nurse and adopted another baby. Then I'd ask myself: How can a mother hate her own daughter? I took tranquillizers, played bridge with my friends, went on shopping sprees, and all to make up for the love I'd given you and which I felt I wasn't getting back.

"A few months ago, when you decided to give up yet another job that was bringing you both money and prestige, I was in despair. I went to the local church. I wanted to make a promise to the Virgin and beg her to bring you back to reality, to force you to change your life and make the most of the chances you were throwing away. I was ready to do anything in exchange for that.

"I stood looking at the Virgin and Child. And I said: 'You're a mother and you know what's happening. Ask anything of me, but save my child, because I think she's bent on self-destruction.'"

I felt Sherine's arms holding me tighter. She was crying again, but her tears were different this time. I was doing my best to control my feelings.

"And do you know what I felt at that moment? I felt that she was talking to me and saying: 'Listen, Samira, that's what I thought too. I suffered for years because my son wouldn't listen to anything I said. I used to worry about his safety, I didn't like the friends he chose, and he showed no respect for laws, customs, religion, or his elders.' Need I go on?"

"Yes, I'd like to hear the rest of the story."

"The Virgin concluded by saying, 'But my son didn't listen to me. And now I'm very glad that he didn't.'"

I gently removed myself from her embrace and got up.

"You two need to eat."

I went to the kitchen, prepared some onion soup and a dish of tabbouleh, warmed up some unleavened bread, put it all on the table, and we had lunch together. We talked about trivial things, which, at such moments, always help to bring us together and justify our pleasure at being there, quietly, even if, outside, a storm is uprooting trees and sowing destruction. Of course, at the end of that afternoon, my daughter and my grandson would walk out of the door to confront the winds, the thunder, and the lightning all over again, but that was their choice.

"Mum, you said that you'd do anything for me, didn't you?"

It was true. I would lay down my life if necessary.

"Don't you think I should be prepared to do anything for Viorel too?"

"I think that's a mother's instinct, but instinct aside, it's the greatest proof of love there is."

She continued eating.

"You know that your father is happy to help with this case being brought against you, if you want him to, that is."

"Of course I do. This is my family we're talking about."

I thought twice, three times, but couldn't hold back my words. "Can I give you some advice? I know you have some influential friends—that journalist, for example. Why don't you ask him to write about your story and tell him your version of events? The press are giving a lot of coverage to that vicar, and people will end up thinking he's right."

"So, as well as accepting what I do, you also want to help me?"

"Yes, Sherine. Even though I may not understand you, even though I sometimes suffer as the Virgin must have suffered all her life, even if you're not Jesus Christ with an all-important message for the world, I'm on your side and I want to see you win."

HERON RYAN, JOURNALIST

Athena arrived while I was frantically making notes for what I imagined would be the ideal interview on the events in Portobello and the rebirth of the Goddess. It was a very, very delicate affair.

What I saw at the warehouse was a woman saying, "You can do it, let the Great Mother teach you—trust in love, and miracles will happen." And the crowd agreed, but that wouldn't last long, because we were living in an age in which slavery was the only path to happiness. Free will demands immense responsibility; it's hard work, it brings with it anguish and suffering.

"I need you to write something about me," she said.

I told her that we should wait a little—after all, the whole affair could fade from view the following week—but that, meanwhile, I'd prepared a few questions about Female Energy.

"At the moment, all the fuss and the fighting is only of interest to people in the immediate area and to the tabloids. No respectable newspaper has published a single line about it. London is full of these little local disturbances, and getting into the broadsheets really isn't advisable. It would be best if the group didn't meet for two or three weeks. However, I think that the business about the Goddess, if treated with the seriousness it deserves, could make a lot of people ask themselves some really important questions."

"Over supper that time, you said that you loved me. And now you're not only telling me you don't want to help me, you're also asking me to give up the things I believe in."

How to interpret those words? Was she finally accepting the love I'd offered her that night, and which accompanied me every minute of my life? According to the Lebanese poet Khalil Gibran, it was more important to give than to receive, but while these were wise words, I was part of what is known as "humanity," with my frailties, my moments of indecision, my desire simply to live in peace, to be the slave of my feelings and to surrender myself without asking any questions, without even knowing if my love was reciprocated. All she had to do was to let me love her; I was sure that Hagia Sofia would agree with me. Athena had been passing through my life now for nearly two years, and I was afraid she might simply continue on her way and disappear over the horizon, without my having even been able to accompany her on part of that journey.

"Are you talking about love?"

"I'm asking for your help."

What to do? Control myself, stay cool, not precipitate things and end up destroying them? Or take the step I needed to take, embrace her and protect her from all dangers?

My head kept telling me to say, "Don't you worry about a thing. I love you," but instead I said, "I want to help. Please trust me. I'd do anything in the world for you, including saying no if I thought that was the right thing to do, even though you might not understand my reasoning."

I told her that the deputy editor on my newspaper had proposed a series of articles about the reawakening of the Goddess, which would include an interview with her. At first it had seemed to me an excellent idea, but now I saw that it would be best to wait a little. I said, "You either carry your mission forward or you defend yourself. You're aware, I know, that what you're doing is more important than how you're seen by other people. Do you agree?"

"I'm thinking of my son. Every day now he gets into some fight or argument at school."

"That will pass. In a week, it'll be forgotten. That will be the moment to act, not in order to defend yourself against idiotic attacks, but to set out, confidently and wisely, the true breadth of your work. And if you have any doubts about my feelings and are determined to continue, then I'll come with you to the next meeting. And we'll see what happens."

The following Monday I went with her to the meeting. I was not now just another person in the crowd; I could see things as she was seeing them.

People crowded into the warehouse; there were flowers and applause, young women calling her "the priestess of the Goddess," a few smartly dressed ladies begging for a private audience because of some illness in the family. The crowd started pushing us and blocking the entrance. We had never imagined that we might need some form of security, and I was frightened. I took her arm, picked up Viorel, and we went in.

Inside the packed room, a very angry Andrea was waiting for us.

"I think you should tell them that you're not performing any miracles today!" she shouted at Athena. "You're allowing yourself to be seduced by vanity! Why doesn't Hagia Sofia tell all these people to go away?"

"Because she can diagnose illnesses," replied Athena defiantly. "And the more people who benefit from that, the better."

She was about to say more, but the crowd was applauding and she stepped up onto the improvised stage. She turned on the small sound system she'd brought from home, gave instructions for people to dance against the rhythm of the music, and the ritual began. At a certain point, Viorel went and sat down in a corner—that was the moment for Hagia Sofia to appear. Athena did as I'd seen her do many times before: she abruptly turned off the music, clutched her head in her hands, and the people waited in silence, as if obeying an invisible command.

The ritual followed its unvarying path: there were questions about love, which were rejected, although she agreed to comment on anxieties, illnesses, and other personal problems. From where I was, I could see that some people had tears in their eyes, others behaved as if they were standing before a saint. Then came the moment for the closing sermon, before the group celebration of the Mother.

Since I knew what would happen next, I started thinking about the best way to get out of there with the minimum of fuss. I hoped that she would take Andrea's advice and tell them not to go looking for miracles there. I went over to where Viorel was sitting, so that we could leave the place as soon as his mother had finished speaking.

And that was when I heard the voice of Hagia Sofia.

"Today, before we close, we're going to talk about diet. Forget all about slimming regimes."

Diet? Forget about slimming regimes?

"We have survived for all these millennia because we have been able to eat. And now that seems to have become a curse. Why? What is it that makes us, at forty years old, want to have the same body we had when we were young? Is it possible to stop time? Of course not. And why should we be thin?"

I heard a kind of murmuring in the crowd. They were probably expecting a more spiritual message.

"We don't need to be thin. We buy books, we go to gyms, we expend a lot of brain power on trying to hold back time, when we should be celebrating the miracle of being here in this world. Instead of thinking about how to live better, we're obsessed with weight.

"Forget all about that. You can read all the books you want, do all the exercise you want, punish yourself as much as you want, but you will still have only two choices—either stop living or get fat.

"Eat in moderation, but take pleasure in eating: it isn't what enters a person's mouth that's evil, but what leaves it. Remember that for millennia we have struggled in order to keep from starving. Whose idea was it that we had to be thin all our lives? I'll tell you: the vampires of the soul, those who are so afraid of the future that they think it's possible to stop the wheel of time. Hagia Sofia can guarantee that it's not possible. Use the energy and effort you put into dieting to nourish yourself with spiritual bread. Know that the Great Mother gives generously and wisely. Respect that and you will get no fatter than passing time demands. Instead of artificially burning those calories, try to transform them into the energy required to fight for your dreams. No one ever stayed slim for very long just because of a diet."

There was complete silence. Athena began the closing ceremony, and we all celebrated the presence of the Mother. I clasped Viorel in my arms, promising myself that next time I would bring a few friends along to provide a little improvised security. We left to the same shouts and applause as when we had arrived.

A shopkeeper grabbed my arm. "This is absurd! If one of my windows gets smashed, I'll sue you!"

Athena was laughing and giving autographs. Viorel seemed happy. I just hoped that no journalist was there that night. When we finally managed to extricate ourselves from the crowd, we hailed a taxi.

I asked if they would like to go somewhere to eat. "Of course," said Athena, "that's just what I've been talking about."

ANTOINE LOCADOUR, HISTORIAN

In this long series of mistakes that came to be known as "the Witch of Portobello affair," what surprises me most is the ingenuousness of Heron Ryan, an international journalist of many years experience. When we spoke, he was horrified by the tabloid headlines:

"The Goddess Diet!" screamed one.

"Get Thin While You Eat, Says Witch of Portobello!" roared another from its front page.

As well as touching on the sensitive topic of religion, Athena had gone further: she had talked about diet, a subject of national interest, more important even than wars, strikes, or natural disasters. We may not all believe in God, but we all want to get thin.

Reporters interviewed local shopkeepers, who all swore blind that, in the days preceding the mass meetings, they'd seen red and black candles being lit during rituals involving only a handful of people. It may have been nothing but cheap sensationalism, but Ryan should have foreseen that, with a court case in progress, the accuser would take every opportunity to bring to the judges' attention what he considered to be not only a calumny, but also an attack on all the values that kept society going.

That same week, one of the most prestigious British newspapers published in its editorial column an article by the Reverend Ian Buck, minister at the Evangelical Church in Kensington. It said, among other things:

> As a good Christian, I have a duty to turn the other cheek when I am wrongly attacked or when my honor is impugned. However, we must not forget that while Jesus may have turned the other cheek, he also used a whip to drive out those wanting to make the Lord's House into a den of thieves. That is what we are seeing at the moment in Portobello Road: unscrupulous people who pass themselves off as savers of souls, giving false hope and promising cures for all ills, even declaring that you can stay thin and elegant if you follow their teachings.
>
> For this reason, I have no alternative but to go to the courts to prevent this situation continuing. The movement's followers swear that they are capable of awakening hitherto unknown gifts and they deny the existence of an All-Powerful God, replacing him with pagan divinities such as Venus and Aphrodite. For them, everything is

permitted, as long as it is done with "love." But what is love? An immoral force that justifies any end? Or a commitment to society's true values, such as the family and tradition?

At the next meeting, foreseeing a repetition of the pitched battle of August, the police brought in half a dozen officers to avoid any confrontations. Athena arrived accompanied by a bodyguard improvised by Ryan, and this time there was not only applause but also booing and cursing too. One woman, seeing that Athena was accompanied by a child, brought a charge two days later under the Children Act 1989, alleging that the mother was inflicting irreversible damage on her child and that custody should be given to the father.

One of the tabloids managed to track down Lukás Jessen-Petersen, who refused to give an interview. He threatened the reporter, saying that if he so much as mentioned Viorel in his articles, he wouldn't be responsible for his actions.

The following day, the tabloid carried the headline: "Witch of Portobello's Ex Would Kill for Son."

That same afternoon, two more charges under the Children Act 1989 were brought before the courts, calling for the child to be taken into care.

There was no meeting after that. Groups of people—for and against—gathered outside the door, and uniformed officers were on hand to keep the peace, but Athena did not appear. The same thing happened the following week, only this time, there were fewer crowds and fewer police.

The third week, there was only the occasional bunch of flowers to be seen and someone handing out photos of Athena to passers-by.

The subject disappeared from the front pages of the London dailies. And when the Reverend Ian Buck announced his decision to withdraw all charges of defamation and calumny, "in the Christian spirit we should show to those who repent of their actions," no major paper was interested in publishing his statement, which turned up instead on the readers' pages of some local rag.

As far as I know, it never became national news but was restricted to the pages that dealt only with London news. I visited Brighton a month after the meetings ended, and when I tried to bring the subject up with my friends there, none of them had the faintest idea what I was talking about.

Ryan could have cleared up the whole business, and what his newspaper said would have been picked up by the rest of the media. To my surprise, though, he never published a line about Sherine Khalil.

In my view, the crime—given its nature—had nothing to do with what happened in Portobello. It was all just a macabre coincidence.

HERON RYAN, JOURNALIST

Athena asked me to turn on the tape recorder. She had brought another one with her, of a type I'd never seen before—very sophisticated and very small.

"First, I wish to state that I've been receiving death threats. Second, I want you to promise that, even if I die, you will wait five years before you allow anyone else to listen to this tape. In the future, people will be able to tell what is true and what is false. Say you agree; that way you will be entering a legally binding agreement."

"I agree, but I think—"

"Don't think anything. Should I be found dead, this will be my testament, on condition that it won't be published now."

I turned off the tape recorder.

"You have nothing to fear. I have friends in government, people who owe me favors, who need or will need me. We can—"

"Have I mentioned before that my boyfriend works for Scotland Yard?"

Not that again. If he really did exist, why wasn't he there when we needed him, when both Athena and Viorel could have been attacked by the mob?

Questions crowded into my mind: Was she trying to test me? What was going through that woman's mind? Was she unbalanced, fickle, one hour wanting to be by my side, the next talking about this nonexistent man?

"Turn on the tape recorder," she said.

I felt terrible. I was beginning to think that she'd been using me all along. I would like to have been able to say: "Go away. Get out of my life. Ever since I first met you, everything has been a hell. All I want is for you to come here, put your arms

around me and kiss me, and say you want to stay with me forever, but that never happens."

"Is there anything wrong?"

She knew there was something wrong. Or, rather, she couldn't
possibly not have known what I was feeling, because I had never
concealed my love for her, even though I'd only spoken openly
of it once. But I would cancel any appointment to see her; I was
always there when she needed me; I was trying to build some
kind of relationship with her son, in the belief that he would
one day call me Dad. I never asked her to stop what she was doing; I accepted her way of life, her decisions; I suffered in silence
when she suffered; I was glad when she triumphed; I was proud
of her determination.

"Why did you turn off the tape recorder?"

I hovered for a second between heaven and hell, between
rebellion and submission, between cold reason and destructive
emotion. In the end, summoning up all my strength, I managed
to control myself. I pressed the button.

"Let's continue."

"As I was saying, I've been receiving death threats. I've been
getting anonymous phone calls. They insult me and say I'm a
menace, that I'm trying to restore the reign of Satan, and that
they can't allow this to happen."

"Have you spoken to the police?"

I deliberately omitted any reference to her boyfriend, showing that I'd never believed that story anyway.

"Yes, I have. They've recorded the calls. They come from

public pay phones, but the police told me not to worry, that they're watching my house. They've arrested one person: he's mentally ill and believes he's the reincarnation of one of the apostles, and that 'this time, he must fight so that Christ is not driven out again.' He's in a psychiatric hospital now. The police explained that he's been in the hospital before for making similar threats to other people."

"If they're on the case, there's no need to worry. Our police are the best in the world."

"I'm not afraid of death. If I were to die today, I would carry with me moments that few people my age have had the chance to experience. What I'm afraid of, and this is why I've asked you to record our conversation today, is that I might kill someone."

"Kill someone?"

"You know that there are legal proceedings under way to remove Viorel from me. I've asked friends, but no one can do anything. We just have to await the verdict. According to them—depending on the judge, of course—these fanatics will get what they want. That's why I've bought a gun. I know what it means for a child to be removed from his mother, because I've experienced it myself. And so, when the first bailiff arrives, I'll shoot, and I'll keep shooting until the bullets run out. If they don't shoot me first, I'll use the knives in my house. If they take the knives, I'll use my teeth and my nails. But no one is going to take Viorel from me, or only over my dead body. Are you recording this?"

"I am. But there are ways——"

"There aren't. My father is following the case. He says that when it comes to family law, there's little that can be done. Now turn off the tape recorder."

"Was that your testament?"

She didn't answer. When I did nothing, she took the initiative. She went over to the sound system and put on that music from the steppes, which I now knew almost by heart. She danced as she did during the rituals, completely out of rhythm, and I knew what she was trying to do. Her tape recorder was still on, a silent witness to everything that was happening there. The afternoon sunlight was pouring in through the windows, but Athena was off in search of another light, one that had been there since the creation of the world.

When she felt the spark from the Mother she stopped dancing, turned off the music, put her head in her hands, and didn't move for some time. Then she raised her head and looked at me.

"You know who is here, don't you?"

"Yes. Athena and her divine side, Hagia Sofia."

"I've grown used to doing this. I don't think it's necessary, but it's the method I've discovered for getting in touch with her, and now it's become a tradition in my life. You know who you're talking to, don't you? To Athena. I am Hagia Sofia."

"Yes, I know. The second time I danced at your house, I discovered that I had a spirit guide too: Philemon. But I don't talk to him very much, I don't listen to what he says. I only know that when he's present, it's as if our two souls have finally met."

"That's right. And today Philemon and Hagia Sofia are going to talk about love."

"Should I dance first?"

"There's no need. Philemon will understand me, because I can see that you were touched by my dance. The man before me suffers for something which he believes he has never received—my love. But the man beyond your self understands that all the pain, anxiety, and feelings of abandonment are unnecessary and childish. I love you. Not in the way that your human side wants, but in the way that the divine spark wants. We inhabit the same tent, which was placed on our path by her. There we understand that we are not the slaves of our feelings, but their masters. We serve and are served, we open the doors of our rooms and we embrace. Perhaps we kiss too, because everything that happens very intensely on earth will have its counterpart on the invisible plane. And you know that I'm not trying to provoke you, that I'm not toying with your feelings when I say that."

"What is love, then?"

"The soul, blood, and body of the Great Mother. I love you as exiled souls love each other when they meet in the middle of the desert. There will never be anything physical between us, but no passion is in vain, no love is ever wasted. If the Mother awoke that love in your heart, she awoke it in mine too, although your heart perhaps accepts it more readily. The energy of love can never be lost—it is more powerful than anything and shows itself in many ways."

"I'm not strong enough for this. Such abstractions only leave me feeling more depressed and alone than ever."

"I'm not strong enough either. I need someone by my side too. But one day, our eyes will open, the different forms of Love will be made manifest, and then suffering will disappear from the face of the earth. It won't be long now, I think. Many of us are returning from a long journey during which we were forced to search for things that were of no interest to us. Now we realize that they were false. But this return cannot be made without pain, because we have been away for a long time and feel that we are strangers in our own land. It will take some time to find the friends who also left, and the places where our roots and our treasures lie. But this will happen."

For some reason, what she said touched me. And that drove me on.

"I want to continue talking about love," I said.

"We are talking. That has always been the aim of everything I've looked for in my life—allowing Love to manifest itself in me without barriers, letting it fill up my blank spaces, making me dance, smile, justify my life, protect my son, get in touch with the heavens, with men and women, with all those who were placed on my path. I tried to control my feelings, saying such things as 'he deserves my love' or 'he doesn't.' Until, that is, I understood my fate, when I saw that I might lose the most important thing in my life."

"Your son."

"Exactly. He is the most complete manifestation of Love. When the possibility arose that he might be taken away from me, then I found myself and realized that I could never have anything or lose anything. I understood this after crying for many hours. It was only after intense suffering that the part of me I call Hagia Sofia said: 'What nonsense! Love always stays, even though, sooner or later, your son will leave.'"

I was beginning to understand.

"Love is not a habit, a commitment, or a debt. It isn't what romantic songs tell us it is—love simply is. That is the testament of Athena or Sherine or Hagia Sofia—love is. No definitions. Love and don't ask too many questions. Just love."

"That's difficult."

"Are you recording?"

"You asked me to turn the machine off."

"Well, turn it on again."

I did as she asked. Athena went on.

"It's difficult for me too. That's why I'm not going back home. I'm going into hiding. The police might protect me from madmen, but not from human justice. I had a mission to fulfill and it took me so far that I even risked the custody of my son. Not that I regret it. I fulfilled my destiny."

"What was your mission?"

"You know what it was. You were there from the start. Preparing the way for the Mother. Continuing a Tradition that has been suppressed for centuries, but which is now beginning to experience a resurgence."

"Perhaps ..."

I stopped, but she didn't say a word until I'd finished my sentence.

"… perhaps you came too early, and people aren't yet ready."

Athena laughed.

"Of course they're not. That's why there were all those confrontations, all that aggression and obscurantism. Because the forces of darkness are dying, and they are thrown back on such things as a last resort. They seem very strong, as animals do before they die, but afterward, they're too exhausted to get to their feet. I sowed the seed in many hearts, and each one will reveal the Renaissance in its own way, but one of those hearts will follow the full Tradition—Andrea."

Andrea.

Who hated her, who blamed her for the collapse of our relationship, who said to anyone who would listen that Athena had been taken over by egotism and vanity, and had destroyed something that had been very hard to create.

Athena got to her feet and picked up her bag—Hagia Sofia was still with her.

"I can see your aura. It's being healed of some needless suffering."

"You know, of course, that Andrea doesn't like you."

"Naturally. But we've been speaking for nearly half an hour about love. Liking has nothing to do with it. Andrea is perfectly capable of fulfilling her mission. She has more experience and more charisma than I do. She learned from my mistakes; she knows that she must be prudent because in an age in which the wild beast of obscurantism is dying, there's bound to be conflict. Andrea may hate me as a person, and that may be why she's developed her gifts so quickly—to prove that she was more able than me. When hatred makes a person grow, it's transformed into one of the many ways of loving."

She picked up her tape recorder, put it in her bag, and left.

At the end of that week, the court gave its verdict: various witnesses were heard, and Sherine Khalil, known as Athena, was given the right to keep custody of her child.

Moreover, the head teacher at the boy's school was officially warned that any kind of discrimination against the boy would be punishable by law.

I knew there was no point in ringing the apartment where she used to live. She'd left the key with Andrea, taken her sound system, some clothes, and said that she would be gone for some time.

I waited for the telephone call to invite me to celebrate that victory together. With each day that passed, my love for Athena ceased being a source of suffering and became a lake of joy and serenity. I no longer felt so alone. At some point in space, our souls—and the souls of all those returning exiles—were joyfully celebrating their reunion.

The first week passed, and I assumed she was trying to recover from the recent tensions. A month later, I assumed she must have gone back to Dubai and taken up her old job; I telephoned and was told that they'd heard nothing more from her, but if I knew where she was, could I please give her a message: the door was always open, and she was greatly missed.

I decided to write a series of articles on the reawakening of the Mother, which provoked a number of offensive letters ac-

cusing me of "promoting paganism," but which were otherwise
a great success with our readership.

Two months later, when I was just about to have lunch, a
colleague at work phoned me. The body of Sherine Khalil, the
Witch of Portobello, had been found in Hampstead. She had
been brutally murdered.

Now that I've finished transcribing all the taped interviews, I'm going to give her the transcript. She's probably gone for a walk in the Snowdonia National Park as she does every afternoon. It's her birthday—or, rather, the date that her parents chose for her birthday when they adopted her—and this is my present to her.

Viorel, who will be coming to the celebration with his grandparents, has also prepared a surprise for her. He's recorded his first composition in a friend's studio and he's going to play it during supper.

She'll ask me afterward: "Why did you do this?"

And I'll say: "Because I needed to understand you." During all the years we've been together, I've only heard what I thought were legends about her, but now I know that the legends are true.

Whenever I suggested going with her, be it to the Monday evening celebrations at her apartment, to Romania, or to get-togethers with friends, she always asked me not to. She wanted to be free, and people, she said, find policemen intimidating. Faced by someone like me, even the innocent feel guilty.

However, I went to the Portobello warehouse twice without her knowledge. Again without her knowledge, I arranged for various colleagues to be around to protect her when she arrived and left, and at least one person, later identified as a militant member of some sect, was arrested for carrying a knife. He said he'd been told by spirits to acquire a little blood from the Witch of Portobello, who was a manifestation of the Great Mother. The blood, he said, was needed to consecrate certain offerings. He didn't intend to kill her, he merely wanted a little blood on a handkerchief. The investigation showed that there really was no intention to murder, but nevertheless, he was charged and sentenced to six months in prison.

It wasn't my idea to make it look as if she'd been murdered. Athena wanted to disappear and asked me if that would be possible. I explained that if the courts decided that the state should have custody of her child, I couldn't go against the law, but when the judge found in her favor, we were free to carry out her plan.

Athena was fully aware that once the meetings at the warehouse became the focus of local gossip, her mission would be ruined for good. There was no point standing up in front of the crowd and denying that she was a queen, a witch, a divine manifestation, because people choose to follow the powerful and they give power to whomever they wish. And that would go against everything she preached—freedom to choose, to consecrate your own bread, to awaken your particular gifts, with no help from guides or shepherds.

Nor was there any point in disappearing. People would interpret such a gesture as a retreat into the wilderness, an ascent into the heavens, a secret pilgrimage to meet teachers in the Himalayas, and they would always be awaiting her return. Legends and possibly a cult could grow up around her. We started to notice this when she stopped going to Portobello. My informants said that, contrary to everyone's expectations, her cult was growing with frightening speed: other similar groups were being created, and people were turning up claiming to be the "heirs" of Hagia Sofia. The newspaper photograph of her holding

Viorel was being sold on the black market, depicting her as a victim, a martyr to intolerance. Occultists started talking about an "Order of Athena," through which—upon payment—one could be put in touch with the founder.

All that remained was "death," but the death had to take place in completely normal circumstances, like the death of any other person murdered in a big city. This obliged us to take certain precautions.

1. The crime could not in any way be associated with martyrdom for religious reasons, because, if it was, we would only aggravate the very situation we were trying to avoid;
2. The victim would have to be so badly disfigured as to be unrecognizable;
3. The murderer could not be arrested;
4. We would need a corpse.

In a city like London, dead, disfigured, burned bodies turn up every day, but normally we find the culprit. So we had to wait nearly two months until the Hampstead murder. We found a murderer too, who was also conveniently dead—he had fled to Portugal and committed suicide by blowing his brains out. Justice had been done, and all I needed was a little cooperation from my closest friends. One hand washes the other: they sometimes asked me to do things that were not entirely orthodox, and as long as no major law was broken, there was—shall we say—a certain degree of flexibility in interpreting the facts.

That is what happened. As soon as the body was found, I and a colleague of many years' standing were given the case, and almost simultaneously, we got news that the Portuguese police had found the body of a suicide in Guimarães, along with a note confessing to a murder whose details fitted the case we were dealing with, and giving instructions for all his money to be donated to charitable institutions. It had been a crime of passion—love often ends like that.

In the note he left behind, the dead man said that he'd brought the woman from one of the ex-Soviet republics and done everything he could to help her. He was prepared to marry her so that she would have the same rights as a British citizen, and then he'd found a letter she was about to send to some German man, who had invited her to spend a few days at his castle.

In the letter, she said she couldn't wait to leave and asked the German to send her a plane ticket at once so that they could meet again as soon as possible. They had met in a London café and had only exchanged two letters.

We had the perfect scenario.

My friend hesitated—no one likes to have an unsolved crime on their files—but when I said that I'd take the blame for this, he agreed.

I went to the place where Athena was in hiding—a delightful house in Oxford. I used a syringe to take some of her blood. I cut off a lock of her hair and singed it slightly. Back at the scene of the crime, I scattered this "evidence" around. I knew that since no one knew the identity of her real mother and father, no DNA identification would be possible, and so all I needed was to cross my fingers and hope the murder didn't get too much coverage in the press.

A few journalists turned up. I told them the story of the murderer's suicide, mentioning only the country, not the town. I said that no motive had been found for the crime, but that we had completely discounted any idea that it was a revenge killing or that there had been some religious motive. As I understood it (after all, the police can make mistakes too), the victim had been raped. She had presumably recognized her attacker, who had then killed and mutilated her.

If the German ever wrote again, his letters would have been sent back marked "Return to sender." Athena's photograph had appeared only once in the newspapers, during the first demonstration in Portobello, and so the chances of *her being recognized were minimal. Apart from me, only three people know this story—her parents and her son. They all attended the burial of "her" remains, and the gravestone bears her name.*

Her son goes to see her every weekend and is doing brilliantly at school.

Of course, Athena may one day tire of this isolated life and decide to return to London. Nevertheless, people have very short memories, and apart from her closest friends, no one will remember her. By then, Andrea will be the catalyst and—to be fair—she is better able than Athena to continue the mission. As well as having all the necessary gifts, she's an actress and knows how to deal with the public.

I understand that Andrea's work is spreading, although without attracting unwanted attention. I hear about people in key positions in society who are in contact with her, and when necessary, when the right critical mass is reached, they will put an end to the hypocrisy of the Reverend Ian Bucks of this world.

And that's what Athena wants, not fame for herself, as many (including Andrea) thought, but that the mission should be completed.

At the start of my investigations, of which this transcript is the result, I thought I was reconstructing her life so that she would see how brave and important she had been. But as the conversations went on, I gradually discovered my own hidden side, even though I don't much believe in these things. And I reached the conclusion that the real reason behind all this work was a desire to answer a question to which I'd never known the answer: Why did Athena love me, when we're so different and when we don't even share the same worldview?

I remember when I kissed her for the first time, in a bar near Victoria Station. She was working for a bank at the time, and I was a detective at Scotland Yard. After we'd been out together a few times, she invited me to go and dance at her landlord's apartment, but I never did—it's not really my style.

And instead of getting annoyed, she said that she respected my decision. When I reread the statements made by her friends, I feel really proud, because Athena doesn't seem to have respected anyone else's decisions.

Months later, before she set off to Dubai, I told her that I loved her. She said that she felt the same way but added that we must be prepared to spend long periods apart. Each of us would work in a different country, but true love could withstand such a separation.

That was the only time I dared to ask her: "Why do you love me?"

She replied: "I don't know and I don't care."

Now, as I put the finishing touches to these pages, I believe I may have found the answer in her last conversation with the journalist.

Love simply is.

February 25, 2006 19:47:00
Revised version completed on St. Expeditus's Day, 2006